T0265511

THE LIONHEART CHRONICLES

The Alchemy of The Beast

Alyssa Noelle Coelho

Saved By Story

The Alchemy of The Beast

THE LIONHEART CHRONICLES

Published by

Saved By Story Publishing, LLC

Prescott, AZ

www.SavedByStory.house

Copyright © 2023 by Alyssa Noelle Coelho

Cover by Alyssa Noelle Coelho

Interior Design by Dawn Teagarden

Photo/Illustrations by Carly Ashdown

Disclaimer: The Publisher and the Author do not guarantee that anyone following the techniques, suggestions, tips, ideas or strategies will become successful. The advice and strategies contained herein may not be suitable for every situation. The Publisher and Author shall have neither liability nor responsibility to anyone with respect to any loss or damage caused, or alleged to be caused, directly or indirectly by the information in this book. Written permission has been obtained to share the identity of each real individual named in this book.

Any citations or a potential source of information from other organizations or websites given herein does not mean that the Author or Publisher endorses the information/content the website or organization provides or recommendations it may make. It is the readers' responsibility to do their own due diligence when researching information. Also, websites listed or referenced herein may have changed or disappeared from the time that this work was created and the time that it is read.

Publisher's Cataloging-in-Publication Data

Names: Coelho, Alyssa Noelle, 1995-.

Title: The alchemy of the beast / Alyssa Noelle Coelho.

Description: Prescott, AZ : Saved By Story Publishing, 2023. | Series: The lionheart chronicles ; 1. | Summary: After experiencing a series of losses, twenty-one-year-old Scarlett V. Leonelli travels to a hidden village in the jungle of Costa Rica where she is guided to learn, heal, and transform the pain of her past into something better.

Identifiers: LCCN 2023912304 | ISBN 9781961336032 (hardback) | ISBN 9781961336049 (ebook)

Subjects: LCSH: Grief – Fiction. | Spirituality – Fiction. | Mental healing – Fiction. |Voyages and travels – Fiction. | Los Angeles (Calif.) – Fiction.| Portland (Or.) –Fiction. | Costa Rica – Fiction. | BISAC: FICTION / Magical Realism. | FICTION /Visionary & Metaphysical. | FICTION / Women.

Classification: LCC PS3603.O45 2023 | DDC 813 C—dc23

LC record available at https://lccn.loc.gov/2023912304

Printed in the United States of America

www.SavedByStory.house

To the Travelers who don't yet know you are so,
and to the Mapmakers you have yet to meet.

To my Papá, you live on.

Contents

Foreword by Joel McKerrow

Sometimes we leave home not really knowing where we are going,
>only that
>>*it is time to go.*
Of course we usually have a destination in mind,
>>but,
>>>I have found that the best journeys are the ones
>>>that choose us.
That when we give ourselves to serendipity,
>>>we find that which we were never searching for.
The offerings on the road gifted
>>from someplace beyond our reach.

And so, if we choose to open our hands as we leave
>>the front door of our ordinary.
If we walk the path,
>>perhaps with a destination in mind,
>>but also with a willingness to be taken off course,
>>then imagine what we might find.
Imagine what you might find… here.

I think that opening a book for the first time
>>is rather the same movement
>>>as walking out the front door to begin a journey.
Crossing the threshold.
This book… it is a threshold for you.
Maybe,
>>if you choose for it to be so.
It is an invitation,
>>onward.

The story of Scarlett might just be
        the story you didn't know you needed,
        until suddenly it is in your hands.
And the journey she goes on
        feels like it's the journey you too are on.
The journey we are all on.
And it will feel disorienting.
And it will feel like opening eyes into the sunlight
        after a long night.
Blink a few times. Let your eyes adjust.
This story is a story,
        but, like all good stories,
        it is so much more.
And, like all good stories,
        like all good journeys,
        all it asks of you is to enter in.
To be present. To choose to be present.

We are urged,
        in the fantastical realm
        of fairy tales read in novels or seen in movies,
        to suspend belief.
That is,
        though your rational mind is telling you
        that magic does not exist,
        to allow yourself to consider for a few moments that
        it just might.
This is important for us humans.
All our deduction and reason and logic convinces us
        that the way in which we are seeing the world is… Truth.
But, perhaps,
        there is truth that can only be found
        in the suspension of belief,
        when we are willing to let down our guards and
        traverse into the fantastical.
To journey into the mythological,
        to take tentative steps into the imaginal.

Friends, what I am saying is,
        there is truth here.

In this story,
   in this adventure into Costa Rica.
There is deep truth.
Ancient truth,
   should you be willing to allow it to speak to you.

So, I urge you NOT to read this book.
   (Great encouragement for a foreword. Ha.)
No. Instead, I urge you,
   to let this book read you,
   to let it name inside you your own resistances,
   to let your own memories surface as they
   knock upon the door of your consciousness.
A journey is never just someone wandering through a land.
A true journey occurs when that someone allows the land,
   the people, the culture
   to wander into them.
To teach them.
To stir up the eddies of the soul.
To breathe upon the embers.

A true journey occurs when the tourist becomes a pilgrim.
The tourist consumes a place,
   the pilgrim allows a place to consume them.

The journey deepens when a pilgrim becomes a traveler.
The pilgrim seeks the sacred unknown once,
   the traveler seeks it again and again.

Be a pilgrim on the paths of this book, let it guide you.
Be a traveler in your life, let it guide you.
Be a pilgrim.
Be a traveler.

Joel McKerrow

Author, Poet, and Creativity Specialist
Director of The School for Creative Development

Dear Traveler,

Ciao. Welcome to what has been one of my greatest adventures!

Although The Lionheart Chronicles is designed to transport you to worlds unseen and dance with the beauty of other cultures, other belief systems, other ways of life and love, it is also crafted to meet you where you are on your journey through the universal realities of your human experience. I endeavor to show you that you are far from alone in the uncertainties you face.

In this first book, Scarlett's journey is that of unimaginable grief and unexpected exploration. As you dare to experience her adventure as your own, I invite you to remember the parts of yourself that you too have forgotten with the big and little losses you've endured.

No matter the type of loss, grief is never a simple journey. It's often tangled with complicated dynamics and it is so important that you are creating the space you need to listen to your body and mind, to breathe, and to move through it at your own pace. And as you witness love and support reveal itself in the many faces of the characters, I encourage you to hold the gaze of the people in your own story who want to support you, even when they don't know how.

I do have a little, not-so-secret agenda here. One of my many hopes for this series is this: When Scarlett's plane lands on foreign ground, so will yours.

You will learn as you read that I refrain from using the word *believe* lightly, so when I tell you that I *believe deeply* in the transformative power of travel, I mean it. I also understand that, for many reasons, these adventures are not easily accessible to everyone, which is why I am bringing it to you here.

In order to bring the fullness of cultural immersion to your hands, I've done my best to preserve the authentic experience of the languages, traditions, and references. You will find a glossary at the back of the book to support you with any of the translations or definitions you might need as you read.

In the spirit of bringing this fiction to life, I have also recorded the poetry you will find on the pages of Scarlett's journal. You can hear and feel Scar's voice by simply scanning the QR code below.

Take comfort. You are now as prepared as you can be, and more prepared than most of us are when life throws us into the jungles of inevitable tragedies. And I want you to know, however lost you might feel, I trust in your process and I *believe* in the magic within you to light your way back to yourself and to the knowing that there is still beauty in existence.

I'm *believing* that the footprints that brought you here know exactly where they are taking you, and that beyond the Beasts you are facing, there is so much life waiting for you.

Thank you for *believing* that maybe… there is more.

I'm lost in divinity

between pages and ink,

shaking the hand of God

in every stranger I meet.

I've kissed heaven so many times,

I write to see it bleed.

And when my pen runs dry,

I dance to hear Love speak.

So if time be my salvation,

then fear be my enemy.

And if my tongue forgets to pray,

all I have to do is breathe.

"

There is a Mystery that many call God,
manifesting as Universal Love,
a set of Laws and a Great Process.
That Process works through each and all of us,
and that Process is perfect.
As we discover this fundamental truth
in the journey of our lives,
we find that wherever we step,
the path appears beneath our feet.

DAN MILLMAN

One

Buenos días! We have initiated our final descent into San José, Costa Rica. It is 5:35 p.m. local time and a rainy seventy-two degrees. Thank you for flying with us today. If you will be connecting to another flight, we wish you safe travels. If San José is your final destination, then bienvenido to the one and only… ¡Costa Rica!"

The pilot's welcome over the intercom echoed faintly somewhere in the distance, but I was fixated on the laughter trickling between the seats on the other side of the aisle. Thin, light blonde hair whipped across the window as a little voice bellowed at the tickles her father sent into her sides.

A single tear rolled from my jaw and onto the words scratched across the page under my hand while my palm grew sweaty and indented by the ring hanging from my neck...

I saw it happen.

I watched her sitting there.

toes in the sand, eyes on the water.

I saw her soul in all its weary.

I watched her fingers recoil,

hair curly and wild in the midnight air.

I saw her give it all away.

I watched her chest rise and fall,

whiskey on her breath, pain in her laugh.

I saw her say her goodbyes.

I watched her whispers trail in the moonlight,

sorry on her tongue, ash in her heart.

I saw her love tear through the trees.

I watched it scream, rage in reckless fury.

Her head fell back, cigarette to the ground.

I saw the moment she let go.

I watched with terror.

Hope vanished into the night.

"*Perdone.*" The smiling stranger next to me spoke sweetly. Her eyes, wilting with concern, snapped me from my trance. My fingers trembled as I unfastened my seatbelt, tucked my journal in my bag, grabbed my luggage, and made my way off the Boeing 737. This was my first time traveling alone internationally. This was my first time accepting a stranger's invitation to a foreign country. This was my first time taking any sort of risk, knowing the one person who always was, wouldn't be there to have my back if any hell broke loose. The family wasn't too thrilled about my decision, of course. Well, everyone but Trix, whose advice had nudged my wandering in this direction.

"So, there is this author…"

"Oh great, another book recommendation." I sighed.

What is it with people trying to fix their lives by reading books? I couldn't get it. They'd quite literally only torn mine apart.

She laughed. "This one is different, Sis. I swear. It changed my life many years ago and it sounds like it might be just the one you need right now. This guy is one of the Masters."

"A Master, huh?" I snickered at the thought of some enlightened guru who might be able to fix my crumbling world with his pen and paper. "Sure, why not? I'm out of school now. Not like I don't have time to read."

Trix laughed… that soft, ominous laugh of hers.

When I stopped to get the mail a few days later, the over-masculated back of some guy stretched out in a landing gymnast pose incited an eye roll. Trix had failed to mention that this seventy-one-year-old author is a former Olympic gymnast. Or maybe she purposely left that part out, knowing damn well I would've discarded the idea immediately.

A week later, I was on a domestic flight to a work event in Oregon, smushed on one side by a large gentleman, who had fallen asleep, his head collapsed on top of his shoulder, now puddled in drool. When I looked up, a frail dainty hand polished with red, wrapped around a half-open book. I crooked my neck as I recognized the book my eldest sister had sent me, the one I'd not-so-accidently left on my shelf before this trip. The coincidence made me flinch.

On my flight home a few days later, I looked up from my aisle seat to see the same wrinkled, red-polished hands wrapped around the same book cover.

No way.

The seatbelt light switched off and I made my way to her row where, to my surprise, there was no one else sitting.

"Hello," I awkwardly ventured. As I gazed down, I noticed her text was in Russian and then greeted her again. "*Zdravstuytye! Kak vas zovut?*"

Her eyebrows raised as she slid her pointy-tipped glasses off, tilted her chin down, and looked up at me. "I am surprised your Russian is so good despite that thick Italian accent."

I sighed at my inability to escape those roots. It was impossible to drop it in English, and my Spanish suffers from it quite a bit as well. "Ah, well. No escaping the Italian." I shrugged. "Do you mind if I sit with you?"

Hesitating only a moment, this older woman grabbed her things from the seat next to her and made room for me.

"I noticed the book you were reading. And actually, I think you were on my flight to Oregon."

"I'm not quite sure if I just flew there." She appeared to be actually contemplating that answer, as if we did not just leave there—on the same plane, together.

Well, I'm not imagining things.

Suddenly hungry for conversation, I probed, "Can I ask you what you think about it?" She stared back at me blankly. "The book?"

"Oh. Ah yes." She shifted in her seat, as if caught off-guard that I sought her opinion. "Well…" Her accent was so thick, it made me miss my mother's family dearly.

I wondered to myself if I might have even known her before, as the rasp in her voice sounded strangely familiar. Her shoulders were tense and I could tell she was hesitant to engage.

"I see you are close to the end?"

"Mmm yes, yes, I am. It's a good book."

It was like pulling teeth. I took a deep breath and shot her a particularly daring glance.

She took a deep breath and pulled her glasses all the way down to hang from their chain on her chest. "Look, you came over here for a reason. I can feel you. You are… you are very broken. Whoever told you to read this book… you should listen to them."

My airway tightened. *I suppose I asked for that one.*

Scrambling to expand my chest, I tried to find some words that might work. I offered my hand, intent on turning this around, "*Menya zovut Scar. Kak vas zovut?*"

Her name was Gelena, and fortunately, the handshake did us well. My Italian blood always forgets: direct, not pushy. We started over and spent the entire two and a half-hour flight talking. While I managed to direct the conversation, so that I didn't have to disclose much information, she opened up quite a bit. She told me how this book had changed her life once upon a time, and how she reads it every so often. She shared some of her lifelong travels—her journeys across the world and those within herself. I marveled and asked as many questions as I could, over the sunrise and our English Breakfast tea.

By the end of the flight, Gelena's laughter filled the aircraft as she recalled fond memories, her hand now squeezing mine as she shared. The pilot landed us and just as everyone began grabbing their luggage, she smiled—a sweet smile with much gratitude—before releasing my hand to reach into her purse. She pulled out what looked to be a folded plane ticket and placed it in my lap, "Come visit me in Costa Rica. There's a special place you need to be. I'll have my finest driver pick you up."

I frowned at her, entirely confused as I unwrapped the piece of paper and found a one-way ticket to San José, dated for August 1, 2017, only two short months in the future, for *Scarlett Vita Leonelli.* My heart sank as I shook my head with confusion. What I read made little sense, but when I looked up, she was gone and those red nails were nowhere to be found in this plane puzzled with people.

Hands moist and throat clenched, I walked through the San José airport, intentionally ignoring the growing crackle in my chest. All the signs were in Spanish and, although growing up in Southern California had taught me to pull some similarities from the languages I was raised with, I had little confidence in my ability to communicate anything of importance. Luckily, I stumbled upon a couple of patient employees who accepted my eyelash-batting and helped me along.

Forgot I had those.

Finally out of the airport, I ducked around the eager friends and family of other passengers and found a wall to lean against while I begged my breath to return.

You can figure this out, Scar.

My skin moistened with oil almost immediately at the brush of the warm water-filled air. I was scanning the crowd when a light shower fell from the sky, sun still shining above. Never in Los Angeles did sun and rain coexist in the same day. A young man with olive skin and a thin black beard, sporting a white fedora, stole my attention.

"Miss Scarlett?" He held a sign that read my name, just as the plane ticket had.

"Ciao. Uh perdóname, hola." I shyly lifted my hand and waved as I approached him. "Me llamo Scar."

With a warm, disarming smile, he reached for my hand. "¡Pura vida! ¡Mucho gusto!" I flinched at his touch. It wasn't hot, but it was... quite strong.

"My name is Ramón. I'll be your driver today. ¿Prefieres inglés o español?"

"Uh..." I looked up to meet his eyes. "Necesito practicar el español, pero el inglés me resulta más fácil."

He smiled wide and bobbed his head. "Entonces, los dos."

Beyond my awkward shock, I immediately felt much calmer in his presence. This must be the gentleman Gelena referred to. I couldn't wait to see her again.

He reached for my luggage and we walked to the car—a very cute, vintage little blue Volkswagen with clunky doors, white leather seats, and stains galore. I couldn't help but smirk at its refreshing simplicity as I considered the escape this experience would be from the never-ending glamour-seeking of LA.

"Is this your first time in Costa Rica?" He had a young, soft voice for his age. My guess was twenty-eight, maybe thirty. His accent was thick, but his voice was clear and easy to understand.

"Yes, it is. I'm very... I'm here." I couldn't decide what I felt, but here I was indeed. The reminder that this was my first time so far from home, and so very on my own, made me straighten my spine a bit.

You're doing this, Scar.

He put my luggage in the trunk and rushed over to open my door before my hand made it to the handle. "Well, bienvenida to Costa Rica, Miss Scarlett. Please let me know if there is anything I can do to make your experience more comfortable." The enthusiasm in his voice was hard to ignore, but I'm sure he spoke to each new visitor with the same silk. And, I'm sure he wore that same beige V-neck with the sleeves rolled up around the curvature of his arms too.

Not that I noticed.

As we drove away through the city, the scenes behind the window reminded me that this was my first time in a less-developed country too. I'd heard stories of my parents' old home in Milan, but never seen the city myself. These buildings stood a pretty stark contrast to the skyscrapers of downtown Los Angeles.

I expected a history lesson from Ramón, but as we exited the more touristy streets, the region began telling me its own stories. The further we traveled from the heart of San José, the sparser the developments became and the tallest concrete reached two stories, maybe a third here and there. The sides of the streets were packed tightly with tractors, bulldozers, and forklifts. Construction everywhere.

There weren't many people out, but the ones who were took shelter from the rain under plastic hole-punctured umbrellas. From the city to the hills, the homes were small with few windows, painted in all the finest colors of the rainbow, and wrapped with gates and barbed wire.

I probably should have researched more before coming. He would be furious.

I could just see my father shaking his head, thumb and index finger pressed on opposite sides of his skull. Here I was, in a strange man's car, on a one-way ticket from an even stranger woman. I quietly spun the charcoal ring on the chain around my neck and let my head fall back a little. Part of me waited patiently, hoping to hear his laugh.

Ramón was quiet for most of the thirty-minute drive. I supposed it was due to his need to concentrate in the rain, which fell harder under the dark clouds awaiting us at the edge of the city. Somehow, we still managed to meet each other's eyes in the mirror a few times.

Scarlett... I haven't been called that in... I can't remember how many years.

I didn't even use that on the plane tickets I'd purchased myself. I shook my head and stared out through the water rolling down the window.

We exited the main highway and turned left on Punta Léona 72 Highway. The concrete disintegrated into the large, unfurled leaves extending from the jungle we were dissolving into, becoming one with. The gates faded to fence posts, tied with thin wire, dividing the portions of land.

Relief washed through me in small waves and, after a few windy and rocky roads, my drowsiness consumed me. Perhaps a crash from all the nervous adrenaline. I set my elbow on the car door, dropped my cheek into my hand, and closed my eyes for much longer than I expected.

When we hit a bump in the road and my head fell from my hand, I bounced up, quickly realizing I'd dozed off. The foggy gray sky had dissolved into a darkness thicker than any night I'd ever seen back home. It was already evening and we were still driving. Ramón heard my shuffle and responded with a soothing morning rasp, "You're alright, Miss Scarlett. You just fell asleep for a few."

"A few?" I asked, puzzled and searching for light, finding only the dim ones illuminating the road ahead.

He chuckled. "Well, about an hour and a half. Did you have a long flight?"

"An hour and a half!?" Panic cracked in my throat. "I hadn't expected Gelena to live so far."

"Oh, you actually aren't going to Gelena's. We have about four more hours to go. Did Gelena forget to tell you?"

I shook my head, my mind racing for what I had missed. "Uhm, perhaps. I… We're not going to Gelena's?" My heart sank into my stomach, my fists tightened, and I felt a sharp pain in my jaw from my grinding teeth. Exhaling a deep breath I didn't know I'd been holding in, I tried to relax and settle myself, so as not to give away the fear coursing through me.

"Really, Miss Scarlett, you're alright. This is going to be an incredible journey for you."

I kinked my neck as I searched for his eyes in the mirror.

Ouch. I really did knock out for a while.

He chuckled when he saw me. "Really, I mean it. This little village, it's incredible."

Little village? A little village—hours into the tropical jungle. IF that is where he is actually taking me. Of course, he is trying to keep me calm. Why would Gelena not…?

"There's a special place you need to visit."

Why am I surprised? I took some strange woman's plane ticket with no direction, or instruction, or any detail about this place she spoke of.

Anxiety tightened my throat. I closed my eyes and wrapped my fist around my necklace. As calming as his voice was, my body was quickly stirring with frenzy.

We drove in my nervous silence for a bit. The curve of the roads ensured I would have no idea how to get back to the city on my own. I considered jumping multiple times, just swinging the door open and jumping out. The black shadows towering above, just barely visible against the sky, told me we had to be hugging the mountains though and provoked my inner control freak to the forefront. The nerves made me nibble on my nails.

"Miss Scarlett." His voice snapped me into focus. "Would you like to hear a story?"

Oh sure, yeah. Tell me a story while you kidnap me.

I extricated the talons gripping my throat.

Don't be rude, Scar.

"Sure."

"When I was a young boy, I'd stay at my grandfather's house for weeks at a time. He spent hours making this delicious, earthy coffee for us. Long before we had organized coffee fields here, we'd hike past the property line of his home deep into the jungle to find just the right beans. He was as original a Rican as they get."

He laughed at the thought.

"It was not a process he rushed, and you can imagine, as a young boy, that part was very boring for me. But it was okay. My parents didn't really like me drinking coffee, so I was happy to be having it at all! But after we found just the right ones—deep green leaves scattered with tiny golden specs—he would take only what we needed. Never too much. We would go home and clean them and pulp them, you know, ferment and dry. My favorite part was roasting them, though! Oh, the house would fill with the aroma. It was so delicious."

The light in his eyes glistened as he glanced back at me.

"We'd grind the beans right before we brewed and then he always gave me the honor of pouring it for us. I'd pack the grounds in the sock and pour the boiling water over it. For him first, and then myself. It was veryyy delicious, but he would not drink fast and, of course, neither could I—as much as I wanted to. It was not just a drink, you know? It was more of… ¿cómo sé dice en inglés…?"

He searched for a bit while I pondered my growing questions.

"Ah, a ceremony. He would tell me stories—mostly history, maybe some myths, you know—but they always had some interesting twists. He talked a lot about the land he grew up on, even deeper there within the jungle. Soil so rich with metallic minerals from the volcanic aftermath, it shone like the scales of… of reptiles when the moonlight fell on them just right."

His animation grew, as he'd periodically lift a hand from the wheel to enhance his story or toss me a quick wink in the mirror.

My lashes fluttered to hide my enjoyment, but I'm certain they failed.

"And the breeze..." His voice softened. "I can still see the goosebumps raised on the old man's wrinkly skin when he spoke of how still the air was—how its soundless voice called to him through the silence, how... how it was filled with so much water, he'd say he was either breathing under the sea some days or... or floating in the heavens."

Serenity paused my thoughts and I felt weightless at the sound of his words.

"And around him, the sunlight, he said, would scatter into rainbows."

Ramón paused for a long moment and his words, despite their little sense, had soothed me into such a state, no exchange was needed.

"He spoke of it as if it was... cleansing, you know? Magical."

I crooked my head in curiosity.

"And the people..." His volume rose with his eyebrows. "Oh, he talked about them as if he knew them all! Well, maybe he did. I don't know for sure!" Every time the car bumped back and forth, I could see his smile in the mirror, his lips saturated with delight while speaking of his grandfather.

This man was feeling a little less scary, and I relaxed even more. My throat opened and grabbing the knob on the door, I circled it clockwise to roll the window down just enough for me to stick my fingers out for some fresh air.

"Oh, Miss Scarlett," I pulled my hand back quickly. "Please roll the window down as much as you need."

I nodded. "So, what did your grandfather say about the people?"

"Shapeshifters, he called them!" He smirked. "Apparently, they were all unique, each with their own powers."

Oh, fantasy. Joy.

I kept my inner eye roll to myself and decided to entertain his imagination with some sweet mockery. "Wow."

"He also said that they were a little backward. They didn't function like many cultures in the world do today. There wasn't so much of a hierarchy and, if there was, it was reversed."

"Reversed?"

"Yes, like you know how children are often told what to do and how to do it? How adults are the bosses?"

"Yes…"

"Well, here, I guess they actually let children make the decisions. In fact, I remember him saying that they actually looked to children for answers."

My eyebrows furrowed at the idea. I don't think I'd ever heard such a thing.

"He always made it seem like children were the epitome of, you know… cómo sé dice… ¡la Présencia! Their experience was fluid and they were really… inside every moment."

Okay, losing me.

"I suppose this was based on the idea that, as we grow up, things happen to us and, we have responsibilities and duties, and we worry about the future."

"Uhm," I coughed, as I tightened my grip on the crackle at my core.

"And, of course, the past. Sometimes, it's difficult to escape regrets… what-ifs."

I gulped at the thought and the spark inside dulled to an ache as I tried to focus on his words.

"And all of those things take us further and further away from being like children. We lose… the moment. We lose the answers."

"Hmmm." My thoughts quickly escaped before I could muster much of a response. Answers. That word really pissed me off.

"And then there were the Guardians! They were tasked with protecting the land."

I adjusted myself into a more focused posture, hoping it would help me stay in the conversation, despite the whirlwind of emotions all of his past and future talk was stirring. "Protecting it from what?"

"Well, those who came for its magic of course."

I felt the arch in my left brow jolt upward at the word. "Magic?" I probed, reigning in the mockery of my tone.

"Yes, when the settlers came, all the indigenous tribes retreated to this land for protection. And the Guardians rose from each tribe and united. They were the ones who kept it invisible from intruders."

"But, what do you mean *the magic*?" I'd only heard tales of magic growing up, and it was never painted in a decent light. The church had always taught that those who practiced magic were witches, followers of the enemy. It wasn't until just recently that I'd even considered the possibility that the word could mean something else, and even that ponderance was only because of the strings in my chest that tugged at the word.

Perhaps he knows.

"Well, there was a lot of magic in this place. From the soil to the Shapeshifters and the children, it was everywhere."

That word again. Shapeshifters. This was starting to sound like just another version of the tales I was told growing up. Adam, Eve, the Garden of Eden. Virgin birth. Holy grail. Fallen angels.

Over it. I'd lived in fantasy long enough.

I leaned back and slowly disengaged. Maybe he didn't know and this was just another myth. His grandfather must have really loved telling stories. I stuck my fingers out the window again—a little further into the rain. It was light, but it looked like a sheet. I drew a gap in the stream and a weightless waterfall appeared. I could hardly feel it though.

How could it be raining so hard?

"Would you like to hear more, Miss Scarlett?" His question intruded my confounding distraction.

"Yes, of course. So, Shapeshifters with powers and Guardians who protected. Please, go on. Were they each born into a role?"

I did my best to behave. I didn't have much patience for myths, especially after the disintegration I'd been in.

Been in. More like been drowning in.

But, I had always been fascinated by cultures—the institutions, systems, and schools of thought which constitute them and influence their development.

Yes, mythology, philosophy… beautiful… until something comes along to show us how full of shit they both are.

I let out a huge sigh as I tried to summon some patience. Perhaps these stories might give me some insight into the culture of this foreign place I would be experiencing soon.

"Nope. You see, they all came into the world with powers, and with the choice to go either way. When children came of age, they could choose which path they wanted. But this was a very serious decision. They could only choose once, and they could never go back."

"Hmm." I let his seriousness sink in a second before I humored his fantasy and dug for some more. "So, if the Guardians protected the land, what did the Shapeshifters do?"

"Well, after a child chose to be a Shapeshifter, they were paired with a Master and would undergo very rigorous training, leaving their village and their families for many years. Eventually, they could come back if they wanted to. But if they did, they had to put their gifts to service for others—to help others heal."

"And the Guardians? How did they develop their powers?" I asked.

He paused for a moment. "Guardians… They didn't get to transform the way Shapeshifters did. Their only devotion was to their land and their people."

"Well, why would someone choose to be a Guardian instead of a Shapeshifter? Magical powers sound much more fun, more adventurous…" It was a snarky giggle that sneaked out before I dropped my chin and tried to recall the days when I believed in superpowers… when I'd felt like I even had them.

When I was a child myself.

His voice grew steady. "Oh, but there was great honor that came with becoming a Guardian. They were trusted with much and were fulfilled with a great sense of duty."

I nodded. *Quite the tale.*

"So, what did your grandfather's people do? Were there hunters, farmers?"

"Well, it sounded like everyone did a little bit of everything. There was equality and harmony. And... a lot of silence."

"What do you mean 'a lot of silence'?"

"The people really valued silence. When it was silent, they remembered."

"Remembered...?" I stuttered, my eyes widening with anticipation.

That sounded like my worst nightmare.

"Yes, then they could be like the children."

I shifted in my seat as a familiar Bible verse skipped across my brain: "Truly, I tell you, unless you change and become like little children, you will never enter the kingdom of heaven" (Matthew 18:3 NIV).

Trailing my whisper, the ache in my chest crept back. My shaking pinky caught my eye and I comforted it with my other hand.

"Tell me more about the magic," I quickly redirected.

Ramón chuckled, as if he knew. "Well, I'm not sure if there were ghosts and goblins, but it did sound like there were fairies."

"Oh, really?"

He was clearly humoring me, but my attention veered as I stuck my fingers further out the window, so I could make designs in the falling sheets of water. I zoned out on the water until I noticed some dancing yellow specs behind it. Actually, it looked as if they were floating in and out of the water, and around it!

I leaned in closer and noticed tons of little specs on the towering shadows we swerved around. Countless, they flickered and shone like... light or gold or...

Too much fantasy fun, Scar.

I pulled my body back from the window.

"Well, like I said, the tale was that the land was full of magic—the kind you can't really describe," he continued.

"*How* though?" I asked eagerly.

"Well, for one, time didn't exist on this land. The sun existed. The moon existed. But no one ever created a system that dictated things like hours or schedules. They didn't function in that type of structure and neither did the land."

"Oh? The land?" My tone revealed my skepticism without my permission.

His eyes flashed to me in the mirror with a playful look about them. "Oh, you have no idea, Miss Scarlett. This land played with all the ways people normally understood their reality."

"Mhm. So, what ever happened to this land your grandfather told you about?"

"Well, he said there was so much violence when those settlers came that when the tribes came from all around seeking refuge, the mountains and the jungle that covered them became just that. And the land grew and expanded for them."

"You said before that they made it invisible?" I did my best to tame my biting sarcasm.

"Yes, Miss Scarlett." His eyes darted to mine with a friendly faith, eagerly seeking to convince its listener. "The land grew and provided everything every single person needed to heal and to learn and to become a child again—to find their eternal moment. Then, it vanished."

This gibberish made me squeak a chuckle out loud, and I quickly covered my mouth, realizing I might appear rude. Ramón smiled and I pulled myself together quickly. "My apologies. This really is such a great story. You must've loved your grandfather."

"Yes, I do love him very much."

"Oh, is he still around?"

"Yes, he is. Not physically, but I definitely feel him and see him everywhere."

I dropped my head and stared into the falling water, my stomach hollowing out. "You believe in spirits, Ramón?"

"Do I believe in them?" His tone twisted with perplexity. "What do you mean?"

"Well, do you believe they exist the same way you believe in magic? Spirits? Souls? Ancestors? Like... your grandfather?"

He laughed lightly, and sincerely, turning his body in his seat to face me. "Do you believe *you* exist?"

I crooked my neck. "What do you mean?"

"Oh, Miss Scarlett, it is not quite a matter of belief."

I frowned.

To believe... is that not the only language for speaking of spirits or any supernatural things, for that matter?

"I don't have to believe. I *know* those things exist."

I gulped.

"You *know*?" My neck cracked in challenge of his response.

After all I'd learned in recent years about religious delusion, the top of the red flags list has "I know" written all over it.

He disarmed my repulsion with a chuckle, "Yes, spirits live everywhere around me. They teach me and talk to me, and they are... a part of me."

I was growing concerned about what cult this man might be taking me to.

"And magic?"

"Magic is not quite a matter of belief either." He winked.

"So, belief, you're saying is... irrelevant?" I clarified, wondering if I'd heard him incorrectly.

All I'd wanted, after these last few years, was a taste of some sort of grounded, objective reality—one that just makes fucking sense. The one I'd been living in for twenty-one years was anything but that. I was so very tired and, frankly, annoyed at having to decipher the psychology and symbology of others' thoughts and language to find some common, coherent ground.

His eyes softened in the mirror and his lips pulled back slightly. Beyond the obvious psychosis in his words, there was a subtlety in the way he spoke. Maybe he felt my frustration. Delusional or not, he was definitely speaking his reality and, despite my animosity for it, the deep profundity of that notion tugged on every heart string I had.

I remembered, for a moment, what it felt like to know Truth, a Truth, the Truth. It didn't matter, because I knew it with all my flesh. And belief, once upon a time was, indeed, irrelevant.

I flashed him a half-assed smile and laid my head against the door once more.

I woke to the heavy rocking of the car a few hours later. Just as I sat up, Ramón turned off the main road and down another on an extreme incline. I wondered if this tiny little car could take it, but he didn't look worried.

As we turned onto the winding road, I saw a faint glow in the distance, hanging in the air a ways from the car. It seemed to continue growing further and further away, until we finally drove right up to it. Perhaps an illusion. How it stayed visible among the turns of the road, I had no idea.

It was a lantern, home to a flaming lump of wax, at a fork in the road, covered by moss and barely visible under the thick trees. Dumbfounded, I stared deeper into the darkness, trying to make out the structure that upheld it. Ramón took the left before I made any headway and kept driving up a hill on an even more narrow one-lane path. It was rocky and the clanky metal frame holding us bobbled as we drove for another long while into the middle of what felt like nowhere.

Fear gripped my shoulders and the crackle in my chest kindled once more. It took all of my sanity to keep my mind from wandering to all the worst places.

The little Volkswagen chugged up the hill and then down and then up, and then slowed under another flaming light, which danced over two large arched wooden gates covered with vines and moss, so hidden by trees that I never would have found them on my own. They took their time opening and as we drove through, those little golden specs returned, bouncing excitedly along the arch and down the aged wood into the bushes.

"Uh Ramón, do you... do you see those little golden things?"

"Oh, don't mind them. They're just happy you're finally here."

I frowned at his joke in the face of my impending frustration.

We rounded a couple more corners and drove right up to an archway, constructed of two thick intertwined trees whose separate trunks had grown into one another. They twisted so tightly, I swore they were one. Their roots seemed to merge into the trunk about ten feet above the ground.

Our headlights shone on the trees, causing lizard-like creatures to quickly scatter for covering—too quickly for me to make them out. The pace of the air quickened around me when, without warning, a white light flashed in the thick forest and illuminated the braided duo at least a hundred feet into the sky. They were even more massive than I could see against the blackness. My body slammed into the seat behind me with shock, but I couldn't pull my eyes away as the light pulsed and fizzled in the shadow of the wrinkled branches. Fireworks of gold flew through the atmosphere in a wild frenzy.

Just as we pulled under the arch, a roar rose from the earth and shook the car. The resounding vibration from the thunder rattled our bundle of metal and glass so violently, I grabbed the door and seat with both hands.

Suddenly, nausea filled my rib cage and my vision warped with confusion. Everything grew blurry, and I couldn't even find my voice. I tried to focus on the swirling headrest in front of me, the rearview mirror, Ramón's head, anything.

Woozy and dizzy, my eyes fell to the floor and I caught a glimpse of my tense little fingers latched onto the white leather for dear life.

Wait. Are those my fingers?

My hands, my legs... they'd never looked so detached... disconnected. The lines which once defined the boundary between my skin and the atoms beyond it twisted into a galaxy of textured oil paint.

Just then, the car came to a sharp halt and my door opened with ease.

"

Losing an illusion makes you wiser
than finding the truth.

LUDWIG BORNE

Two

Everything finally still, I looked up to see Ramón's smile coming into focus. He reached his hand out to me.

"Bienvenida à La Présencia, Miss Scarlett." The sultry in his voice accentuated his chivalry, but I was much too preoccupied with my confusion to do more than notice.

I gulped and placed my flaccid hand into his for comfort. His was still hot, but soft. And when I looked at it, I saw mine in it—in full form again. He practically pulled my limp, disoriented body from the car and steadied it down a broken stone path illuminated by those wonderous, animated golden fliers. As he guided me through the yard to a tiny makeshift wooden desk under a dimly lit white canopy, exhaustion took my knees out.

"Oh, cuidado. Cuidado. I got you. I got you." Ramón's arms swooped beneath mine and cradled my rib cage. He steadied me in a basket-like chair and paused to make eye contact. "Just one moment, Miss Scarlett. Someone will be here to greet you shortly." Then, he disappeared before I could turn to ask what the hell was going on.

I was a second away from the crackle in my chest exploding when I noticed the silence. Everything was so… still. Despite the darkness, there was an ominous sense of calm all around me, enveloping me. The air was even warmer here than in the city, stickier too, but a light breeze swept around me and through my hair.

"Vita…"

I turned quickly at the sound of my name but didn't see where the faint, almost genderless voice had come from.

I'm losing it.

I slammed my eyes shut and tried to shake myself awake.

I must be drowsy still. From the nap, yes, that's it.

When I opened my eyes and looked around, I couldn't help but question my reality. I was in the middle of what was surely nowhere, hidden by enormous trees with leaves as large as umbrellas and roots trailing with embers. Not to mention, there was no one around.

Where on earth is Gelena!

I was beginning to question the woman's actual existence. Had I completely imagined her? I couldn't have. Ramón knew her.

Although this place felt deserted, I didn't quite feel danger. In fact, the ground around me seemed to vibrate with a certain, indescribable energy, one that reminded me of… what home used to feel like.

Certainly not the home I came from. Los Angeles was an entirely different jungle, concrete and covered in lights, lined with salty beaches. The only green there was the small portion landscapers were asked to groom along Pasadena's streets or Santa Monica's.

I sat there sort of aimlessly, questioning the distant familiarity of the moment: the vigor of the plants around me, the withered purple flowers sprinkled at my feet, and the mud puddled and rippling with the light rainfall, somehow melting on my skin but not soaking me.

Slowly, and perhaps with a bit of delusion, I stuck my tongue out to taste it dripping off the edge of the canopy.

"Miss Scarlett, welcome. Let me get you set up with your bungalow." I jumped and spun around to see Ramón behind the wooden counter, this time dressed in a uniform with a baseball cap that read *La Presencia.*

"It's okay. You can taste the rain if you'd like!" he snickered. "No judgment."

"You are the guest concierge, too?"

He smiled and tilted his head down. "I am many things here." Turning from the thick, tattered, and surely ancient book in front of him, he grabbed a key from those hanging below the desk. "You are in bungalow number four. I just need you to sign here and then I'll show you the way."

Four.

Of course I was. I felt the ache return to my center and I cradled it with my hand. It was his favorite number.

Too tired to read the form in front of me, I signed quickly. At this point, I didn't care.

Once more reaching for the handle on my suitcase, the handsome man led me down the broken stone path that laid beneath the arch of many more trees. I lifted my head to find that the dim warm light saturating the ground was the glow of small balls of fire burning at least ten feet above my head. They hung like little exploding stars between the overhanging trees and illuminated their colorful fruit.

I was captivated and tried desperately to understand, until I realized I'd fallen behind and picked up my pace.

I can't lose him.

We approached a large brown teepee-looking structure.

"Here you are. Bungalow number four. The bathrooms are right around that corner. Should you need anything else, you know where the front desk is. I will be there all night."

I had so many questions.

"You'll be there all night…" was apparently all I could muster. "You don't go home?"

He looked around and back at me. "This is my home." He offered me a sweet smile as he turned away. "Descansa, Miss Scarlett."

My name had never sounded so… *Stop, Scar.*

"Oh, Ramón?" I caught him with my failed attempt at a whisper before he walked away.

"Yes, Miss Scarlett?"

Mio dio, Is there any getting used to that?

"What time do I need to be up tomorrow?"

"You'll know." He winked and turned once more.

I crooked my neck in confusion. "Oh uh, Ramón?"

He turned again and lifted his chin.

"Is there any sort of bath here or pool?"

He pulled a map from his back pocket and pointed to a secluded area in the corner of the village. In the fading light, a faint illustration of some rocks rippled across the page, but that was it. The rest was empty.

"It's no Jacuzzi, but it does have a great view."

It was far and I was airplane-and-long-windy-road worn, but some bubbling water sounded perfect for my achy bones right now. I thanked him, resisting the temptation to invite him to join me.

"Ramón!" I gulped. "Gracias por todo."

"Pura vida, Miss Scarlett." He winked as he disappeared into the night.

I unfastened the lock and zipped the small tent-like structure open from bottom to top. I was surprised to see enough space for a table and two chairs, two clothes hangers, and two twin-beds—one of which was already occupied.

Long blonde hair fell over the pillow, and I wondered what it would be like to meet my roommate in the morning.

Not taking any more time to observe the bungalow in the faint light, I quietly changed into my black one-piece bathing suit and a sweater, grabbed the towel at the foot of the bed, and headed in the direction Ramón had pointed me. I had to pass the front desk to get there and noticed he was nowhere to be found.

The path was carved around tree roots bubbled with little neon upside-down plungers. The tiny mushrooms lined every crevice of the trunks and lit the way in the darkness. Stones were scattered atop the rooted steps and between them, forming a perfect jungle staircase. After a few wrong turns at the intersecting walkways, I looked down to see the map's path, still faint on this wrinkled paper, leading off to the side into the dirt.

That couldn't be right.

I stepped forward and my toes sank into something warm. Whipping the map aside, I lifted my feet to see the very brown, very wet mud I'd plunged into.

Cazzo.

I almost turned back, but just then, a familiar gust of air encircled me and disappeared the other way. I pushed the leaves back and forth to make a way through. Sighing and sticking my other foot forward and deeper, and then the other, my weight squished very loudly into the mud as I followed the map and wondered which critters' homes I was invading.

Crickets and cicadas filled the air with a harmonious symphony, the loudest I'd ever heard. Frustrated and weary of bugs, I fought against the vines and the roots clearly determined to trip me as I sunk deeper. Suddenly afraid I'd get lost in the dark, I looked back and found no signs or lights anywhere.

How the hell am I supposed to find the... Oh.

I looked up as the mud thinned out to a watery texture. Cradled on the edges by large stones, miniature boulders really, a cloud of steam swirled over the water in the moonlight. Hesitantly, I inched forward with fear of something slimy slithering past me. I continued and, despite expecting to sit in some mud, found the water to be clear enough to show me the tortured expression of my own face reflected across the ripples.

I set my dry towel down on one of the large stones and sank into the nearly scalding water bubbling from the spring. Tilting my head back in relaxation, I opened my eyes to perhaps the most beautiful view I'd ever seen—a practically architectured circular carving in the trees where my old, nocturnal friend hung full and golden in all her glory.

"Well, Ciao, Luna."

The night was crisp and dark around me, very dark, as I laid my head back and eased into the frequency radiating from the earth around me.

"Do you mind if I join you?" A very strong voice surprised me from the dark. I jumped and looked up to see an older gentleman standing directly in front of me.

"I'm so sorry. I didn't mean to startle you," his voice softened. As I settled my core, I met his big wide eyes and immediately felt relieved. Something about his shoulders and the silver locks falling down the sides of his face disarmed me.

"Oh no, no, of course not. Please, have a seat."

"Thanks." He smiled and then hung his robe on the rock. The brown of his skin glistened in the moonlight. I managed to turn my stare to the landscape as he sank into the hot water.

"My name is Scar," I offered.

"Ah, well, that is a fascinating name. Pleasure to meet you, Scarlett. How are you?" My eyebrow twitched at his sure assumption. The indigo in his eyes glowed as he entered the moonlight. They were captivating, dripping of... royalty, a birthright. Instantly, a vibration foreign to me washed over my head. I dropped my chin and fought the odd urge to bow to him as he melted into the rocks as though he was one with them.

"I'm good, thanks. How are you?"

"Really? You are good in this moment?" His Rican accent was thick, but his words crisp.

His rephrase made me think twice. "Uhm, tired. Long flight, you know. Currently trying to get the airport smell off me." Chuckling, I tried to buffer the discomfort of his pointed question.

His eyes remained fixed on mine and, if it weren't for the sincerity in his relaxed smile, I might have felt uneasy. "Good. That is good to hear. Tired and airport-smelly isn't half bad." He stopped speaking to look around, taking obvious deep breaths as if to greet the nature encapsulating us. "So, what do you do in Los Angeles, Traveler?"

"Oh, well, uhm, a few things. I'm a..."

Did I mention where I was from?

"I'm a full-time student right now, an author, and a business owner. I also…"

His chuckle interrupted my scripted introduction.

"Mmm, my apologies, I didn't ask you *who you are*," he started, tilting his head and smiling. "I asked what you *do*." Had his intention not felt genuine, I might've thought he was mocking me.

"Oh, well, a few things. I study full-time, although right now, I'm in a gap year before I transfer to a university. My parents are… uhm," I choked on my tenses.

Come on, Scar.

"They're first-generation immigrants, so… very excited to see me going to college," I redirected.

His smiling pause let on that he was waiting for more.

"And I run a small business to support entrepreneurs and authors. I left work and had to figure something out that I could do remotely so…"

"And, you're a writer yourself?"

"Ah, yes, but not professionally. Poetry for the most part, but I have a novel on my mind."

"Well, publishing a book is no easy feat, Traveler. That isn't professional to you?"

"Mmm, I'm not sure. Poetry is different."

"How so?"

I looked around the night while I searched for the words, "It has sort of… always been there for me, if that makes sense. The words find me when they want to and I either pick up my pen or I don't. It's a gift when it comes, not quite something I can claim as my own."

"Ah, I see. So, who is the owner?"

"Well," I snickered, "I'll let you know when I find out where the words come from."

We belly-laughed in unison.

"And your family?"

"Big Italian family. My mother's side is mostly Russian. We are all pretty close…"

"You're a busy young woman."

"Yes, I do like to keep busy."

"Well, you won't find busy here." It was hard to see in the dark, but I'm positive his grin reached from ear to ear.

I returned his humor with a chuckle. "That sounds like… medicine."

"You know, I've found… in all these years…" He sighed as he sank deeper. "The best place to be is just… here… and the best time is… now."

It sounded like an original Socrates fortune cookie, and I barely managed to pull my lips back into a smile despite the complexity rising within, which seemed to be bubbling faster than the hot spring we sat in.

"So, now, who *are* you?"

Confusion tilted my head and furrowed my brows. I'd just said more than I ever do to strangers.

"I'm sorry? I'm not sure I understand," I stuttered.

"Well, you just told me of the beautiful parts of your life—the things you do. But, who are *you*?"

Stunned, I watched the question swirl in his indigo eyes as I disappeared, feeling the tension in the strings tying me to each of those things tighten with friction.

He held my eyes for a long moment. "Well, I think I am just about toasted. Probably best to get some rest. Thank you for the wonderful company, Traveler."

"Oh, of course. I should probably get going, too." I pulled myself up and out and reached for my towel. "You know, I'm so sorry. I didn't get your…" I turned but he'd already vanished. "…name."

I shook my head. The first person I'd met in this village and they disappeared.

I hurried back through the dark and broken, critter-filled mud trench mapped out for me, following the stunning golden creatures that wound up around every tree trunk as I passed, following me... ushering me... welcoming me...

Calm down, Scar. They're not alive.

"

A knowledge of the path cannot be substituted
for putting one foot in front of the other.

M. C. RICHARDS

Three

"Coo Coo! Coo Coo!"

I jumped from my pillow.

"Coo Coo! Coo Coo!"

Disoriented by the hurricane of red-lored parrots circling our bungalow, I rubbed my eyes in the pitch black tent until I remembered where I was. When I pulled the tarp to open the little window next to my cot, the light blinded me. I closed it shut and decided I'd rather suffer the light of my phone.

Cazzo!

It was 6:15 a.m. I jumped out of bed, pulled my jeans over my cold legs and a sweater over my head, and was frantically searching for socks when the door zipped open.

"Hey, Roomie!" A tall, slender woman with sparkly gray eyes that shined like my mamma's strolled in. Peaceful as ever, with two coconuts in hand, she sat yogi style on her bed, hair tethered in a towel.

"Um, hi, how are you?" I cracked in my half-asleep rasp.

"Oh, I'm good. How'd you sleep? I slept surprisingly well for a first night in the jungle. Here you go!" She handed me one of the coconuts. "Where are you rushing to?"

"Oh, thank you! Uhm, that's a good question." I realized I didn't actually know. "I just uhm, I thought it was late and to be honest, I don't really know what I'm doing here. Or... what here is for that matter." I breathed a sigh of confusion as I checked my phone, realizing I probably sounded like a lost moron.

There was no service, of course, and the time was incorrect anyway. Now, it read 6:12 a.m. I held down the power button.

"Oh, you're brave. I can't bring myself to do it. I don't even have kids." We laughed. "I'm Jenna, by the way!" The twang in her voice clued me in to a southern origin.

She picked up on my confusion as I shook her hand.

"Oh, you really don't know where you are. This is _La Presencia._" She said it so matter-of-factly that it almost seemed I should know exactly what that meant. "People travel from all over in hopes of finding this place, but very few ever find it. I had to do a ridiculous amount of research and, even then, I couldn't. Wasn't until some strange man at the library slipped me a one-way ticket. Apparently, this is an invitation only thing."

Huh.

"Fancy that. I was also slipped a one-way ticket." I paused, wondering if she might have some answers. "I'm Scar. Nice to meet you. So, this place is famous?" I climbed on my bed to face her. Attempting to match her expert yogi pose, my tense joints quickly aborted, and I sat sideways on my knees instead.

"Um, not quite. More like… top secret. Think, forbidden."

"Oh wow, that makes sense why it was so quiet here last night. I didn't get in bed until around, well… I'm not sure, but it was late. Hope I didn't miss anything important. I don't really know what to expect here."

"Oh no, you didn't, Girl. Don't worry. It's very relaxed here. A group of us got in yesterday. Some folks'll be headin' out soon." I found it fascinating that in only a few minutes of conversation, her enthused verbiage ranged from that of a teen to a middle-aged woman. It was disorienting at first, until I realized just how disarmed I felt. "We mostly just introduced ourselves and then got settled. This place is sooo relaxing."

"Yeah, I've never been surrounded by so much lush green in my whole life. Hey, do you by chance know a woman named Gelena?"

She chuckled and bit her lip, "Hm. Nope! Don't believe so. I ain't ever seen this much green in my dreams, and I'm from

Tennessee." Suddenly, the woman before me made more sense. "Where are you from?"

"Los Angeles, actually."

Her big blue eyes stretched with excitement. "Oh, wow. I've always wanted to go there."

"Trust me, this is much more beautiful. Well, except for the sunsets. Can't really beat California sunsets."

How he loved those sunsets. "Find me on the golf course with the sunset, Kid. That's where I'll be."

I grabbed for the ring at my neck and winced at the memory, quickly shoving it to the back of my mind.

"I can only imagine, and pictures never do anythin' justice." This woman had a particular pep in her voice that I couldn't quite put my finger on. An eagerness, a joy, I marveled at while I searched for a similar memory. "So, what brought you here?"

I shared with her my story, skimming over the unnecessary details, which ended up being pretty much all of them. "Oh, had a hard year and my sister gave me his book and it led me to this woman who told me I needed to come here... yeah, it was all very strange. But I'm happy I'm here. And, you?" Distant from my body, I heard my totally discombobulated answer and I cringed. I was not here to dive into my sob story. This would be the story everyone would hear.

"What book was it?" When I told her it was Dan Millman's, her eyes lit up. Jenna went on to tell me how she had found one of his other books and stalked him on social media, because she was so obsessed with his work. She marveled at his martial arts and coaching journey, going on and on about him.

Wow, this girl can talk.

I managed to persuade her in the direction of the bathrooms as she talked so we could get ready and find our way.

It was refreshing—tiresome, but refreshing. I had been locked in my home, away from outsiders, for quite some time now. Luckily, she just about carried the conversation on her own.

She pulled a map from her pocket and unfolded it. When I gazed over her shoulder, I saw only the words La Transparencia and the path to it suddenly sketched out right before us. "Did you see that!?"

"Uh, you mean how the sketch just magically appeared on the paper? What the heck?" Her eyes lit with curiosity.

That word again. Well, it couldn't be the same map I'd had last night.

A map with only one place on it?

We looked at one another a bit baffled but agreed to shake off the superstition together.

"We must be seeing things," I offered.

"Yup!"

Of course, the hall was on the other side of the village. We hustled past a pretty little pond I seemed to have overlooked in the dark the night before. The sunlight tunneled on it and followed me as I walked past. It reminded me of those curious little lights I'd seen hanging last night. We were on the same path, but I couldn't make out any wires in the trees around or above me.

A low-pitched growl interrupted Jenna in mid-sentence and we slowed but didn't sense any immediate danger. The hum rolled through the jungle and elicited others like it for a good long time.

"I think those are the howler monkeys I read about!"

"Those are monkeys!?" I couldn't believe it. Our eyes were wide as we searched the trees for the origin of the strange call, to no avail.

As Jenna told me about her trip, my gaze was totally enraptured by the vibrancy in the gardens around us, coloring the opening and rounding some of the huts behind her. There were bushels of rambutans, red and orange with their porcupine-like skins hanging from the trees. Dragon fruit and guava plants colored the garden with gradients of pink and green. Draping overhead were the large brown and hairy coconuts from their mother palms and plantain trees. The rush of color alone made me salivate. Strange, considering the rather serious lack of appetite for months now.

A few feet from the hut, across from the front desk canopy, the sunlight bounced off a subtle gray moving in the garden. Looking closer, I saw silver hair and dark skin. An older man sat on his knees in the dirt, tending to the plants. I strained to see if it was the gentleman from the hot spring, but this man was younger, with darker eyes and a much less welcoming expression. He stilled as we walked by and then glanced our way with an all-too-steady stare, piercing straight through me. His body remained relaxed, but his eyes held a very particular intensity that made it hard for me to look away.

We quickened our pace through the front canopy and past the makeshift wooden desk where Ramón was smiling patiently. I tried not to make too much eye contact, but it was difficult when his big brown morning eyes clearly settled on mine. The joy in his eyes could give the sun a run for her money.

"Buenos días," I offered shyly, barely lifting my chin.

"Buenos días, Miss Scarlett. Would you like some coffee?"

I hesitated. "Uhm sure." I shyly glanced at Jenna, feeling her eyes on me and, frankly, feeling a little awkward that he had only offered it to me.

"Black with honey, right?" He smiled, nodding toward the cup filled to the brim in front of him.

My head tilted of its own whim. "Uhm, yes please."

"Here you go." He slid the cup to me. "Enjoy your orientation."

"Thank you," I replied, confused but grateful for the warm cup to offset the crisp morning.

Orientation… I wondered silently as Jenna and I started in the direction he'd nodded.

"Isn't he sweet?" Jenna sighed. "He had some ready for me this morning, too."

That made more sense and put me at ease, although I didn't remember putting my coffee preference down on the form I signed the night before.

"So, your full name is Scarlett? That's so beautiful!"

That either.

I whispered a quick *thank you* as we scuttled toward a building, just barely visible, tucked halfway underground.

"Well, this is the only building the map is showing here. I guess we should have asked him."

We continued under a small wooden peak wedged between a few trees and into the back of the building with *La Transparencia* carved in its wooden beams. Grabbing a mat at the door, we joined the group of about a dozen other people seated on the floor. In front sat a row of tranquil faces, all dressed in beige garments and facing the group with welcoming expressions.

Surprisingly, we weren't late. Once seated, I realized the building was structured on all four sides with floor-to-ceiling glass, topped with a log-like roof. Every window was wrapped on the outside with hibiscus flowers larger than any I'd ever seen. They were at least three times the size of my head in full bloom. Bursts of every color—violet and blue, red, and fuchsia pink. The flowers climbed all over the glass and looked as if...

No...

They were, in fact, penetrating the glass, some of them actually inside the room. The glass was so transparent, I could hardly tell where the inside ended and the outside began.

While the group remained silent, I scanned the room, searching for what could be the back of the head that held those royal indigo gems from the hot spring.

The silence began creeping up my spine, and I wondered what we were waiting for as I took my first sip of the hot drink and nearly spilled it all over myself. I pulled the cup back from my lips. Creamy and robust and beyond anything I'd tasted before. I shifted uncomfortably in my second failed attempt at a yogi position that morning.

"Good morning, everyone!" Startled, I managed to hit my tooth with the coffee mug as a young voice broke the stillness and began her introduction.

"My name is Gitana. Most of you have already met my brother, Ramón. I am the experience coordinator here. I hope all of your travels and transitions went smoothly and you are settling in nicely here at *La Presencia*. I am thrilled to finally see all your faces and I know the villagers here are as well. I'm going to hand off the introductions to the Awapa, but I just want to say that I really encourage you all to take advantage of the opportunity to work with these shamans. They are each so gifted. Trust them. They are truly in touch with their innate abilities."

One by one, each Awa introduced themselves and their specific therapeutic modality. One was a fire-cupping therapist, another a water therapist, another an acupuncturist. A reiki healer, an ayahuasca guide, and so on. I was fascinated by their unique descriptions of their work, but I hadn't planned on doing anything crazy here.

Shoot, I hadn't even planned on *here*.

They continued down the line, and I was only half-listening until the massage therapist began speaking. Her hair was pulled to one side around her bare, plump cheekbones, draped over her chest and around her wide hips. Her tone sultry and steady, I couldn't pull my eyes away.

The woman next in line tugged my attention further. Her voice was soft and raspy, and oozing with familiarity, like I'd known it so intimately in another life. This fair woman, with transparent eyes and caramel hair, introduced herself as Rebecca. She explained her role as the lead shaman and, although it was difficult to make out her every word, something in her melted me. My throat tightened at the swelling in my eyes. When she wrapped up her introduction, I gulped my emotion down with another mouthful of coffee.

Following the introductions, Gitana went on to summarize the basic structure for our time together and briefed us on the location of the different halls. Every day would begin with a morning meditation here in *La Transparencia,* followed by breakfast together at the tables in *El Placer.*

We would then have some free time to ourselves for the pool, sessions with Awapa, or exploration in the jungle. We would have an afternoon excursion that would last several hours and then an evening workshop and meditation at *La Encarnada* before dinner. The activities were designed to end fairly early each night to allow time for debrief from the day. I wasn't sure exactly what we would need so much debrief time for. After all she'd just shared, it seemed these days were designed for rest and recovery.

I mean, we are in Costa Rica.

She thanked everyone for their presence once again and dismissed us to an early breakfast. Everyone stood and began rolling their mats, introducing themselves to one another, and swarming to *El Placer.* I've never been one for crowds and figured I'd wait this one out... that is, until I started to get stepped on. It was a practice of patience until my coffee was kicked over.

I hustled my way through the swarm of yogi bees to the door and, as I lifted my gaze from the ground, I noticed the caramel hair draped over the beige garment in front of me.

"Rebecca!" Her name shot out of my mouth before I could think twice, and her quick turn and raised eyebrows reflected the panic in my tone.

Dio Santo. I'd practically screamed at her.

"Yes?" she asked with a surprised, inquiring smile.

We both stopped to face each other.

Stuttering, I shot my hand out. "My name is Scar."

She received it and a look of concern washed over her face as her eyes fell and the entirety of her being sank. She furrowed her brow and wiped something off it.

"Hi, Scar." Her smile faded to a solemn distress and I wasn't sure if I'd done something wrong.

You know, other than directly yelling to get her attention.

"I'd introduce myself but you... clearly know my name. I..."

I tightened my lips and put my chin down. "I was... touched during your intro. What days are best to schedule with you?"

"For you, any time will be perfect. You can sign up in the front canopy."

"Ah, okay, perfect. Thank you."

She relaxed her expression as she looked at my hand once more. Giving it a quick squeeze, she managed a smile with a tilt of her head.

"¡Pura vida!" she said as she sent me on my way.

Perhaps she was confused at the insignificance of my question after I'd literally shouted at her. I couldn't say what came over me.

I scratched my head and exited *La Transparencia*. I grabbed the map Ramón had given me, only to see a different sketch of a building off to the right and a set of words trickled across the corner: *El Placer.* I sighed, wondering how I would remember how to get around this entire village.

Okay, Magic Map. Take me where I need to go.

I took my time, admiring the layers of green that constructed the new world around me. I couldn't see but glimpses of the sky through the trees, and I quickly realized how true my words to Jenna were. I'd really never seen this much natural lush in my entire life.

Life. There was life everywhere and it reflected off the dewy crystals which, as the sun peeked through, awakened an array of colors that bounced through the air. I turned as I followed the painted mist in a full 360 around me. I was walking through a rainbow, and couldn't fight a creeping smile as I delighted in its profundity in the midst of my pitiful presence.

A weightlessness swept through my being.

My stomach rumbled and I cradled it, racking my brain for the last time I heard it ask me for food.

I approached the building, this one raised from the ground but still cradled on every edge by trees. I struggled to swing open one of the massive brown doors that towered over me, entered a room full of people, grabbed a plate on the table to my left, and joined the line that filed around the back.

Mango. Pineapple. Bananas. Rambutans. Handmade almond butter. And sweet jam. Scrambled eggs. Green juice and coconuts.

My mouth salivated with such fury, I actually reached to check for drool on my chin. The ache in my tummy was roaring now, and I grabbed my stomach to shush it. Having filled my plate with much more than I knew my tiny self could handle, I looked up just in time to see her.

"¿Quieres beber algo?" A petite dark-haired woman had rounded the corner. The happy lines around her eyes indicated she was around her late forties, but her energy shined like that of a blossoming twenty-five-year-old. Her name tag rested below her left shoulder.

How fitting.

"Uh si, prefiero un coco si tienes, por favor, Sol."

Her eyebrows raised with surprise at my response, as she nodded a smile and turned to walk back to the kitchen. The door swung back and forth and, like stiffened wind, music whistled lightly through. My knees tingled at the sound and my eyes were transfixed on the faint glow that seeped through the cracks around the door and flashed brighter as it swung.

I turned back to the food and continued filling my plate until I heard it again. Those instruments. My ear couldn't identify them. Despite Papà playing his cello, following supper each night, the only music I'd paid much attention to was in the studio.

"Aquí tienes, Señorita." Sol appeared in front of me with a coconut in her palm.

"Muchas gracias, Sol." She nodded her head, but I tried to stop her before she turned. "¿Oh ,Sol, hablas inglés?"

"No, lo siento."

I gulped. "Oh, okay, una pregunta. ¿Qué música es?"

She straightened her posture and her eyebrows bounced again. "¿La salsa?"

I shook my head. "Um, no. No quiero salsa. ¿La música, qué es?"

She chuckled into her hands. "Esta es Salsa, Señorita."

After questioning whether my Spanish was off or not, a memory of a brief Latin music class at my dance academy fluttered to the forefront. I managed a confused smile, thanked her, and went to find an open table as I combed through the old genres I hadn't heard since I was young.

I settled at one in the corner of the empty patio outside, nestled in the elephant-ear-like leaves of the overhanging trees. I marveled at the architecture of these buildings, either built around nature or by it.

Stillness paused me and I let my eyelids fall as a familiar peace washed over me. Ramón's story unfolded behind my eyelids until a splatter toppled my nose. Then, my hand. I opened and watched the rain begin its descent. No wonder everyone was packed inside. Despite the late morning and sunny, clear skies, my body didn't twitch one bit at the water landing on me. It did occur to me the judgment behind the windows should anyone have seen my hardlined lips soften as I quickly wilted with water.

This time, it got me wet. I couldn't help but chuckle at its apparent playfulness. An old church song rang through my memory about letting rain wash away the pain of yesterday.

My tummy full, I strode back through the sprinkles to the front canopy where I found a paper sitting on the desk, waiting just for me. Strangely, no time slots. I just signed my name on one of the lines next to Rebecca's.

The same excitement that coursed through my hands when I cashed Gelena's one-way ticket in for this trip pulsed its way back to my fingertips.

Perhaps that is how I know what a right move feels like.

I pondered the paralysis I'd felt for the past few years in the face of making decisions and fearing the outcomes I might be responsible for.

"How was your coffee this morning?"

I jumped. "You people literally appear like magicians around here."

He smiled back at me.

"Um the coffee... Oh, that was delicious actually. How did you make that?"

"Just as you like it... black with honey."

"But that was... creamy and rich, and it tasted like so much more."

That one stood a contest against Mamma's espresso, and that was saying something.

Another sweet smile before he pulled another mug from behind the counter and slid it over to me. "I heard your last one spilled over this morning."

"Oh... I..."

When the desk's satellite phone rang, he held a finger up and reached for it. "Perdóname, Miss Scarlett."

I hesitantly reached for the mug, and mouthed a *thank you* to him, winning another sweet smile. I shook my head at this oddly sweet man, who somehow knew so much more about me than I'd divulged.

Following the stone path, I came upon the pond once more and paused to soak in the light dancing over it, tickling my insides as I watched the show. Bubbles rippled in the water as a long, curved nose surfaced, followed by a six-foot reptilian body. I jumped back but the crocodile disappeared beneath the muddy water as quickly as he'd surfaced. I gulped and looked around, wondering if I'd imagined the sneaky creature.

A few out-of-place stones scattered to the left of the pond were puzzled around more tree roots, and I pushed through a canopy of vines, dodging the hanging webs with their giant yellow-legged and black-backed, football-sized monsters.

Eventually, I came upon a small round pool, clearly constructed by nature with more stone than the hot spring from last night. An elegantly-arched and light-blue tiled gazebo towered over it with two rocking chairs on the far side.

La Conexión.

My fingertips traced the words carved into the wooden side of the white pillar before I wandered through the gazebo and admired the native, mission-like structure and neared what appeared to be hand-woven chairs. Just beyond the chairs, the edge of the cliff.

A violet haze hovered over the chasm and through the crystallized sprinkles that buzzed in the morning air. Light emulated from the clouds, suddenly eye-level with me now, as I realized how high up the mountain we were.

This was the first spot on these grounds I'd been able to see beyond the trees, anything beyond the thick of this jungle.

I gasped as I stretched my neck to see an entire city past the mountains and the jungle that barricaded this cliff. Squinting harder, I could even make out the ocean line in the far distance.

Not as far from civilization as I'd imagined.

I inched a bit closer to the edge in an effort to calculate just how high I was, surmising it was at least a thousand feet. My eyes scanned everything and, after making their way downward to the loose rubble at my toes, a crackle kindled behind my rib cage again. Teetering on the edge, with nothing below me but a sea of trees and their critters, I turned to see the pillar of the gazebo a few feet away.

I backed up to it, dropped my head against it, and slid to the ground. Although I chose a limited view, I could still see the clouds, and my fingers were content to play in the dirt beside me.

A spark lit in my chest as I marveled at the scenery. I pulled my journal from my bag and sighed as words spilled aimlessly from my fingertips.

I watched it fall.

I felt the solidarity slip

like sand through my fingers.

Before my eyes,

the matrix crumbled to granules

that stuck to my skin

like stars on a map,

that led me nowhere,

but everywhere,

with no destination,

but onward, and through,

and into

the Unknown.

"

The important thing is this:
To be ready at any moment to
sacrifice what you are
for what you could become.

CHARLES DUBOIS

Four

After staring at the rocking chairs for far too long, I pulled one of them back about a foot, grabbing for some comfort. It must have been at least a century old, rickety and splintering. The whole thing creaked as I struggled to settle my body into it, totally distrusting it to catch me.

"Worry is a funny thing, isn't it?" I turned at the sound of the soft familiar voice resounding in the gazebo. "It's almost impossible to feel present when we're always thinking in the future."

I actually wasn't sure if I'd heard it or felt it. I tried not to swivel too fast in my chair, so as not to collapse it.

"Hi! How are you? Wow, you caught me off-guard. It's so… quiet here."

"Might I join you?" he asked with an eager gentleness.

"Of course, please." I extended my hand to the second chair.

He smiled kindly, walked over to it and, grabbing the two arms with firm trust, rocked back into it with more grace than a dainty aerialist could have managed. No hesitation. No fear. No moans. Didn't even pull it back from the edge of death as he answered me, "I am doing well. How has your first morning here treated you? Aren't you glad you came in the rainy season?"

"It's treating me well. This land is really… something else." I relaxed at the ease of this foreigner's presence, despite his odd questions. I wouldn't guess rainy season would be more appealing than its alternative for most. "You know, I didn't get your name last night."

He turned to face me, eyes an even deeper indigo in the sunlight. "Hmm…" A brief pause later, he offered, "You can call me Sibú."

I frowned as he seemed to actually think about which name to use with me. "Oh, I… I can? Is that your real name?"

"Real enough," he said, dashing a wink my way.

My cheeks stretched an awkward acknowledgment at his mystery. Had he thrown on some white hair and a mechanic's suit, I might've mistaken him for Dan Millman's enigmatic service station mentor. "Well, it is a pleasure, Sibú."

Eyes closed, he took several deep breaths in and out. Naturally, I followed. Something about this gentleman's demeanor soothed the air around him.

"Isn't the light remarkable?" he asked quietly.

I opened my eyes to see his wandering over the cliff below us, noticing the goosebumps that flickered down his wrinkled brown skin.

"Everything it touches, it awakens."

I followed his gaze from the clouds to the mountains and the wildlife around us as the shadows under the mist lifted. The sprinkling lightened and the sun made its way into the gazebo, greeting my toes and legs, then slowly, moving over and up my body as if on cue.

"Do you ever feel awake, Traveler?" He shifted in his chair to face me.

I lifted my chin. Pupils stung by the light, I took a deep breath to gather my thoughts. "Awake? Like alive?"

"Sure." The white of his teeth twinkled in response.

"Mmm." I squinted and watched my memory fill with an old green, a much lighter shade than Costa Rica's. "Sure. I remember feeling awake once."

"Tell me about it," he coaxed.

Fighting the rising fear, I took some time to sink into the memory.

"Growing up, my parents could never afford summer camp. So, my papà would… take me on the golf course every day that he worked. I was a pretty quiet kid, so he could do that. All I needed were my books."

I cracked open one eye and shot a glance his way.

"It's one of… Well, it's my only memory, really, that I can recall with such vivid detail. Perhaps, the last time I'd been around this much nature. We'd leave early every morning and be out there all day. He'd wrap me up in his windbreakers: hat, jackets, pants, the whole shebang. He'd set me up with a box of french fries and a cup of Sprite." I giggled. "Mmm. I remember everything. The crisp morning air. The dew. The freshly cut grass. The scratch of the wind on my jacket. The tiny things he would do to make me laugh."

When my voice cracked, I paused to fill my lungs.

Sibú synchronized his breath with mine and gave me time to catch up. "You know, there are times we watch parts of ourselves die. We're forced to surrender to it, accept it, because we have no other choice. And we resist. Of course, we resist. It hurts like hell."

I waited without words, blinking the tears back at this stranger's choice of chit-chat.

"What do you think follows death, Traveler?"

I shook my head, ignoring my rising irritation.

"Can I ask you something, that might be just a bit forward?" he tried again.

Lips hardened to a line, I nodded.

"What if… we stopped resisting and just kept watching? This cycle, these seasons… this thing we call existence. Imagine… what could we see come to life if we stopped resisting? Imagine what we could… remember."

I found myself in pause, letting his words sink past my annoyance. I didn't want to talk about any of this.

When I finally opened my eyes, all that surrounded me were rainbows, multiples of the one I'd walked through earlier. Now filling the entire sky, they sparkled in the vast light.

I'm not sure where Sibú had gone, or when exactly he had left, or just how long my eyes were shut, but I assumed he'd left me to savor my memory—to ponder his words.

My interactions with this man were starting to feel imaginary.

I sat there, sun-soaked in silence and let the warmth nourish my skin. Cracking my right eye open, I stared into its intensity.

Where have you been?

Slowly, and partially without realizing it, I started imitating those slow deep breaths I'd watched Sibú take. The quiet around me was unnerving and, somehow, peaceful.

Inhale. Exhale. Inhale. Exhale. For a moment, I let the stillness in.

A quick moment.

It was all I had before a quake rose from my stomach and a familiar shakiness crawled over my goosebumps to my fingers and toes. My palms grew clammy and my throat tightened. I slammed my eyelids open, shocked it was happening, at this moment, in this stillness. I stared at my hands and knees, tremors coursing through them.

This hadn't happened since that day.

There was a light knock on my door, but my bones refused to uncurl from my fetal position under my desk. Chin tucked into my knees, I didn't even look up.

"Sweetie? What happened?" Mamma cracked the door behind her and came to sit in front of me. "Scar? Talk to me."

I just stared back at her through blurry eyes. The tears flowed heavily with each shaky heave of my breath. My throat strained so tightly, I couldn't produce any words. All I could muster was a shake of my head. As she wrapped her arms in a cradle around me, she tried desperately to steady the tremoring of my tiny body. I heaved for air and tried to regulate my intake and calm my heart. But as my vision kept going in and out, my breathing just worsened. Her tears fell softly on me as she sat in the silence while we waited together for the panic to subside.

As soon as my mind calmed and my airway opened, I tried to talk to her. "Mamma, I can't do this. I just... I don't know what to do. Everything was fine. It was manageable... and then, it just wasn't." I stopped to focus on my breath so it wouldn't pick up pace and spiral me again.

"Did something happen at the doctor's office?"

"No. I thought it went fine. We went over the list I wrote with him. But then... we left, and I guess he forgot something that wasn't on the list. And he just... he just got so frustrated. He hit the window. And hurt his wrist... and he got mad that he hurt his wrist. And then... we pulled into the grocery store. And he was... he wasn't walking well. And he tripped over his shoe. And... then we couldn't find the right groceries. And his wrist... he just kept cursing about his wrist. And I... I just wanted to get the grocery list done, you know? I was just trying to focus and I just... broke. In the middle of the aisle, I just melted down. I couldn't control the shaking. I... I don't know how to do this Mamma."

She pulled me in closer. "I know, Scar. I know. I'm going to try to be there more. I'm sorry, Honey. I know this isn't easy."

"Mamma, I don't mind. I want to be there. I just... I don't understand what is happening to him. And I just... that's my papà. He's always been the dad, my dad. And I just broke today. I couldn't handle it. I don't even know how we got home. Mamma,

I've always been able to handle it, to pull myself together when I need to. But, I…" I unfolded my hands from under my arms and held them out. "I can't stop shaking."

Her grip grew tighter around me and I knew she understood. I'd finally popped.

The months of driving here and driving there… and trying to remember this and trying not to forget that… and making sure the blankets were switched out every time he woke up with night sweats… and waiting at the drug store counter at midnight… and sitting with him in front of the television until his pain subsided around 4 a.m.… and checking to make sure his pulse was steady while he finally slept through the mornings and afternoons.

This was my papà. This was the man who had carried me to bed when I fell asleep on Mamma's tummy. This was the man who had held an umbrella over my head and walked me to my classroom door every winter. This was the man who had wrapped me up in all his golf gear to make sure I was warm on the course.

This was the man who had stuck a key into the bridge of my braces every night for eight years to tighten them. This was the man who had rolled the windows down, blared Andrea Bocelli, and used his whistle and finger like an orchestra director to my singing on all of our long drives. This was the man who had showed up and yelled and clapped the loudest for all of my honor roll ceremonies.

This was the man who had tucked me into his side of the bed in a pillow fort with a bowl of cheerios every time I stayed home sick. This was the man who had snuck me Del Taco after school three times a week behind Mamma's back and then tossed the evidence in the garbage down the street and sprayed the car with air freshener.

This was the man who had kept *Ice Age* always running in the background as we played Blackjack in bed after homework was done. This was the man who had chipped golf balls with me in the living room as we stayed up into the early hours of the morning talking about love and life and all the lessons in between.

This man… he was my best friend. He was my protector. He was *my* caretaker.

And now… I couldn't wrap my head around this exchange of roles. I never thought twice about leaving work to stay home with him. It was my desire to give back to him all I felt he gave to me my whole life. But… this was my papà and in all the busyness of appointments and prescriptions and schedules, I just forgot that. I shut down and made it work.

Until… *I popped.*

Enough fucking silence.

I bounced out of the rocking chair much quicker than I'd eased into it. And without thanking or saying goodbye to the sun, I trudged heavy-footed through the mist and focused myself back down the path.

I was delighted to hear Jenna's perky, distracting voice when I reached my tent.

"Hey! I was lookin' for ya. A few of us are heading to the coffee fields at the edge of the village. Do you want to come?"

Without contemplating, I agreed. "Sure!"

Anything to keep me out of my head right now.

I changed into a long white skirt and comfy light sweater since the rain was slowing and the sun was peeking through more intensely now. I grabbed my bag and stuffed it with my camera, my journal, and some of my favorite chocolate that I'd brought, leaving my phone on the bedside.

We walked past the empty front desk and around the pond, arriving at the big wooden gates we'd driven through the night before.

I sought those two twisted trees, to no avail. They were nowhere in sight.

"

Do not wait for the teachings from others,
the words of the scriptures,
the principles of enlightenment.
We are born in the morning and
we die in the evening;
the one we saw yesterday is
no longer with us today.

BODHIN KJOLHEDE

Five

Ramón stood with a hat and a handful of maps.

"Buenas tardes, mujeres, here is a map. Be careful not to get lost. The fields are... extensive. I recommend staying together. The entrance is down that road and to the left. Enjoy!"

"You're not coming with us?" When the question slipped out, I saw Jenna, in the corner of my eye, crook her head toward me.

"No, I will be staying here, but the fields are beautiful and the sky just cleared for the day. When the sun begins to set, we will be starting our evening meal."

I shot a *thank you* in his direction and he nodded. When I looked down at the map, I was grateful to see a static one.

Finally.

We walked down the pebbled road and made a left through the rusted vintage gate to a walkway covered by palm trees. Still no clear sky, just lots and lots of green, and I soaked it all in. My eyes were finally drinking again. The walkway dumped us into a lane between bushels hanging with clumps of green coffee beans. I ran my fingers over the lumpy beans and inhaled the robust aroma that filled the lanes.

We followed the map, sloppily but together, as we separated from the group a bit and wound our way through the maze of fields.

Jenna was charming. She was really good at small talk and, although I was only half-paying attention, she made it very easy to listen.

"So, are you in a relationship?" She brought her blur of conversation to a halt.

It was easy until that question. I could tell she wanted to get to know me more. After all, by now, I knew where she was from, what she did for a living, and how she liked her morning juice.

"No." I cleared my throat. "Uh… I was, but I ended it a few months ago."

"Ah." I'm not sure if she respected the soreness with which I spoke or if she just wanted to chat about her situation. Regardless, I appreciated her redirection. "Well, I've been married for five years. We've been together for eight."

"Oh wow, that's great," I replied lightly.

"Yeah." She dropped her chin a little and I sensed by the change in her energy that there was more to the story.

So, I probed a bit. "Are you… happy?"

She looked up at me and then back down toward her feet. "Um, yeah. I… I'm happy. I mean, I don't have a reason not to be. I just…" She paused and I took my eyes off her to relieve some pressure. "We just got married so young, you know?" I nodded. "I mean, I love him so much. He is really there for me, in so many more ways than I ever expected a husband to be. I just… eight years is a long time, you know?"

"Yeah, my relationship was only three and it felt like a lifetime. I can't imagine eight."

We rounded a bushy corner and stumbled into the space Ramón must have been referring to. It was an open field filled with the sun's favorite colors dancing wild across the sky. I was grateful to see a view beyond the towering trees. Pink, purple, and orange… it was a sight for nostalgic eyes.

A hidden part of me missed sunsets dearly. They'd been painful of late, so I stayed away.

"It's a looong freakin' time." She laughed nervously.

"Can I maybe say something? Just a reflection?" I asked.

She looked up a bit surprised, but nodded.

"You have a sadness in your tone when you talk about it. I mean… you've told me about your work, your hobbies, your family.

But there's a sadness around your hubby." She paused and caressed some of the nearby beans. "I'm sorry... I don't mean to overstep. You totally don't have to talk about it if you don't want to."

"No," she whispered. "I do want to talk about it. I just haven't yet."

I waited until she was ready.

"I almost went out on him. I'm really... I'm all tore up about it."

"Oh?" I quickly adjusted my tone before I responded and immediately tightened all my facial muscles in an effort to control my expression. I knew it wouldn't be good if it matched the pit her words hollowed out in my tummy.

"Yeah, about a month ago. I just... I wanted to so badly. I just... I met this guy and he made me feel things I haven't felt in... years." She sighed. "If I'm being honest with myself, I still want to, and I regret not taking advantage of the opportunity." Her remorse hung like a cloud over her head, but her fondness and exhilaration at the memory was palpable. "Gosh, I am an awful person, aren't I?"

I stayed silent, trying to tread carefully and listen intently.

"I feel terrible. I love my husband and he's away a lot. He's in the military, you know. But, that's not really why. We do fine with distance. It's just... I'm not sure. Maybe it was the thrill of it all. That was the first time I've felt... alive... in... years."

"Mmm."

"You must think I'm dumber than a sack o' rocks."

I furrowed my brows at her Tennessee slang as I tried to decode it while her eyes fell and face flushed.

I shook my head, remembering that the man I'd just left had treated me like I hung the stars in the sky for most of our relationship.

"I get it. Nothing's ever simple. There's no black and white with relationships." I gulped my own memories down as I searched for the right words to support her despite my bias.

"Ain't that the truth! Have you ever... you know, cheated?"

"No, I haven't. But, I've been on the other side."

"Really?"

I hesitated. "I know it can be complicated." Dark clouds rolled in and the breeze picked up a little too intensely, coaxing a flare of goosebumps down my arms, as I resisted my growing scorn for my new friend.

"Ugh. I'm sorry to hear that, girl. I know, I know, it would break his heart so much." Her voice cracked with pain.

"You haven't told him?"

"No. god, no. I can't even imagine. It would shatter him. I don't want to hurt him. I just... I don't know if I want to be together anymore. I just really want to live and feel alive. And, I don't know... I don't know if he can be part of that for me."

Jenna described their dynamics in detail, and I couldn't help but resign myself to half-paying attention again. I couldn't help it. Her question had shoved my aching heart back to the second day of last August.

I'd just launched my business and gotten my book on the market the day before, and it was going to be a big month for me. The following Friday, I would be in New York, performing a slam poem to launch the bestseller campaign for the book and then touring throughout the month, while managing my very first six clients from my computer as I traveled. Most importantly, this was the first month I was going to be away from my ailing papà in about three years.

Julian and I had just finished watching a movie, and I'd opened my laptop to get some work done while he slept. When his phone vibrated on the desk next to me, I'd glanced quickly and seen the name Megan. I only knew of one Megan, and it was an ex.

I never wanted to be one to invade privacy. But in that moment, I realized I'd never had a reason to until then. I slid his lock screen open to a stream of messages filled with naked photos and frisky emoji.

"Get out." I threw his phone at him and he stared at me through sleepy, confused eyes. That is, until they filled with guilt when he quickly came to.

"Scar..."

"Get out."

Head down, he gathered his things and slumped his shoulders as he left my home—the home I'd welcomed him into, the home I'd made him a part of, the home I'd opened to him, that I'd loved him in.

This was the night our love ended and the truth is that it should have been the night our relationship ended, but it wasn't.

The lane narrowed to another rusty gate, and we headed through it back to the center of the village. Turns out, neither of us were very good with maps, even ones that weren't constantly shifting and changing. But the wind led us forward, and after I packed away my judgments, the tender conversation opened up a very sweet, very much needed artery for us.

"Oh shoot! Look! Jenna look!" A giant spiky-haired iguana raced across the grass in front of us. It was at least five feet long.

"Oh, that is really somethin'! I just love animals. You ever look up their meanin'?"

"Ah, no I don't. Not really the nature-loving type, to be honest."

"Girl! You're in Costa Rica. You best be gettin' used to the critters round here. I can't actually remember though what those things are all 'bout." Neither of us had ever seen one in person, let alone so close. It's dinosaur-like jog disappeared quickly into the trees and left us in stitches.

Laughter. I missed it.

We actually made it in time for dinner, which looked even more incredible than breakfast. Just the sight saturated my mouth and I stood frozen in line for several minutes, trying to figure out what to put on my plate and in what proportion. I wanted everything and mountains of it. My appetite suddenly expanded under my rib cage.

"¡Buenas tardes!" I savored that sweet, lively voice.

"¡Hola, Sol! ¿Cómo estás?" I wondered if she ever took a break.

"¡Bien, bien! ¡Dime si hay algo que puedo conseguir para ti, pequeña bailarina!" Her smile glowed with sincerity and I desperately chased her Spanish.

Bailarina? I looked around.

"Ok, si, muchas gracias!"

"¡Pura vida!" I watched her bounce away from the counter, amazed that she was so light on her feet. Glancing back down at the food, my head shot up when that sultry music spilled through the door, tugging on my ears. Again, the light teased me.

But my stomach won. I packed my plate thick with grilled Tafaya chicken, mixed greens, and plantains, and then topped them with all sorts of fruits—ones I wasn't even sure I ever knew existed.

Jenna and I were joined by a couple. Nick, about six foot with a healthy build and blue eyes, held his wife's hand. Aileen had long, stunning red hair, and her green eyes shone bright above the freckles scattered across her nose and cheeks. I guessed they were in about their late thirties and felt comforted by their calm, easy way as we spoke softly in the intervals between moaning over our dinner.

I found out they're nomads. Sold everything they had four years earlier and packed their lives into what they could carry on their backs to travel the world. They run a joint business where he does videography and she does primarily marketing for travel agencies, and they manage it all from their laptops wherever they are in the world. They were headed to Switzerland after this trip, and then Scotland and Ireland, before they'd go down to Colombia the following summer.

I tried to pick up my jaw, now sloppily crunching leaves, bewildered and so very envious.

"Wow! What inspired you guys? That's such a massive life change!" I was too curious not to ask more.

"Well..." Aileen looked at Nick with a soft smile as if to reflect a tender agreement, "...life inspired us." There was clearly more to be understood beneath that sheltered response. But I didn't push, especially when I saw Nick's eyes recoil back to his plate.

"Cheers to life!" Jenna raised her wine glass and the rest of us our waters and coconuts.

"Salud." As I raised my glass, I noticed a man over Jenna's shoulder in the corner of the hall, sitting beneath the same elephant-ear-like leaves I had that morning, alone.

We cleaned our plates and hustled to our evening workshop in what now appeared on the map as *La Encarnada*. Jenna and I followed Nick and Aileen this time, grateful we had made friends with people who had much more developed magic map reading abilities.

We approached yet another practically-underground cabin, toppled with brush-like hojas de palma suita and surrounded on all four walls with floor-to-ceiling mirrors.

My heartbeat quickened at a faint memory of my old dance studio as we each grabbed a yoga mat and blanket and completed the circle made of bodies.

I'd forgotten to use the restroom and jumped to run quickly outside and to the front desk.

"Hi, Ramón! Where's the nearest bathroom?"

"On the side of the building." He pointed in the direction.

"Thank you!" His availability was quite convenient. I hustled to release all the coffee and coconut water from the day.

Walking briskly back to the studio, I stifled a yawn.

"Miss Scarlett." I turned around, surprised to hear my name. "Here is your..."

"Coffee!" I looked up confused as he handed me yet another cup. "But how did you—"

"Oh!" Ramón's hands clasped my shoulders and gently turned me in a circle. "¡Mira!" He whispered as he lifted one finger to the trees above. I squinted, unable to find what he was pointing to until I saw a slight movement between the branches.

"Un perezoso."

I finally spotted the beige ball of fur with a brown spot in the middle of his back. It was so high in the tree, I could barely make it out. His limbs moved slowly as he crawled through the treetops.

"Está despierto."

We watched in silent awe while the sloth slowly made its way through the tree branches, eventually disappearing into the leaves behind the building.

Ramón's hands fell with ease from my arms as he whispered again, in my ear this time, "The workshop is starting." He smiled and shifted his eyes toward the entrance.

I took the cup with gratitude and walked into the studio-like hall. As I cuddled back under my blanket and sipped on my coffee, I purred.

Hay dios mío.

There was an older gentleman sitting at the front of the room, silent and still. Legs wrapped one around another beneath him, his hands relaxed around the round belly in his lap. He was a slender but muscular man, very content in his skin. His eyes were open but focused on the ground before him. Cheekbones high and plump, his expression seemed to be settled in a smile, tucked in a thick coarse beard which stood in stark contrast to his olive brown skin. It was a light beige, similar to what I'd seen a moment ago. He wore the same white garment as the Awapa from orientation, but I didn't recognize him from that lineup.

The room settled and everyone waited patiently. Because I was in the back corner, I couldn't see any faces, but I took the opportunity to scan the heads and bodies around me. There seemed to be a striking variation among the men and women, a mixture of young and old, as well as white, black, and brown skin. I became increasingly curious where everyone was from and how they'd stumbled on their invitations to this forbidden gem.

"So, when I was young..." the beige-haired gentleman began with a rasp in his voice. "I thought it was pretty cool to be able to do things like this..." Slowly, he extended his arm and stretched three fingers out to a center point in front of him on the ground.

We waited with anticipation as this older man very intentionally shifted the weight of his entire body onto his three fingers. He took his time but, without one groan, the veins in his arm protruded and his biceps grew with tension as he moved all of his weight to a perpendicular plank. I leaned forward, joining the collective jaw drop.

Still balancing on his fingers, his legs slowly curled in and then extended up into the air. Completely relaxed and vacant of any tension or shaking, he held that position for a good five minutes while we all sat in wonder.

The awe was real. We watched in dumbfounded silence as he brought his body gracefully back down and folded his legs beneath him.

"But then..." He steadied his breath and spoke as slowly as he'd just performed. "Then, I grew up. And I realized that doing tricks such as these didn't help me much with the other areas of my life, with my real-world problems. It didn't help me when I left my job. It didn't help me when I lost my grandparents. It didn't help me when I crashed my car and shattered my spine. It didn't help me when I was faced with wondering what the rest of the life before me would look like, what it could look like."

From curiosity to bewilderment, the energy in the room leveled out pretty quickly at his words.

"I'd been doing things like this since I was young—training seriously since the age of eight. But after these tragedies, my sense of self crumbled and doubt filled my vision. I no longer saw anything more for myself.

Eventually, I started asking bigger questions. How much of what we know is innate? What truly determines our ability to bounce back, to heal and recover? To reclaim our bodies and our gifts? Is there a foundation that can be trained and developed in us to become better... at life? At... this whole human thing? How much say does our will have in this?"

Still, from head to toe, he made eye contact with each person in the room as he continued to share. He spoke so slowly, I wondered if he was forgetting his next words.

"I studied closely, everything that allowed me to become as skilled as I was: strength, flexibility, coordination, timing, rhythm, balance, trust. I returned to these basic principles. And really, that was the beginning of ever truly learning them. And not for anyone else but myself. I realized, similar to how I'd developed these skills for my craft, that it might be possible to develop these skills for living as well."

He paused while we hung on his every word.

"What if... it was possible to teach the muscles we need to change with life as it changes around us? And to do so with grace and ease, acceptance and understanding? What if?"

His words froze me.

"Would you raise a hand if you have experienced any sort of mental, emotional, or physical pain in your life?" Everyone paused and hesitated, as if that was such a ridiculous question we didn't know if he actually wanted us to answer it. We looked around at each other and after Nick's lead, one by one, raised our hands.

The beige-haired gentleman let a small smirk slip through his already resting grin, as if to acknowledge the ridicule everyone was feeling.

"Would you agree that because of that adversity, regardless of how you responded or handled it initially, that you are now a little bit stronger? A little bit wiser? And maybe you even have a little bigger capacity for compassion and perspective about what you went through? Perhaps you see yourself a little more able to handle a similar circumstance again?"

The words were banging against my dam, filling my mind with memories, and I gulped at the thought of losing him… *again.*

"You see, we don't need to pretend to like difficulties when they come, but we need to keep that thread of attention to the fact that there are gifts to be unraveled from them, depending on how we learn to respond to them."

He paused again, letting his words sink in.

"There are times when life's circumstances demand we put forth a lion's heart—a brave spirit. And there are times when life's circumstances demand that we turn inward, get quiet, and listen. How do we do both? This is the golden ticket… learning to live with our head in the clouds and our feet, or fingers…" he winked, "on the ground."

I could hear the gears in everyone's minds grinding, but just barely above the sound of my own.

I really had no idea what I was coming here for when I accepted that plane ticket, but tools for living, for navigating these tragedies that have begun the unraveling of my twenty-one years of identity, sounded like a good start.

If there is a god, he knows I need those.

He answered a few questions around the room and then wrapped up for the night with a quick meditation and slow movement to process his words in silence. As we collected our belongings and headed to the door, he invited everyone to the hot springs to get to know one another.

I walked alone back to my bungalow and debated whether or not to accept. Socializing was always the worst part. But after I rolled my eyes at my inner introvert, I forced myself to slip my one-piece on and wrap my towel around me. Leaving my tent, I managed to find the same stone path to the other side of the village by memory this time, marveling at the little balls of fire that had reappeared above my head.

They really didn't offer very much light and I was struggling to make out the stones in the dark. Then suddenly, I saw a white mist between my toes. I slowed and tried to understand. Every time I pressed the ball of my foot harder, the white steam-like glow actually expanded outward through the soil, like microscopic bacterial critters or something. They seemed to move forward and, as I followed their trail, they lit the entire path before me with a scaley luminescence.

I searched up and around, until the moon peeked through some holes in the trees and I stumbled into the same mud from the night before.

Weary of the webs I'd seen in the daylight, I covered my head and brushed a couple branches aside, following the whispers in the distance.

About three-quarters of the group had changed into their suits and were immersed in the hot spring lit dimly by fire balls all around.

Apparently, I was the only one who thinks those fixtures bizarre. I unraveled my towel, hunching over a bit in an effort to hide my skeletal frame, and slipped by a couple chatty folks onto the first step.

The faces surrounding me through the steam quickly revealed I was the youngest among them. Nothing new there. This was only the first day, but I hadn't paid nearly as much attention to the other people at this retreat as they had clearly paid to each other.

Nonetheless, it was clear that everyone was engaged and excited to get to know one another. I sank into the bubbles and turned my ears up a little. While I heard shallow information exchanged—where they were from, how many kids they had, where they had traveled—I was astonished to hear just how deep several of these strangers, who had only just met this day, were diving into conversation.

"Yes, well, I got fired from my job…"

"Actually, my wife left me recently…"

Something in my throat started screaming. The bubbles slipping from the stones soothed my back but didn't help to slow the rolling crackle in my chest.

"I actually just sold my home and have no idea where I'm going or what I'm doing next…"

"Well, I was caring for my grandmother for some time, but I just couldn't do it anymore…"

That was my cue. I scuttled to grab my things, but felt someone's eyes on me as I hurried to leave just as quickly as I'd come. As I wrapped back up, I noticed the gentleman from dinner standing between two hedges at the corner of the hot spring, opposite the direction I'd come from. He was clearly surveying the scene and hesitant to join.

His skeleton-like frame had such a familiar hollow, and a distant part of my psyche wondered if I was looking into a mirror.

I bent down to grab my bag and, when I looked up again, he was gone. I scanned the group, but he was not in the water or with anyone standing around.

I skipped over the stones and hurried around the hovering trees to see if I could find him. I looked down the path to the right and the path in front of me. I even walked a few feet down each to see if I might catch him anywhere, but I didn't.

Silently, I hoped I'd see him the next day, while I took the path to the left back through the front canopy and to my bungalow.

"

Then the time came when the risk it took to
remain tight in a bud was more painful
than the risk it took to blossom.

ANAÏS NIN

Six

It was the juiciest ricotta gnocchi East LA had to offer, and I thoroughly enjoyed it every time. The last time I'd been there was with my papà, enjoying the first day I'd gotten him out of the house and eating a whole meal in months.

I looked across the table and smiled at Mamma, my rock. We ate in peace until panic sparked in the air around us. Confusion cycloned around us and we noticed others on the street staring up at the hot-air balloons that sprinkled the sky. Shining like sirens, they reflected the sunlight and, somewhere, a distant alarm sounded. I squinted at what looked like wings, white and large swaying in the balloon baskets.

Butterflies? One. Two. Three. Huh...

I stood and walked around the patio to the other side of the restaurant.

Four. Five. Six. Seven... Whoa.

I couldn't count anymore. There were too many and they were so close! Hot-air balloons out in wine country are common, but not here in the city. My attempt to reason was soon washed away by a splash of rain on my face, then my hands. Before I knew it, water poured around me.

I turned around at the vibration of a large thump. One balloon had hit the ground in the lot across from the restaurant. A man in a white coat whirled out of the basket with such grace, it seemed he flew. Wiping the rain from my face, I peered closer. Body stiff and eyes bloodshot, the man in white grabbed a nearby father whose wife screamed when he pushed their two kids toward her. He wrapped his arms around the husband who struggled in confusion to both protect his family and get away.

Thunderous blasts pounded through the air and vibrated the water falling around it. As a cloud rose from the exploding fire, both men turned to swirling ash while sparks flew in every direction. The family shrieked in horror, frozen where they stood. Another red siren landed and another man in white rushed out, eyes fixed on the woman and her young ones. I found myself running, without thinking, toward them, yelling for them to escape. But their shock paralyzed them and the man exploded just as he reached the two-foot radius of them.

I was blown back on my tailbone from the impact of the blast. Adrenaline pulsed hot in my blood as I watched the fire dissipate and illuminate nothing but the silhouette of scorched corpses piled on the ground. Panicked, I scanned the horizon, only to see more shining balloons bleed from the sky as fire and smoke filled the street around me.

I turned back to see Mamma, still and staring at me with puddled eyes. I picked my jaw up with as much courage as I could muster, ran to her, and yanked her arm.

"Let's go!" We began running through the red around us. The balloons, the blood. The white men and their wings. I couldn't make out the difference.

We were almost at the car when she tripped on the curb and fell to her knees. I hadn't realized she'd fallen until she screamed my name.

I turned back and rushed to her when I saw a white coat, quick as the wind, skidding to her as well.

"No!" I grabbed her and we struggled to run together until I felt the gravity of his tug on her arm.

She pushed me away from her with all the force she could muster. "Go, Scar! Leave! Go!" She thrusted me away.

I looked up from the ground and screamed. Fireworks detonated my vision and my entire body tremored in shock while I watched my mother disappear in the flames before me.

"*MAMMMAAAAAA*!" I shot perpendicular in my bed, throwing off my wet sheets, and heaving for air. My vision bounced and ping-ponged around the dark space.

I panted and tried to find some saliva to soothe the dryness in my throat and mouth.

"Scar! Scar, are you okay?" Jenna's voice echoed somewhere in the distance.

"Uhm! Uhm!" I coughed and breathed, coughed and breathed, trying desperately to focus my vision.

"Scar!" My sweet roommate grasped my shoulders and centered herself between my eyes.

"Yes! I uhm. I… I'm so sorry!" We both looked down at my shaking hands. I struggled to breathe deeply and steady myself. "I'm so… sorry! I…"

"Scar, don't apologize. What were you…? I mean, are you…?"

I just looked down and clasped my clammy hands together, fighting the shame for my lack of control.

I couldn't believe this was happening. I reached for my phone but heard my brother's words, the ones he repeated every time I called panicking after this recurring night terror.

"Scar, the mind is a powerful force. Your brain is just trying to work out what happened. You know, make sense of it all. You've never… experienced death before. Your inner wiring is trying to

*understand it, make peace with it. It's okay. You're not broken.
You're just... you're still trying to figure it all out."*

I dropped my phone on the bedside table and took a deep breath.

"Uhm, I'm going to uh... I need to use the restroom."

Concerned, Jenna nodded and hesitantly retreated to her side of the tent while I turned in my bed to touch the sweat stain outline of my body. It was drenched.

I felt her care, and her eyes on me, as I gathered my bathroom bag, towel, and a change of clothes and hustled out.

I found the shower just around the corner. They were half-outside bathrooms built right into the trees, stalls to the right and showers to the left with gorgeous beige bamboo doors. I picked the one at the far end, started the water, stripped, and jumped in before it got warm.

Dropping my face into my hands, I let the water stream in the cracks. After a few frozen minutes, I melted to the floor, face still in my palms. My back found the bamboo wall and I let the shakes move from my limbs, through my chest, and to my eyes.

"Scar... Scar, honey..." I felt her dainty hands trace through my hair as my ears struggled to find her voice. Her words. My name.

"Scar, will you come downstairs, please? We need to do this together, as a family." I lifted my head up to see Mamma sitting over me, tucked in the crevice of my fetal position. She continued to nervously caress my hair, eyes blistered red and swollen with tears.

It had never been this difficult to make out the gorgeous slate gray of her eyes. Teardrop eyes, he used to call them. Through her muffled sniffles and cracked tone, I wondered if they'd ever reclaim that shape he loved so much.

"Scar... it's okay. We'll be here. Take your time, okay?" Her lips pressed to my forehead and a stray tear ran down the side of my face. I watched her tiny frail frame make its way to the door where she paused.

Several deep breaths later, my saint of a mother gathered all her strength to walk out of the bedroom and face what was next... as she always did.

This bedroom. This bedroom that had felt more like a prison these last three years. His prison... that became my prison. Long days of awaiting doctor's calls and pharmacy texts. Late nights of anxious pacing, waiting for those little white pills or big brown patches to kick in. Early mornings of nervous sweats and jaw clenching, waiting for the episodes to pass. Waiting, just waiting. It was all one vicious waiting game—a prison.

It was one I was happy to sit with him in. I felt blessed to be able to share in his pain, in fighting his depression by getting lost in movies together and playing cards, in distracting him from his body's shortcomings. Even if I'd known at the beginning the toll it would take on me by the end, I wouldn't have done anything differently.

But my mamma... she always managed to gather her strength, put on a smile, and make it through that bedroom door each day. She was my hero for that.

I understood the need for me to go downstairs. I was part of this family, of his family. I knew this was the only way we would get through this—as a family, as the family he loved. It's the only way he would have wished for us to.

Focusing solely on that thought, I channeled all my willpower to follow Mamma's example and push myself from the sunken mold of his body shape in their bed. As I unfixed my eyes from the wall, I gazed at his bedside table filled with pictures—all of me at every age—and love notes from my mamma and I begging him to stay strong for one more day.

My eye caught the glimmer of something under one of the notes. It was a ring I'd given him three years before on his sixtieth birthday. A brushed charcoal with a piece that spun around the middle. I remember thinking how great it would be when his anxiety made his hands twitch and they needed something to do. On one side of the chain, it read, "Is. 54:17, No weapon formed against me shall prosper." And on the other side, it read, "Eph. 6:11, Put on the full armor of God that you may be able to stand firm against the schemes of the Enemy."

It wasn't long after I gave him this ring that I realized his story was less about a god and an enemy and more about imprisonment, the imprisonment of humanity—his humanity. And, when I say I realized it, I really mean it was only me. Eighteen years in a Christian household, raised around the teachings of an almighty god. Both gracious and jealous, both all-powerful and intimate, both inexplicable yet defined in doctrine. Quite the contradiction this god was to me until I realized the range of those descriptions were extraordinarily close to those of humans. I'd been told the mind is a powerful thing, but never fully understood just how powerful the myths and stories it creates—it believes—can be. Until I witnessed them torture him in his darkest hours.

I watched one of these stories firsthand. I watched him, the most devoted and faith-driven man I'd known, struggle to understand the story his *god* had written for him. Little did he know, by doing so, he was forsaking his own pen.

The long days, I could take. The late nights, I could take. The early mornings, I could take. But watching him unconsciously create a story about what god was orchestrating, and what he was consequently helpless to prevent or solve, broke my heart.

Where was the strength of our will? Of our purpose? Of our potential? Who decided what we make of this life? I refused to believe it was some being in the sky, amplified by our perceptions of humanity and capable of all the same good and evil, deciding the fate of our existence based on the purity of our hearts and the actions of our hands. All according to this ancient and entirely outdated text canonized centuries ago by men of the time.

I grabbed an old chain from the bathroom drawer, strung it through the ring, and slid it around my neck. Looking up, I caught a quick glimpse of my reflection through the love notes on his mirror.

Minus the vacancy of expression, I was sure there was still some shock inside me somewhere. This was the first time I could see what everyone had been telling me the last three years. I started to understand why all their pitiful concerns never ceased.

Perhaps I shouldn't have brushed off their comments.

Now 103 pounds, my jeans practically hung around my waist, clinging only to the protruding hip bones on either side. My stomach caved up to meet my flat chest and rigid collar bone. My once voluminous golden curls now hung like lifeless threads around my pale face and bony shoulders. I couldn't recall when my skin began sinking back into my jaw's frame, but my Kolesnikoff cheekbones had never looked more pronounced. I could probably trace the timeline of the dark circles around my eyes to figure it out. My eyes, so empty—so hollow.

Stop, Scar. None of that mattered today.

Before walking out the door, I grabbed his favorite beige sweater and draped it over my tiny frame. As I approached the stairs, I mused that I'd never heard a house so full be so quiet. I slowly made my way down the staircase, where I immediately felt more than forty pairs of sad and curious eyes fall on me.

This was the last thing I wanted to do. I couldn't even feel the pain my own body was writhing in. How was I supposed to handle being around everyone else's?

I lifted my chin and, of course, the first pair to meet mine were blue and dripping tenderness. Julian made his way across the room to catch me, no doubt. Because… that's just what we did. We caught each other.

Unstable from the start, our dysfunctional relationship added up to three years of broken promises and sworn apologies stitched together by one constant—catching each other. Catching each other when it didn't make sense to. Catching each other when we should've caught ourselves. Catching each other when it stole all the strength from our own reservoir. Catching each other when we should've walked away.

It's not that we didn't want to love or let go. I think it was more that neither of us knew how to do either.

His hands wrapped behind my neck as his thumbs traced my cheekbones. "I'm here, okay. Please let me know if you need anything." His lips kissed my forehead and I wondered silently to myself when I stopped feeling those, when I stopped caring to.

Behind him, the front door opened and relief collapsed the tension in my shoulders as Enzo shuffled in, removing his coat and making his way to Mamma. She tucked her face in his shoulder and thanked him for coming. Chest firm, he held her tightly as a tear streamed from the green eyes and down the pale skin I'd known my whole life. I slid past Julian and made my way to his familiar arms through the crowded bodies. He pulled me in. No words were exchanged as his embrace swallowed me and I melted into him. His lips pressed on the top of my head and I breathed his grief in with mine.

Moving my hair behind my ear, he guided me to the living room of my 2400 sq. ft. home where the entirety of my rather large Russian and Italian family waited. The first warm hand on my lower back made me jump and I turned to see my aunt Caroline.

"Scar, I'm so so sorry." She pulled me in and I knew the dam broke when my shoulder puddled. "I just, I don't understand. We were just with him Saturday night and he was fine. He was more than fine! He was kicking all of our asses at cards. I just, I'm so sorry."

I nodded and leaned in for another hug.

What am I supposed to say to her? I couldn't understand either. I'd been trying to do just that... at least to even understand what had transpired these last three days.

As I moved through the crowd, all sorts of hands fell on me. One after another, they took turns sobbing through their "I'm so sorry's" and "I can't imagine's."

They must have thought me cold. I couldn't even muster a response. No words. No tears. I'd wondered too.

As soon as I spotted the open seat next to Mamma, I put my head down and made my way to it. My second-to-eldest sister, Bella, pulled up a chair on the other side of Mamma and Trix pulled one up next to me. Here we were, his four girls, all together, hands gripping one another's. If we were going to pull through this, this was the only way—sharing whatever strength and courage we could each gather, moment to moment.

The room's whispers fell to a deep silence as my brother approached center stage, coffee in one hand, 151 in the other.

That about summed up what I could remember of the last three days.

"I want to thank you all for coming on such short notice. I know there is still a lot of confusion and shock. I will do my best to clarify all that happened, but please, know that we..." Alex's watery brown eyes shifted to us, "are in the same boat. We don't expect that this sadness will be easily shaken nor will this vacancy be easily forgotten. Three days ago, on Sunday, the eighth of January..."

I pushed the echoes of my mother's screams from that morning as far out of my consciousness as I could and came back when the story was over.

"So, as my sisters, my mother, and I have tried to figure out the best way to honor him, we have decided that inviting you all here is how we will start. My father, as everyone is well aware, was a storyteller and the best of his kind. Tonight, through our tears, we will do our best to share our most precious stories of him with all of you and we would be touched if, through your tears, you could do the same."

And so, the tale lived on...

"Gabriel was one of a kind..."

"You could hear his laugh from down the block..."

"I remember the first time he put a golf club in my hand..."

"And that's how he hustled me out of six month's-worth of allowance..."

"Gabriel was the most generous man I've ever met..."

"His laughter brought life to everyone around him..."

"He was one hell of a storyteller, an enchanter..."

"Jacket? Check. Charger? Check. Keys? Check. Ass?"

"What a mouth! That man had a gift for talking..."

"I remember his laughter..."

"I'll never forget the wisdom he shared..."

"He told me his voice would be the last I'd hear..."

"And even when he didn't have an answer, he did..."

"But damn... that laugh."

"He taught me..."

"He gave me..."

"He showed me..."

"He believed in me..."

"He supported me..."

"He bewildered me..."

"He got me to think..."

"He mentored me..."

"He took me in..."

"He cared for me..."

"He held me..."

"He loved me..."

I couldn't separate the shower water from my tears. All I knew was I was drowning in both. It was impressive, after so many months of crying, how my body had learned to do it without making a sound. I heaved in the corner of the shower for what felt like hours, in a deafening silence, begging with all of my tightening muscles, for the pain to leave.

The water was suddenly falling with more force, and I looked up to see it was coming from the sky. I closed my eyes and imagined it washing all of this pain from my eyes and down my skin, from my protruding ribs, and over my bony knees, into the ground beneath me.

Some time passed by and the shakes calmed to a tremor. I looked up again and forced my aching eyes open to see the lightening lavender sky. Listening to the leaves rustle as the water toppled them, I remembered Sibú's comment and focused my attention on filling my diaphragm with air… over and over. My body calmed. I watched the water spots that stuck to their bubbles, and followed the ones that rolled down my ankles.

The same old church melody filled my mind and tugged on my heart, and I wondered if the rain might really be able to take it all away.

I missed my mamma.

Scrubbed down and finally steady enough, I wrapped my body and hair in a towel and made my way to the mirror, where I doused my face with more water and stared into the eyes looking back at me, dark with exhaustion. I reminded myself where I was, the beautiful land I was standing on, and how I'd made it here... on my own will, answering every call, however strange, that led me here.

"Coo Coo! Coo Coo!"

I shook my head at the ridiculous decisions I'd made over the course of my few years on this planet and started to get ready, smiling at the newness of this experience: I hadn't exactly made this decision. In so many ways, the decision to come here had been made for me.

Unraveling the towel on my head and grabbing my brush, I looked up in the mirror and jumped when I saw the man's face in the distance. I turned around to see... Nothing. It was the man from last night, the one who sat alone at dinner and then dodged the hot spring gathering. I stared into the distance, confused and unsure whether I'd imagined him.

This day was off to one hell of a start.

When I unzipped the bungalow, I saw Jenna propped up on her pillow, reading Dan Millman's *Laws of Spirit.*

"Hey..." I half-smiled and made my way to my bed, which had a pile of fresh sheets at the foot. "Thank you."

"Course. How ya feelin'?" She closed her book to give me her full attention.

I busied myself with tidying my things and stripping my sheets. "I'm good. The showers are amazing here!"

She dropped her chin and gave me *the look.* "What's got your panties in a wad, Hun?"

"I'm okay, really."

"Oookay," I could tell she was curious but it was sweet of her not to press. "I brought you the coffee Ramón made you. It's almost time. Do you want to walk over to the hall together?"

"Oh! Thank you. Sure, let's go!"

I didn't need dry hair here anyway. I just hoped my frizzy mane didn't scare anyone.

We strolled past the village children, and their resounding laughter, into *La Transparencia.* Jenna was totally a front-row person and said good morning to everyone on her way to the front. There was one spot next to her and she probably assumed I'd take it, but I scuttled to the back row and laid my mat out in the corner next to the mirror. Sitting down, I tried to stretch through the tension now buzzing between my limbs and joints.

One by one, participants strolled in. There were still many unfamiliar faces, and I realized I should probably make a better effort to get to know everyone.

Aileen flashed a sweet good morning smile my way as she walked behind Nick who seemed so internally preoccupied, he didn't raise his chin. I smiled back and searched for the mystery man, to no avail.

"It's so good to see everyone. Please get comfortable and relax in any position you'd like." I was surprised to hear Rebecca's beautiful raspy voice float through the crowd. I let my search go and focused on her. It was hard not to.

"We're going to focus on meditation today. Let's start with some deep breaths. Inhale. Exhale." She modeled. "Go ahead and close your eyes. Elongate your spine so that it's straight. Inhale. Exhale. Relax your muscles. Relax your throat. Relax your mind. Inhale. Exhale." She spoke slowly and the room breathed together in unison.

I closed my eyes. Then I opened them. Then I closed them, and opened them again.

Focus, Scar. Relax.

Inhale. Exhale. I decided to watch my breath's journey. Perhaps, that would help me. I opened my mouth and felt the air I sucked in fall through my throat. I followed it down and placed all my attention on my diaphragm as it filled. I held it there, disregarding Rebecca's instructions. When I felt a sharp pain in my tailbone, my concentration shattered.

I hated sitting like this. I could never keep my back straight. Despite my years of formal training, my posture was terrible. I could never keep my shoulders back long enough for them to really set into a comfortable frame. My spine hunched and my butt curled in. This stupid yogi position didn't help.

"Inhale. Exhale. Inhale. Exhale," Rebecca continued, interrupting my internal tantrum.

I refocused again, trying to relax all of my now frustrated muscles. I followed her voice and my breath once more, right down to my tummy and then noticed my shoulders slouching. I kept breathing as I corrected the little nuances.

"Feel the air within you. Acknowledge it. Follow it. Cherish it. Thank it. Release it." Her calmness was truly antagonizing my inner perfectionist.

It baffled me how something so simple could be so damn difficult.

Isn't my mind supposed to be quiet through this?

Inhale, exhale. I could do this.

I wonder what they will have for breakfast this morning... Ah, cazzo.

I opened my eyes and searched for a clock while everyone else continued in unison.

Why is there no clock in this room? That's stupid.

I let my fake posture deflate and fell down to my back.

Maybe meditation was supposed to turn you into a toddler. I resolved to rest my eyelids for a bit and laid there silently, passing into a light sleep for about twenty more minutes while the group finished.

"Coming back now. Inhale. Exhale. Open your eyes when you're ready."

I sprang up from my mat as erect in my cross-legged position as I could. As I peeled my eyelids open, I felt a bit of guilt gnaw at me for not taking full advantage of this experience by really trying. I'd always hated meditation. I could never do it right.

"Great session, everyone. Let's head to breakfast."

Thank god.

I rolled my mat up faster than everyone else, propped it on top of the stack, grabbed my creamy coffee, and headed to the door before anyone could smell my fraudulence.

The morning air was crisp and filled with moisture. I followed the stone path to *El Placer* and pulled with all my might to open the large wooden door, wiggling my way through to the empty room. The food was laid out as it was the previous morning, and the aroma of fresh toast filled the air.

But, where is everyone?

I heard a faint high voice singing from the kitchen and then, as I listened closer, I heard familiar instruments. They echoed through the empty hall.

"Sol?" I repeated a couple more times. "Sol?"

The silver door swung so far open, the brightness behind it practically blinded my foggy morning vision. I hadn't thought it possible but Sol's smile glowed brighter today than ever before.

"Señorita! ¡Buenos días! ¿Cómo estás mi bailarina pequeña?"

My whole chest brimmed with excitement at her pitch. There was something effortlessly contagious about her. I felt lighter after just her greeting.

"Sol? ¿Por qué me llamas bailarina? No soy una bailarina."

"Pero siii, Señorita. Tú eres una bailarina. ¡Tú eres una bailarina increíble!" She threw an Italian gesture into the air!

She must be confused.

I intentionally laughed so as not to make her feel ridiculous, "No, Sol, yo no bailo. No he bailado en mucho tiempo."

That was a lifetime ago.

The woman's smile faded and she looked me straight in the eyes as she reached her hand across the counter and rested it on mine. It was so hot, I glanced at it to see if I was imagining the steam.

"Lo siento. Linda, no puedes cambiar tú destino." Her smile reappeared and she turned around to grab something behind the counter.

I smiled at the coconut in her hand and then at her. "Estás loca, pero muchas gracias."

She rolled her eyes with one of those obnoxious, all-knowing smiles and I suddenly missed Trix. It was clear this bundle of joy had no idea what she was saying, but she was so sweet to me that I didn't mind her confusion one bit.

When the group filed in through the double doors and began filling their plates, Sol winked at me as she turned to get back to work.

I filled my plate more with fruit and found a seat on the patio where I could enjoy the dewy air. I was so lost in the godsent meal that I hardly noticed Nick place his orange juice next to mine and settle in.

"Good morning," I peeped through a mouthful of plátano.

"Good morning, Scar. Hope you don't mind if we sit with you."

He put his jacket on the chair next to him to save it for Aileen.

"Of course not."

I glanced in silence through the left corner of my eye to watch Nick, unable to ignore the heaviness in his composure—in the way he hunched over the table, in the delayed speed with which he brought food to his mouth, in the lackluster movement of his pupils. I knew those subtleties.

There was more to their story.

"¡Buenos días!" Aileen joined us with a friend trailing right behind. "Aye, have you guys met Sybil?" Nick and I looked up to see a white-haired woman with a plate in one hand and a cane in the other, wobbling to join us.

"Morning, Nick." She looked right at me. "Well, hello! I don't think we've met yet!"

"Hi, Sybil. My name is Scar." I smiled and continued to enjoy my breakfast. We exchanged small talk, but it didn't take long for me to wonder if I was losing her attention or if there was another reason for her odd behavior. She seemed to be looking around me every time I spoke. Perhaps she was just uninterested.

I learned that she was from Portland, where Trix recently relocated. She has a couple kids who are all older and moving on with their lives, taking new jobs and starting families. Although she had a ring on her left hand, she didn't mention a husband in all her life changes and new plans. I quickly got the impression that coming all the way here was a big step for her, one of many that she would take alone going forward.

Then again, what did I know?

A petite brunette bounced up the stairs and through the draping palms. "¡Buenos días, everyone!" Gitana spoke to all the tables at once with her dreamy accent and crisp English, "We have our first excursion today through *Bosque Nuboso*. We will make a couple stops along the way to try some of our local strawberries and coffee. Please make sure to bring your passport and small change for whatever you would like to buy. We will provide you with water on the bus, so meet us at the front after you finish your breakfast. And please find me if you have any questions!"

"It was a pleasure meeting you, Sybil." I smiled at the group, cleared my plate, and headed for the stairs to my bungalow. I was hoping to lay my head down for a few minutes. That dream had really taken it out of me.

I passed a couple of the landscapers along the stone path who politely nodded at me. "Buenos días."

"¡Buenos días, Señorita!" One of the men tipped their hats and I smiled in return.

I continued steadily through the morning fog, but a cackle stopped me in my tracks. I looked down at the ring hanging from my neck.

I know that cackle.

It was a laugh that I'd known all my life. I turned around and peered in all directions to see where it might have come from, but there was no one in sight. Everyone was still in *El Placer,* and that was not a sound those quiet workers would have made. I decided to keep walking, but slower this time, so my footsteps didn't drown out any sounds.

I heard it again.

This time, it came from the trees to my left. It was so faint, it seemed I was catching only residual echoes. I deserted the stone path and followed it. Eyes wide, I peeled through the bamboo and hanging vines, practically wrestling them apart to make my way. About fifteen feet in, I found another path outlined by more neon glowing tree roots, covered by so much brush it must have been there longer than all the others.

It resounded once more.

I pressed on through the draping leaves, now swirling beneath me. Before I knew it, I had lost all orientation to where I'd started. Direction eluded me. Then through the fog, I saw a shape take form. It was large with sharp corners. I raced toward it and, as I parted the fog, a tiny gazebo with a well in the middle puzzled into formation, materializing before my eyes. On either side, there was a hammock, strung around the poles of the tiny structure. Two hammocks. One well. No one in sight.

Frustration pulled me to my knees next to the well between the two hammocks, surrounded by large shelled and half-eaten nuts. I waited, trying to sort my confusion. Fog engulfed the tiny gazebo until I searched and realized I could no longer see the stones that led me here.

Fear rushed through me, but it didn't shake me enough to get me on my feet. Instead, I sat there on the clammy stone of the gazebo and stared deep into the well.

No laugh. No sounds. No one.

My head ached with exhaustion as I remembered my dream from this morning. I stared deeper into the well until I could've sworn I saw sparks fly, like the explosions from the white hot-air balloon men. Red painted the sides of the stone well. Tiny detonations in the same golden dust that chased me around here.

I grabbed the edges and leaned over further.

There in the beyond, in the very depths, there was... green. Bright green with freshly cut grass. The green that stored drops of morning dew and blew through the crisp, early morning breeze with Papà's laughter.

I leaned further, and further.

"

Be humble for you are made of earth.
Be noble for you are made of stars.

SERBIAN PROVERB

Seven

"Scar!" The dark tunnel held me captive. "Scar! Wake up! Scar, are you coming?"

"Jenna?" Her big blue eyes locked on mine as the room slowed its spin around her. I pushed off from my bed. My hand was heavy as I dragged it to the charcoal ring hanging from my neck.

"Hey, sorry, I can totally let you sleep if you don't want to go! I just thought you were planning on coming. Didn't want ya to miss out!"

"No! Thank you for waking me! I'm definitely coming." Still fuzzy, I threw my wallet and my journal into my bag, changed into leggings, put my sneakers and cap on, and headed out to the front desk with Jenna, shaking my head free of the nonsensical dream that had felt so real.

We joined the line of people filing onto the old vintage bus, where Ramón stood with his clipboard, wearing a dark green baseball cap I hadn't seen on him yet.

He looked up at me and smiled. "Hi, Miss Scarlett. You are checked in."

I nodded sleepily and headed to a seat in the back of the bus. I wandered, looking for the perfect spot, after Jenna found a new friend to sit next to. I think she picked up on my need for some space.

I always found corners to cuddle up in. They were safer.

Huddling up on the seat, I brought my knees into my chest and tilted my forehead against the cool window while we waited for the bus to start. Once moving, we drove through the tunnel of jungle trees and my inner pessimist took over, reviewing all the night terrors, the silence, the anxiety...

I just... I wanted to find some sort of healing—some semblance of peace—here, not rattle all of my broken pieces.

I rolled my eyes and searched for the large, intertwined trees that we'd driven through upon my arrival. They should be right there, right before the gates, but they were nowhere to be found.

This place was fucking with my head.

The big brown wooden gates creaked open and a couple village locals waved us off. Everyone on the bus beamed for this venture and, once again, I really had no idea what to expect.

Something about a forest. I was really just along for the ride.

I tilted my cap down over my eyes and relaxed into my familiar fetal position while we bumped along the dirt road to the main street. It was a windy paved route under a clearing sky at about forty miles per hour and I tried to take in the landscape.

Everything was slower here. Everything was vibrant, too, but slow. So slow. There were pockets full of the same giant flowers I'd seen in *La Transparencia,* nestled between the trees and along the stone mountain as they flashed by, radiating all sorts of different auric glows. Some a mix of turquoise and purple. Others a combination of yellow and orange.

I wished Southern California had this much natural beauty. Well, maybe it did... I mean, it had to. Maybe I just hadn't noticed. Maybe it had something to do with the fact that I was always indoors at my desk or at a coffee shop, zoned into my screen. Always working. Always studying. And what for? Numbers, numbers, numbers. It always came back to numbers. The higher, the better. The more zeros, the more smiles. The higher my grade point average, the more credibility. The more certificates and degrees, the better my curriculum vitae.

But for what? What fucking difference is any of this actually making?

I sighed with all the will in me. The weight on my shoulders made me ache to just disappear. I tucked my cap deep into my hoodie and cradled my head with my hands as I silently begged the endless stream of bullshit to just shut the fuck up already.

"It's beautiful out there, isn't it?" Sibú rounded the corner of the seat in front of me and extended his hand out in question. "Mind if I join you, Traveler?"

"Sure." I hadn't noticed him sitting in any of the aisles when I walked in. I was clearly too preoccupied to care.

"How was meditation this morning?" He slid in next to me.

I gulped and hesitated to look at him, my eyes darting this way and that. There was no hiding my dissonance today.

"Mmm, I'm not very good at it. Just… can't do it."

When he sighed an understanding, judgment-free smile, relief loosened my shoulders a bit.

"Breath is a funny thing, isn't it?"

I stayed quiet. I didn't have the energy for rhetorical questions. He'd elaborate if he wanted to.

"It's the greatest gift we have. Our greatest tool. And yet, it's the easiest thing to forget to use." He stared out the window with me, lost in the carousel of flashing colors.

"I suppose you're right," I grunted, hoping he'd save his fortune cookies today.

"You know, the first person who tried to teach me about meditation… Oh boy, I grew to resent him so much. I know *hate* is a pretty strong word, but I was tipping that iceberg. I had so much to do all the time and this ol' man wanted me to sit down and be quiet… and not think… and not do… and just… breathe. I laughed at him, scoffed, thought he was crazy." He chuckled at the memory.

"What changed?"

"Death changed."

The word punched through my chest. Gulping and intentionally trying to push through the stone wall that had just shot up somewhere between the thump in my chest and the spin in my head, I looked at him.

"Death?"

He nodded. "Yeah, it had always been something I'd just heard a bit about. Burials were a normal part of our traditions here, but I'd never lost anyone close to me. Then one day, it was on my doorstep. No announcement. No invitation. No heads up. Death has a way of putting things in perspective for us—what matters, what doesn't."

He paused and let the silence hollow out the words between us for a few minutes. We stared out the window and watched life's movie loop before us. Up and up we went around this mountain.

"There's nothing like death to make us understand just how real life is... you know? How precious the force behind it..." He took a deep breath and shifted his shoulders back. "The breath."

I sat in silence, his words somersaulting through my brain.

"What changed? I think I started treating my breath as less of an annoyance, a burden, something I had to tend to or develop... and started to truly understand that it was all I had. When the meaning of everything else fell away, my breath was all that was really, truly mine. It was... me."

I sunk into his words—his thoughtful, carefully crafted words. Sibú was indeed a man of words. A writer at heart, if I was being honest with myself, I resonated with the weight they carried.

"It's all we really have," he whispered under his breath.

I looked up at him and smiled, "Sibú, you have a way with words, you know?" That elicited another snicker. "Where are you from, if you don't mind my asking?"

He returned my smile with his big lucid eyes. "In this lifetime or the last?"

I frowned at his question just as the bus jolted to a stop.

"¡Estamos aquí!" Gitana shouted with excitement, and everyone began shuffling toward the door.

Sibú looked back to me with raised eyebrows. "Come on, Traveler. Let's go see what life has for us today."

"

This is your reminder to
rip off the muzzle.
You have teeth that are meant to
sink into the marrow of life.

ALLIE MICHELLE

Eight

We followed the crowd off the bus and into a cabin where three men stood, waiting with harnesses and hooks.

I'd seriously missed a memo.

Hesitantly, I stepped into one of the harnesses and the man buckled it around me. My heart fell as I realized what this equipment might be for.

"Estás lista." He smiled and pointed me toward the table at the exit of the cabin, stacked with red helmets. I slowly grabbed one and joined the rest of the group just outside of the door for the quick tutorial.

When I looked up, I saw Ramón giving a demo on the correct positioning of the harness hook and hand placement on the handle that hung from a horizontal wire attached between two poles. Immediately, my palms were drenched.

Ziplining.

Mio dio. I really should ask more questions.

"You ready for this?" A young man from the group anxiously whispered in my ear as he slid next to me.

"Not quite," I said and offered my hand. "I'm Scar."

"Jake!" He smiled and thrust his hand into mine enthusiastically. I managed to get a decent look at him without being too obvious, but my guess was mid-thirties. He sported jeans and a flannel over a plain white shirt. His young spirit beamed through his big, genuine smile.

We both turned our attention back to the demo which in total was only about ten minutes. My sweaty everything was telling me there was something to be concerned about here.

"There are five lines in total. They start out short and each one is double the length of the last." Ramón hopped down the steps from the demo stage. "Okay, let's start forming a line. Who wants to go first?"

I shot my hand in the air and he tilted his head in my direction. "Okay, Miss Scarlett. Follow me."

Let's get this shit over with.

There was no way I was going to wait and watch everyone go before me. That would just worsen my nerves.

"Everyone, go ahead and stream in behind us!" Ramón instructed.

Jake jumped behind me. "You're literally the only person who raised a hand," he joked. "We are... in a jungle. You do know that, right?"

"Trust me, I am just as surprised as you are. I'd just rather get it over with! I mean, shoot, we have to do this regardless, right? We're already here."

"Get it over with? I think the point is to enjoy it." His brows arched with pity as he laughed.

I shot him a quick contemplative glance and kept walking behind Ramón.

Enjoy it. Enjoy what? The terror? Psycho.

We hiked up the broken, jungle-covered staircases and across a few small, very sketchy bridges lined with rope that appeared to have all the buoyancy of floss.

Perfect.

Trudging deeper into the dark moss, my intimidation twisted into a quickly-growing whirlwind. Under the bridges and all around us was muddled, murky water—home to god-knew-what. As we passed, movement rippled across the water in all directions. I gulped.

"You know what they say: The one who walks in front goes home with the ecosystem in their hair!" Jake teased, noticing me mercilessly swatting at the insects, ducking under low branches, and spitting out what I was sure were gnats.

Not exactly a nature-lover was an understatement.

We moved at a decent pace until a loud crack echoed through the trees and, faster than we could look up or around, a furry brown ball plummeted into the earth just five feet from where Ramón and I stood. The reverberation of a body slamming into the ground clapped like that of a mini boulder. The group gasped in unison at the scene. A baby spider monkey had fallen at least fifty feet through the air.

"Oh my god!" Jake rushed forward, but was halted at the chest by Ramón's hand.

"No, no, no. He's okay. We can't touch them."

"What! Are you sure? He... what if he's hurt?" Jake was confused.

"He's okay. Just give him a moment. We can't interfere with certain parts of nature. He was learning up there. This is part of his process." Beyond the firmness in his response, Ramón's quickened breath reflected his concern for the little guy.

We waited until the disoriented monkey's body uncurled, and his spinning eyes looked up and around at us. Eyebrows arched in confusion, whimpers of fear and likely pain squeaked from him as he searched for familiarity. Responses came from the trees as two older mahogany-painted, female monkeys swung at high speed toward the nearest and lowest tree.

Once he noticed them, he rolled to his feet, limping until he got to the trunk and lifted himself up through the branches. He swung to the next tree where his Guardians met him, pulled him up, and cradled him in their arms before leaving us.

The group, still stunned, finally breathed a little easier as they debriefed the experience.

"Alright, let's move on." Ramón ushered us onward.

Hesitant, my feet slowed without any conscious permission and Jake noticed.

"Hey, you good, Scar?"

"Mhm." I nodded in an effort to convince us both.

We reached our first platform.

"Careful, Sweetie." Ramón stuck his hand out to caution me around the hooks in the ground. I looked up to see a charcoal twist of deadly wire that spiraled out of visibility, the landing platform at the other end where one of the gentlemen from the cabin waited to catch me.

The baby spider monkey's fall echoed in my mind, but this time to the depths beneath the platform.

Ramón threw some ropes through some hoops, and then looked back to me. "You ready?"

"Uhm. Are you going to help me if I fall, or leave it up to nature?" I looked back at him, eyeballs surely rolling.

He chuckled until his gaze dropped to my nervous fingers, spinning the ring that hung around my neck. My fear was so potent, he could probably taste it.

"Would it make you feel better if I was the one who caught you at the end?"

I paused to think that over. I hated making a big deal of things, but he did offer. So, I nodded in agreement.

He turned to whistle to the man on the other platform and motioned for him to come our way. The man hopped on the line and glided to us. Ramón helped unhook him and then hooked himself. When he looked to me, he reached to the rope around my neck and used it to lift the ring up into the neck of my shirt. My heart fluttered at his tender touch and I dropped my chin.

"I'll be there to catch you, okay?"

I smiled a thank you through my chattering teeth and tremoring lips.

He glided down to the next platform and then shot the trolley back up to his helper who grabbed it and hooked my harness to it. The crackle, behind the bones in my chest, was creeping back as I tried to foresee the next—or last—moment of my existence.

"You got this!" Jake cheered me on from the stairs of the platform.

I took a deep breath and nodded for the man to release me. He gently pushed me off and I glided a decent speed down the line. In an upright position with my knees curled up, I clung to the handles as if my life depended on the solidarity of my grip. My whole body tensed. It wasn't until I felt arms around me that I realized I'd landed at the end.

"You did it!" He laughed as he helped me settle onto the platform and unhooked my harness.

"I did? I... I don't even remember it." I looked back.

He chuckled as if he knew something I didn't. While he continued resetting the ropes and ushered the other participants onto the platform, I walked to the other side. A few minutes passed, and I felt his hands on my waist as he tried to maneuver around to me.

"Okay, I'm going to go to the end again to catch you."

"Okay. Uh, Ramón..."

He looked up from my harness where he had checked me after the last run.

"Thank you." I hoped he could hear the sincerity in my voice. This was very sweet of him.

He smiled back at me, "Claro. Oh and Amor, open your eyes this time. It'll be worth it, I promise."

Oh snap, that's why I don't remember anything. My fucking eyes were closed!

He handed the rope to the other man and jumped on the trolley down to the next platform, which I could still see in the distance, though it was definitely further than the last.

I caught myself locking my breath in again.

What was it that Sibú said about the breath? It's not just a gift...

The rest of the group had joined the platform and the trolley came flying back up the line.

"¿Lista?" the man asked. I could barely hear him over the pounding in my chest as I hopped up to the ledge, and looked over.

I didn't know how to estimate feet, but the space between me and the ground allowed for a good fuck ton of them. I desperately searched my memory for Sibú's words.

"It's all we really have."

Inhaling as deeply as I could, the man pushed me off with a little more power this time, and I swear my stomach fell out of me when my heels slid off the wood.

I breathed through clenched teeth and quickly realized my eyes were closed again. I pried them open through the wind that grazed my cheeks. I was flying.

Light flickered through the trees and shot a whole new thrill through my veins. I couldn't get myself to look down but looking around was enough. I glided into Ramón's arms.

He held me with strength, with steadiness. My eyes were wide open, just as he'd instructed, and I couldn't help but feel wide awake there... in his embrace.

He smiled and reached for the rope to secure me.

"Beautiful, isn't it?"

All I could do was smile and nod, distracted by the surge of energy that pulsed through my bones. A high of sorts.

He walked me over to the other end of the platform, where I could wait while he filed the other guests down the line.

The energy puddled in my chest and tightened my throat.

Whoa, no. Please, no.

I sat on the edge to try to calm myself before the shaking in my core made its way to my limbs. My fingertips creeped around the curve of the wood and I slowly peeked over at the vast forest below.

"It's all we have," I repeated to myself as I took gulps of air in and out, in and out.

"Are you ready, Love?" I looked up to see Ramón reaching his hand down to me. He helped me up and readied my harness once more before hopping on the line down to the other platform, which was so far hidden in the trees that I could only really see an outline of its shape. My heart thudded. When the trolley came back up the line, the other man hooked my harness up and pushed me off with way more force than the last time.

The puddle of energy in my chest exploded, as if someone had thrown a stick of dynamite right into it.

"Dio Santo!" I clung to the handles above my head and felt the shakes pulse from my core through my limbs.

Through, not to. That was it. They kept going. And then, they were gone. I suddenly felt... light. I felt... release. I felt... excited. I was flying.

What did that psycho say about enjoying the fear?

My grip loosened and I looked up at my hands, then past them to the baby blue peeking through the treetops above. I tilted my head back and let my hair drop into the fog that trailed through the forest. The sun flashed across my face and my mouth opened. I could actually feel my taste buds playing with this...

Freedom.

Tension vacated my body, and my knees uncurled from my chest. I stared into the wildlife that twirled around me. I was spinning. Pretty sure this wasn't in the demo, but I gave zero fucks at this moment.

Just then, I crashed into Ramón. I didn't even see him because I had totally spun around and lost my destination point.

"Ayyye!" He let out a giant gasp as my body punched the air out of him and we both toppled backward.

"Oh! I'm so sorry! ¡Perdóname!"

We both laughed in unison, uncontrollably. He struggled to steady us next to the wooden post that held the platform. I turned to help and his eyes caught me, locked me.

We both stopped. Time stopped. Everything stopped.

"Uhm." He coughed. "I... uh... here..." He turned my waist and helped steady my feet onto the platform. "You, uh, you got the hang of it."

I smiled and looked down while blood flushed my cheeks red.

"That was... remarkable."

He looked up at me with confused eyebrows as he readied the rope.

"Remarkable?" His English was so great, I'd forgotten it wasn't his first language.

I smiled, "Cómo... increíble."

"Ah." He nodded and smiled. "Yes, you are."

I don't think he understood.

I looked down, sinking like quicksand into the warmth of this man, and made my way to the other end of the platform. Staring down at my hands, I marveled. They were... still. They were light. Not one sign of shaking. No clammy nervousness.

Excited to share my highlight of this doomed day, I jumped to the side rail and looked through the faces for Sibú's, to no avail.

Tiptoeing to the edge of the platform, I curled my toes until the tips of my shoes curved over the wood, and gazed into the vastness and the stunning craze of every shade of green There was life everywhere: scarlet-rumped tanagers hopping from branch to branch, red-crowned woodpeckers hunting for lunch, tent-making bats cozied up to nap.

The air was crisp and cool. There was no breeze and yet, the leaves and the flowers and the moss all seemed to pulse like the beating of a heart, like the breath that pumped oxygen through it.

Life. Everywhere. All around me.

Pura vida.

Without looking for it, I reached up and latched one bare hand around the metal line and then the other.

"Vita... Remember..." That soft ominous voice carried a breeze through my hair.

A light pushed through my vision and a childlike wonder filled my chest.

I do remember. I frowned.

My toes slid past the edge as the arches of my feet balanced on the wood and I became distracted again. It was all so beautiful. I wanted to dive in. I wanted to...

"Miss Scarlett!" The intensity in Ramón's voice made me jump backward and I turned to see the group of guests staring at me wide-eyed with shock while he walked over to me. "Is everything alright?"

"Yes, of course!" I couldn't contain my excitement. "Ramón, what else can I do?"

"What do you mean?"

"I mean... Can I go backward?"

His face froze for a moment. Then, he cocked his head and chuckled to himself. "You were terrified of this a few minutes ago and now you want to go backward?"

He had a point. Bashful, I tucked my chin in and looked up at him.

He laughed and started arranging the rope. "You really are something else, Miss Scarlett."

"Sooo... is that a yes?"

He shook his head as he busied himself. "Is it possible to say no to you?"

I blushed but my embarrassment was quickly replaced with frenzy. Most of the guests seemed to be distracted with conversation, but I could feel a few of them watching me intently.

Ramón gave instructions in Spanish to the man pushing me off and then he looked at me and shook his head before he jumped on the line and glided away. I rushed back to the edge. This time, I couldn't see the platform—just the curtain of bamboo he'd disappeared into. There was no final destination in sight.

The man plopped me up on the line, turned me back to face the other participants, and hooked my harness to the trolley. "¿Lista?"

"Si," I nodded, wondering where the hell this newfound confidence was coming from. Nervous, I focused on my breath. Inhale. Exhale. Inhale. Ex...

"Wooooooooo..." I couldn't help but scream. He really pushed me this time and I was flying through the air at high speed. The group cheered me on as they grew tiny in the growing distance.

I weaved through the trees, trusting the line that attached me to the end of my route. No clue where I was going, I didn't care and fought the urge to release my hands from the handle and instead just let my eyes get lost in the scenery.

All was quiet and I was alone in the expanse of life that surrounded me… in the wind that carried me. I could disappear right here and not think twice.

"I got you. I got you." Ramón's subtle whisper surprised me when I found myself in his arms again. He stabilized me on the platform and quietly maneuvered around my harness to unhook me. "Estás loca, you know that."

"That was amazing!"

We both giggled as he whistled down the line to announce his readiness for the next guest.

Stepping aside, I focused on getting my bearings. I couldn't help but notice how open my chest felt, how weightless my arms and legs were. Opening and closing my knuckles several times, I tested whether they were really there or not.

This must have been edging euphoria. I'd read books on this in my degree prep… about the flow state, about transcendence. I'd just never thought I was capable of actually experiencing it. A faint memory of the healing mysteries I'd attended when I was younger crept to the forefront of my mind as I recalled the sensation of those moments. I stretched my arms out and peered into the treetops above me. I twirled a couple times, but my balance must have been really off.

"Cuidado, por favor." Ramón monitored me out of the corner of his eye, so I settled myself next to the wooden post at the end so as not to concern him. After he was finished, he walked back over to me.

"Alright." He took a deep breath and arranged the rope. "What this time, mujer?"

I laughed and then realized there might be more. "Really? Can I choose?"

He looked at me with all the fear of someone rolling open the stone door of a lion's den.

"This is the last line, right? Can I go upside-down?" I covered my mouth with my hands, wondering if I could suck the question back in.

He took a deep breath, let out a big sigh, and wiped the shock and sweat from his face with his hands, as if silently pep-talking himself. I stayed quiet as he readied the rope again. The other gentleman came over and, once more, Ramón gave him instructions in Spanish. Eyes full of confusion, he clearly wondered why Ramón was letting me do this.

Before he zipped ahead of me, he came over to me, his nervous energy palpable.

"Okay, if you go upside-down, you cannot hold the handle the whole time, or the resistance won't let your weight push you down the line. You'll have to let go. Can you do that?"

I nodded with so much energy, I thought my eyes would pop out of my head. My insides were screaming like a giddy schoolgirl. This was the last line and the longest, and I wanted to make it worth it.

He just stared at me, as if reassuring himself he could trust me.

"Okay." He hopped on the line and hooked his harness to slide to the other end. "Miss Scarlett, be careful, okay?"

I smiled a thank you and clapped my hands quietly. There was absolutely no sign of the last platform and I wondered if I would care while I hung like a bat in a cave. The group watched carefully now after hearing my joyful yelps in the last run. The trolley swung back up the line and the helper caught it and then grabbed my elbow to steady me so he could hook my harness.

"Reclinarse, por favor." He put his hand on my shoulder and tipped me upside-down. "Déjalo." Then he tapped my hands, which were still attached to the handles. "Déjalo."

Slowly, I slid my hands off the handle and he pulled me up to the wooden post to gain some momentum.

Gasps swept through the group.

"Wait! Can we go upside-down, too?"

"OMG! I want to go backward like her!"

When he both released and pushed me, my entire body jolted with inertia. Fear shot through my core like lightning, and my abdomen tensed to hold my body together. I reached for the handle but couldn't find it with the impact of the wind forcing my body down.

Cazzo, what did I do?

"It's all we have!" Sibú's voice reverberated between my ears.

Closing my eyes, I located my breath, letting it climb backward through my mouth and up my body to my diaphragm as I zipped through the air. I exhaled and opened my eyes. Upside-down and spinning in the vastness around me, my arms fell below my head and relinquished control of any steadiness, any stability, any certainty my body had been fighting for.

I exhaled the last of the tension and watched it escape in the breeze behind me. Time slowed and suddenly, I could see it all. I could *feel* it all.

The sun that slashed streaks across the earth and the plants and leaves that uncurled at its touch. The light that sparkled and rainbowed in the mist, dancing above the tiny stream that toppled over the mountain's rocks. It rose through the air and played in my fingertips. The monkeys, the squirrels, even the water was running over and under the laid logs, chasing me as I flew over, laughing at the freedom that radiated in my body for the first time in… ever. The breath that pumped life through all matter was carrying me in the wind, swimming in my blood. I could feel it.

I could feel *all* of it. I'd never been… *closer*, more *one* with the world around me.

There I hung, upside-down, a caterpillar in the cocoon of the universe. Vacant of fear. Desolate of certainty. All I knew was this natural and undeniable embrace of the life force that flowed through all that surrounded me.

The only emotion separating me from that force was the reckless adrenaline now pulsing hot through my veins, the carelessness, the faith in my unfolding, in my landing, in my timing.

My feelers transcended the boundaries of my skin and soaked in the silence, the peace, that my being pirouetted in. I was at the whim of the cosmos, defying the gravity of fear, of pain, of all that weighed me down on this planet, of all that made me human, that kept me human.

This... the unknown.

My body thrusted into a wall of flesh, and Ramón heaved as my knees knocked the air completely out of him. He quickly flipped me right side up and unhooked me before my momentum threw me backward off the platform and before I could steady my vision or my feet.

Stumbling, I fell into his chest and we toppled to the floor, nose to nose, and all at once. I couldn't tell whose breath was whose.

I was so out of my body and yet, so entirely inside it. I was here. I was still. I was present... with him. On top of him.

And strangely, I could feel more than the mountains of his arms cradling me, more than his beard scratching my cheek. I could feel his insides, the light radiating from the center of his chest, the frenzied energy that shot to his limbs, the desire that tickled goosebumps to the surface of my skin. The strength, the duty, that called the fibers of his being into one.

"Uhm." He fake-coughed to break the silence, eyes still locked on mine.

I shifted my knees to find the ground and used my wobbly arms to push myself off him.

"¡Oh perdóname!" I rolled over and grabbed the metal rail on the platform to pull myself up. He used one arm to sit himself up and stared out at the trees for a good half a minute before looking at me and shaking his head with a confused smile. The man on the other platform yelled something to him in Spanish through the trees, and he rustled to stand himself up and send a ready whistle back.

While he raised his elbows above his head and wiped his face with both hands, I walked shyly over to the other side of the platform, simmering with the confusion of everything I'd just experienced. Locating the exit sign, I headed down the stairs to which it pointed.

The rope that was piled next to the stairs started whipping away and my eyes followed it back when I heard the trolley zipping down the line. Sybil screamed with excitement as she, too, landed in Ramón's arms... backward.

"Oh, that was just fantastic!" She laughed through Ramón's clearly distracted attention. I smiled, as the next guest who came after her rolled down the line upside-down.

They're... copying me.

I looked down at my chest, trying to understand the heat filling it. A smile spread across my face at the realization.

I think I assumed the group had followed me in single file after they each finished their run; but as I approached the cabin, I realized they waited for the rest of the group. I sat in the corner and tried to unbuckle my harness the best I could. My head felt so distant, like I had left it swinging in the branches somewhere.

The ride back to the grounds was quiet for me despite the excited chattiness of the bus. Everyone raved about their experiences and while Jenna attempted to exchange with me, I wanted to keep this one for myself. For some reason, I feared that speaking of it would strip it of its... *magic.*

Recalling my near-interrogation of this word Ramón used in the car ride and my slightly indecent interrogation about his faith in it, I wondered what ever happened to his grandfather's land after the settlers came—what ever happened to his people, to his grandfather.

"

That I feed the hungry,
forgive an insult, and love my enemy—
these are great virtues.
But what if I should discover that
the poorest of the beggars and most
impudent of offenders are all within me,
and that I stand in need of the
alms of my own kindness;
that I myself am the enemy
who must be loved—
what then?

C.G. JUNG

Nine

The big wooden doors swung open and we came to a stop next to the fountain outside the canopy housing the front desk. Ramón ushered us off the bus and announced it was time for dinner. My stomach growled in agreement and I ducked past him, following the group to *El Placer* where we filed into line to begin serving ourselves.

I kept my eyes peeled for Sol and my ears strained to hear her tapping feet and the music that usually followed, but I failed to locate her as I packed my plate. I asked one of the young boys behind the counter for a coconut and he happily helped me.

But Sol was nowhere to be found today. Neither was her music. The hall felt empty... hollow... compared to the other days.

We ate in silence for the most part. Everyone was clearly tired from the adventure, and obviously preoccupied with their full plates. The food in Costa Rica must be grown and raised with some special ingredients. I swore I'd never tasted fruit or vegetables this scrumptious. I could taste all the vibrancy of their colors and had to go back for seconds and thirds of my favorites. The seasoned broccoli and brussels with the roasted potato strips were the priority this meal.

One by one, we cleaned our plates and made our way down the stone path to *La Encarnada* until Gitana intercepted us and explained that tonight's session would be held in *La Transparencia*.

Feeling my eyes drooping and sinking into my skull, I wondered about the time. While rubbing my eyes, I stepped on a large lump, slid forward, and stumbled to catch myself. I looked down to see the same half-cracked open nut shells I'd sat with around the well.

"Beach almonds." I looked up at the sound of his voice. "The guacamayas eat them." Ramón pointed to the treetops where a bright turquoise bird with a long ruby-feathered tail swung above us. It shifted quite a bit, rotating in a circle as it disappeared behind *La Transparencia.*

"Here you go." He gifted me with another warm cup of creamy rich glory. His smile twitched with nerves as he leaned in to press his lips on my forehead. "Gracias por hoy."

His tenderness shot lightning through my chest. Clearly in a rush to get to wherever he was needed, he hustled past me as the walkie talkie on his hip jabbered into the darkness. Baffled, I stared into the steaming cup between my fingers, noticing that the gratitude growing in my chest was competing with its heat.

I walked through the door, grabbed a yoga mat, a blanket, and an open spot in the circle. Looking around, I realized I wasn't the only one with tired eyes and a yawning mouth.

"I'm grateful, despite the exertion of energy today, that you all showed up tonight. I'm guessing not many of you will make it to the salsa class tonight. I'll keep this evening's workshop on the shorter side, so we can all get some rest." An older woman at the front sat with her straight red hair draped from her ears to her crossed knees. She chuckled, and I noticed her earrings, necklace, and lips were all a shiny aquamarine, a striking contrast to her fair skin.

Salsa class, like the salsa Sol spoke of...

The strength in her voice snapped me into attention.

"I want to share a story with you."

The dainty red-haired woman reached her right hand into the draping left sleeve of her loosely fit garment and carefully slid out a beautifully cut piece of silver. As she turned it to an upright position, I realized it was no ordinary piece of silver. Too long to be a knife, I quickly saw the two handles near the top carved with symbols around a diamond-shaped ruby at the center, from which light emanated to every corner of the room.

Besides the candles that bordered our mats, the light pouring from the ruby was the only in the space and it shone bright enough to reflect the intention in her eyes. The room fell quiet as the older woman inhaled deeply and stared at the weapon before her with a particular reverence, almost as if she were waiting for the sword to tell the story.

"When I was young, I was betrayed. I will spare your beautiful day the details, but in short, I was betrayed in one of the worst ways a young girl can be betrayed. Our village was invaded and one of the invaders robbed me. Not of my family's belongings or wealth, but of my innocence, of my choice, and of my light."

I gulped as her carefully chosen words mitigated the heaviness hovering in the room, so it would not fall.

"And the worst part is that I was too young to realize any of that. I was too young to realize all the ways that act of theft had violated my heart, my mind, my body, and my spirit."

Her gaze fixed on the ruby, she placed her two fingers at the top of the sword and rotated it slowly, shifting the light across the room until every shade of scarlet poured forth.

"I wouldn't know until much later in my conscious years just how those wounds stayed trapped in my body, hidden beneath shame and resentment, anger, and despair. I wouldn't know until I tried to love again—to connect again."

With just a slight tap of her index finger, she increased the momentum of the sword's dance, twirling it quicker and quicker as its light illuminated the faces in the room.

"We are all here, at *La Presencia,* to return to our ever-evolving now, to our eternal moment, to our only choice. The problem…" She tilted her head, "is that when we get quiet and settle within ourselves, if we can, we are usually met with the clouds of these memories—these pains. And it stops us."

Violet and fuchsia and pink scattered in glorious flares over our skin and through the glass walls beyond us, seeping into nature.

"Whether we are aware of it or not, it is the trapping of these wounds and, more often than not, our inability or unwillingness to recognize them which keep us from moving deeper, from settling in the silence of our soul, into the memory of who we really are."

In the flashes of light, we became one. Raveled in the weight of her spoken truth, our gazes met through the flashes of color.

The sword stopped. All was still.

I shook my head and rubbed my eyes, looking up to see the others just as dazed as I was, trying to digest her story and her pain with my own.

A hand slowly worked its way into the air on the opposite side of the circle. It was Jake's. The red-haired woman nodded her head in invitation for him to speak.

"So, I think… I'm confused," Jake started. "How exactly do we move through those clouds? To the wounds? How do we… find them? Heal them?"

I gulped at his question as I realized my wounds were no secret to me. They weren't something I had to journey within to find. The blue Caribbean of Julian's eyes filled my vision and the ache of betrayal crawled back through my spine to my chest.

"I'm glad you asked, Jake." A steady smile stretched from her lips and her gaze met the other eyes in the room. "These wounds, covered in the energy of our emotions, will stay trapped within, dictating the trajectory of our thoughts, our feelings, our choices for the rest of our lives if we don't find them. _How_ we find them will look differently for all of us. Unfortunately, there is not a single approach. But if we do find them, when we do, and I have no doubt everyone in here will, it is important to remember this: Meet those wounds with forgiveness and you will find peace."

Forgiveness? Part of me was about to search the room for cameras. This had to be a joke. The magnitude of the violation this red-haired sorceress had experienced clearly far exceeded my own and yet, I still couldn't fathom the thought of forgiving Julian.

I slid my hand over my heart, feeling the wound throb, feeling the fog of energy wrapped so tightly around it. I raged silently. And as she stared back at me, her silent words struck my core, "If you don't forgive this, how will you ever trust again? How will you ever love again? Connect again?"

Forgiveness. I cringed.

My other hand fell to my hip as the pained memories on the wood of my dance studio floor surged behind my eyes. I felt the wound cut like a knife at the muscles and tendons that held my hip together.

If I don't forgive this...

Beyond my control, the tears surged.

"This," I looked up during her pause to see her gaze fixed on my unmoving hands, now hugging my body. Her eyes met mine with tenderness, with understanding, "will be your freedom from the past... and from the future. Forgiveness lies at the door to your here and now."

Some time passed and, as I eased out of my internal storm, I noticed the others around me consumed in their own. Despite the hurricanes of thought swirling through the room, the heaviness had dissolved. In its place, a mercy—a compassion—was palpable. We breathed together, bound by the inevitability of human experience, of suffering.

Inhale. Exhale.

The time was approaching an obvious conclusion.

"I would caution you all to be very wary of falling under the common misconception and even the culturally-reinforced notion that meditation, or going within, is the only way. Everyone's door has a different painting on it—a different carving in it. I know this journey is not for the faint of heart, but I promise you: The present moment, when finally found, can become quite magical and the self can become... quite limitless."

She slipped the sword back into her sleeve, settled her arms in her lap, and bowed, letting us know the session had come to a close.

"

When one is willing and eager,
the gods join in.

AESCHYLUS

Ten

Jenna and I gravitated to each other and walked back to our bungalow. We passed the empty front canopy and walked around the pond, reflecting on our experiences from the last few days. We were mid-conversation when a dark shadow dove through the trees above us and sped with fury right toward us. We gasped with fear and froze. Before we could duck, the leathery creature grazed Jenna's arm and then slapped me with its bony membraned wing on the cheek before disappearing behind us. Our screams hushed the symphony of cicadas, and everything quieted as Jenna and I found each other's wide eyes.

I grabbed my cheek and we fell to our knees, twisted in laughter at the realization that I had literally just been slapped by a bat. Tortured by the braiding of our abdomen, our shrieks filled the misty night air and we stayed on the ground for a good long time.

"Oh my god! Girl!" Jenna tried desperately to speak between her cackling. "You know what bats symbolize, right?"

I wiped the tears from my cheek as I tried to respond, "No." I wheezed, "I have no idea!"

"Death and rebirth!" Her answer quickly sobered my insides. "They're actually… In a lot of regions, they're even called Guardians of the night! It's actually a really great omen you just got slapped by one." That little calculation toppled her over with more laughter and I couldn't help but join in.

We reveled in the moment until music floated on the wind through the trees. That same music from the kitchen again. But this time, it wasn't coming from the kitchen.

"Whoa, did you hear that?"

"The music? Yeah." Jenna seemed unfazed by it.

"Where do you think that's coming from?"

"Uh, I think that's the Salsa class they scheduled for us tonight," she answered matter-of-factly.

I looked back at her confused. "Salsa… it's a dance, right?"

Jenna's nose scrunched and her cheeks twisted with another painful grin. "Scar, I'm from Tennessee and even *I* know what salsa is."

I smiled shyly, still looking around for the location of those clanging instruments.

"Silly, go find out! I'll head back. You should check it out. They said it's in *La Encarnada* tonight."

"Hmm, you want to come with me?" I asked.

"Oh no, this white girl cannot move her hips like that. I'd rather go soak them in the hot spring before bed."

"Okay, *La Encarnada* is over that way, right?" I pointed to the left and she nodded.

"See you later," she chirped as she headed back to the bungalow.

I looked for a stone path in the falling darkness and eventually, found one with a mini bamboo sign popping from the ground that pointed to *La Encarnada*. The music grew louder as I got closer and my pace quickened with focus, as if some sort of hypnosis was underway.

"1, 2, 3… 5, 6, 7…" A familiar raspy female voice rose above the music with a thick accent. I hopped up the steps and peeked through the door to see Sol in a beautiful white dress that curved tightly around her body and had ruffled red and orange flowers over the left breast and shoulder. Her hair was down and her black curls bounced with every step she took,

"1, 2, 3… 5, 6, 7…" Her eyes found me in the mirror and her smile grew even brighter. "¡Mi bailarina! ¡Vente! ¡Por favor, vente!"

Timid as ever, I slid through the door, took off my shoes, hopped down the stairs, and walked to the back of the class of only three people. Two men and one woman from our group had shown up, clearly intent on pushing through their exhaustion. I joined in and stared at her feet to figure out her pattern, "1, 2, 3… 5, 6, 7…" For not speaking English, she sure knew her numbers. Perhaps this was why.

I mimicked the movement of her feet with mine until I was in sync. Forgetting the hips, I focused on just the feet. Left foot forward, right foot back. 1, 2, 3… 5, 6, 7…

"¡Ok, entonces, escucha la música! 1, 2, 3… 5, 6, 7…" She broke from the pattern but continued repeating the numbers. She clearly wanted us to follow her lead as she walked over to her bag in front of the mirror. She grabbed a little metal triangular-looking bucket and a wooden stick.

"1, 2, 3… 5, 6, 7…" She banged the stick to the metal in sync with the counts. Listening carefully, I caught on. She emphasized the one and the five by hitting on the side of the triangular bucket that echoed louder and the other numbers on the quieter side.

"1, 2, 3… 5, 6, 7… ¡Esssoooo!" I looked around the room at the weary smiles. The man and woman with whiter skin looked more confused than the African American gentleman whose attention was narrowed in on Sol.

I was focused too, but despite my intimidation, this felt very familiar to my feet. I followed Sol and noticed our right foot landing back on one and our left forward on 5, with a nice smooth switch in the middle. I was ready for more and smiled to her in the mirror.

"¿Lista? ¡Ahora, una vuelta!"

Vuelta, vuelta, what is a vuelta again?

"1, 2, 3… 5, vuelta a la derecha." She went first and no one followed.

Ah, a turn!

She smiled. "¡Otra vez! ¡1, 2, 3… 5, vuelta a la derecha!"

I turned with her and syncopated right back with the basic step. She clapped with excitement. We did it again and again until everyone caught up.

"¡Que buenooo! ¡Ahora! ¡Vuelta a la izquierda!" She turned to the left and lined right back up with her basic.

I listened as the songs flowed right into one another and watched her steps carefully to catch up with her. She introduced a few more basic patterns. A crossover with the left foot. A crossover with the right foot. Then, a step from the middle to the left and from the middle to the right. A right turn. A left turn.

She smiled and showed us again and again and we repeated until everyone was able to join in.

She continued with the basic and then alternated the turns, but I stopped focusing on the counts and her verbal instructions.

My feet took the lead as if they'd known these patterns for years. The music was drowning out her voice now. It was beautiful. I flashed from her bright smile in the mirror to her hips, swaying with ease and grace. I tried to mimic her movement and moved left to right as my feet switched back and forth.

They sunk into an infinity shape with corners that fell heavy with her metal clangs still echoing in the background on one and five. My eyes focused on her arms, and I mirrored their perpendicular positioning, as they moved in a circle around her abdomen. Her shoulders were set back strong, and I copied.

I swear her smile grew brighter with every step. My eyes bounced back to my reflection and I was pleasantly surprised to see my frame looking very similar to hers.

The pace of the song picked up and a few more instruments were introduced. They sounded like drums, but I couldn't tell. I watched Sol, instructing less now but still doing the basic patterns, moving her shoulders with much more flavor and bouncing her knees high on each 1 and 5. Her hands circled her head and combed through her hair during her turns.

Her energy was contagious, and I felt the music zing through my bones as I danced alongside her. I attempted all of her styling and did so until they matched perfectly with the music. Her eyes were on me, too. I could see her yelling some Spanish words with enthusiasm, but I couldn't hear them over the music still rattling my skull. Awe overcame me as her arms raised to the side and swayed back and forth with the rhythm in her shoulders.

My feet, my legs, my hips hadn't felt this much energy move through them in I don't know how long. We danced and danced as the song reached its peak and, with a final explosion of musical orchestration, we ended with a last turn and our arms in the air.

We all clapped and celebrated our accomplishment together.

It wasn't until all had calmed and we exchanged smiles and hugs that I realized I couldn't tell my sweat from theirs. I was drenched. In fact, I wasn't just drenched. I was heated and drenched and the humidity did nothing to dry my skin. It was on fire and I panted for air as if I hadn't breathed for the last… I looked for a clock.

How long was that anyway?

I caught a glimpse of myself in the mirror and saw my skin flushed red. I collapsed against the mirror and, when Sol finished speaking to one of the men, she began packing her bag just a few feet away from where I continued panting.

Her smile was still bright and glowing with energy, "¡Hermosa! ¡Tú eres increíble!"

I laughed and shook my head.

"¡No, no, usted! ¿De dónde sacas toda tú energía?"

Only a small trail of beaded sweat lined the edges of her forehead. Balancing on her bent knees, she laughed.

"¡El baile es vida, mi Corazón! ¡Te lo dije!"

"¿Que? ¿Tú me dijiste qué?" I asked confused.

"Tú eres una bailarina. ¡Vive en ti!" She slapped my knee with the back of her hand.

I smiled softly and after a long pause, she bounced from her squat, blew me a kiss goodnight, and disappeared. My head fell against the mirror, but not with exhaustion. I was overcome. I don't think my body had ever felt as alive as it had today.

And the last time I danced?

I racked my brain for the moment, but couldn't recall. I marveled at the empty room, the wood floors, and the carousel of mirrors. Suddenly inspired, I walked over to the speaker and grabbed the outlet to connect it to my phone. I scrolled to an old playlist I hadn't touched in years. The first song was Ed Sheeran's *I See Fire.*

Realizing how drenched I was, I stripped to my bralette and shorts. Throwing my sweaty t-shirt and skirt to the floor next to my stuff, I laid the ring that hung around my neck on top and walked to the middle of the room.

I started with my feet.

First position. I opened my knees and collected my heels to one another, stretching the tension in my hamstrings.

Second position. I spread my heels out to shoulder width.

Third position. I brought my right heel directly in front of my left, toes pointing outward to the sides of my body.

Fourth position. I moved my right foot about six inches in front of my left.

Fifth position. I stood with my feet tucked tightly together under me. I cringed at the pain shooting through my shins as I tried desperately to keep my legs straight. Prep. And again. I let my hands trace my feet this time, painting arches over my head.

It had been ages, and yet I didn't even have to think. Fifth. Fourth. Third. Prep. Turn. Fail. I tumbled backward. Maybe it wasn't like riding a bike.

I got back up and stared at myself in the mirror.

Okay, let's just stretch, Scar.

Feet spread wide and arms extended straight to my left and right, I swayed back and forth. I leaned all the way to the right and felt the strain up the left side of my body.

"Dio Santo!" I hadn't even leaned very far. I breathed through the pain and leaned to the left. An even stronger pain shot up my right side.

My poor body. What have I done to you?

I centered myself and let my chest fall to the ground between my legs. My arms folded behind my back and fell. I rolled out the pressure as my shoulders creaked. Upside-down, I focused on my breath and caught my mind wandering to the years in between now and the last time I'd been in a studio.

High school. Senior year, but, I couldn't place it exactly. Suppression is tricky like that.

I dropped my arms around my torso and secured a steady grip on the wood, and then lifted my heels to balance on my toes and let my legs fall to either side. Slowly. Very slowly. I grinded my teeth as I squeezed my abdomen and pain shot through my hamstrings and up my groin while I fell into the splits. I released my jaw as best I could and focused on filling my lungs with air.

Inhale. Exhale. Inhale. Exhale.

"Do you ever feel awake, Traveler?" Sibú's voice rang through my head.

"Awake, likę alive?" Our conversation replayed.

The pain radiated through my right hip and throbbed down my thigh. My head fell to the wood and water rolled down my cheeks. I was determined to reclaim my splits.

I growled and used my elbows to hold myself up and roll my hip bones out.

"There are times we watch parts of ourselves die."

Part of myself had surely died.

The pain was not subsiding. If I remembered right, the therapist had told me every session that stretching was the only way to soothe the pain. But this wasn't going away. This pain was so different. The tears kept rolling and my skin shuddered all over. It was demanding to be felt. There was no denying that.

"We're forced to surrender to it, accept it, because we have no other choice. And we resist. Of course, we resist. It can hurt like hell."

Inhale. Exhale. Inhale. Exhale.

I could get myself up, I could push myself off, but I wouldn't.

"Imagine... what could we see come to life if we stopped resisting?"

There was so much... sensation. It hurt. It hurt like hell. But... I felt it. I felt it all.

Inhale. Exhale. Inhale. Exhale. I focused on Ed Sheeran, on his voice, his melody, his tale... of fire and burning, watching flames rise into the night.

Finallyyy. The heat coursing through my muscles began to cool. My steady breaths turned to pants as I pushed myself back to sit on my butt. I leaned in full extension of my torso to each foot and a venomous sting shot through my arms and legs. I fell back to the ground and pulled my knees into fetal position.

"I'm so sorry," I whispered to my body. "I'm so so sorry." I laid there, cradling my sore bones into a heaping pile.

With a few last tears, I let my body unfold as the burning subsided and a steady heartbeat pulsed in its wake. I focused on his words again.

Inhale. Exhale. Inhale. Exhale.

I rolled over and pushed my body up off the ground as the song concluded and the playlist transitioned into Mumford and Son's *Awake My Soul.*

Once more.

Fifth position. Fourth position. Third. Prep. I paused and repeated it several times before I attempted a turn. This time, I focused on my breath. One turn. Two turns. Three turns. Four turns. I stumbled out of them and, with every attempt, I stumbled out of time.

Again!

Four turns. Five turns. I solidified my landing and caught my eyes in the mirror. They were seething with determination. Unencapsulated by a past or a future, not even a semblance of an ache or a crackle.

"This will be your freedom from the past... and from the future." The ruby-haired sorceress's words skipped like rocks in my blood. *"Forgiveness lies at the door to your here and now." This is my time stop... It always was... Dance, how did I ever forget you?*

Mumford's words sang my soul awake and I thought of Sibú telling me of my breath, of it living in this body, of it dying in this body.

I looked my body up and down. For the first time in forever... I was looking at it from the inside out. The music pulled me. It tugged my arms into the air and wound me around in circles, and... I followed it, searching for the Maker Mumford spoke of.

A kick, ball change, I relevéd and threw my right leg into the air, high above my head. And again. I turned. And turned. And turned. From one corner of the room to the next, I split my turns with a fan kick and then an arabesque.

I jetéd in a mid-split, thrusting my arms high to pull my body into the air. I landed in a lunge with my arms arched in a halo over me, and my back slowly curved to the ground where I rolled over my shoulders and threw my legs high above my head in a switch kick. I pushed off and found myself on my toes, knees locked, and arms posed.

Like riding a bike.

I paused when I saw two dark legs hanging in the mirror out of the corner of my eye. Panicked, I stumbled from my demi-pointe and turned to see Ramón sitting on the platform in front of the door. His legs dangled over the wall under the staircase.

Gulping for breath, I walked to where my phone was plugged in, grabbed my shirt, and wiped the sweat from my forehead.

"How long have you been there?"

He tilted his head.

"Long enough." His smile showcased sweet surprise and I fought the butterflies in my chest. "Where did you learn to do all that?"

I leaned my back against the mirror and faced him. "All what?"
He shot back a condescending glance.
"Uhm, I used to, uh… I used to dance."
His blank stare was clearly waiting for more. "Used to…"
"Twelve years. Contemporary. Ballet. A little hip-hop, but mostly contemporary."
"Ah." He nodded his head. "Well, you're incredible."
I dropped my chin. "Oh no, not really. I used to be. I think my body just about hates me now."
"Why do you say that?" His eyebrows fell to a genuinely curious angle.
I tilted my head back to the dim lights that hung from the ceiling. "Ah, I just haven't used it. I haven't danced in… I think it's been three years now." I chuckled. "All that actually hurt pretty bad."
"Why did you stop dancing? If I moved like you, I would never stop." His sincerity touched me and I took a nice deep breath to contemplate. I smiled and searched for words, resolving not to bring the conversation down with the sob story though. Coming up empty, I shook my head.
"Hmm, okay… why did you start?"
"Why did I start dancing?"
He nodded.
"I've never thought about that. I was so young. I guess… it's just all I knew. It was just *inside* me." I laughed at the memory that surfaced. "Mamma used to tell me, 'Don't ever let anyone take your dance, Scar.'"
"Your mamma sounds like a wise woman. Did someone take it?"
Death took it.
I shook the realization from my head and looked at him, shrugging my shoulders to forfeit answering that one, too.
"Well…" He waited, an obvious effort to give me space. "You should take it back."

I smiled. "You know who is really incredible? That Sol! My god, I wish I could move like her! Her energy is astonishing."

He laughed. "Yeah, Sol is pretty great. She is our own in-house salsera."

"Salsera?"

"Yes, it's what we call female salsa dancers, salseras. Males are salseros. Pretty much anyone who loooves salsa the way she does."

"Well... that shit is rough!" We laughed. "But exhilarating!"

Ramón was clearly getting a kick out of my expressiveness. "I'm sure you were great, Miss Scarlett."

"There's something very different about that dance. I vaguely remember an intro class when I was young. I mean, I've always loved ballet, but that was... And the music! Wow, the music."

"You like it?" His tone danced with excitement.

"Ah it was... it was..." I wanted the perfect word. "FIRE. I didn't want to stop."

"So, if tonight was your first time and she just taught basics, then you've never danced it with a partner, correct?"

"A partner? It's a partner dance?" Intimidation coursed quickly to my palms and I wiped them on the back of my shorts, trying to recall that from the only class I'd ever taken.

Ramón dropped his head in laughter.

"You are adorable."

"Don't patronize me," I half-joked, snapping my shirt in his direction.

"Yes, Miss Scarlett, it is a partner dance. And you're lucky I don't know what that word means."

I laughed. "But, it's so fast!"

He blushed as he stared at me and then pushed himself off the platform and hopped down to the floor. Placing the front desk phone that was attached to his belt on the floor where he'd sat, he walked over to me and extended a hand.

Without permission, my eyebrows and heart rate raised in surprise. Swallowing the knot in my throat, I put my hand in his and he guided me out to the center of the room.

"So, you already learned the basics, right? Chest out, shoulders back, elbows never go past your back?" I nodded in agreement and adjusted my body.

"...and?" He looked at me with wide eyes as if I was supposed to finish his sentence. I crooked my head to the right and waited for him to feel the gust of sarcasm I sent his way.

"And... relax." He shook my hands out playfully and his smile disarmed me, enticing one of my own.

He held both my hands in open position. Turning his wrist in, he unfolded my palms so that our hands were against each other. His voice was subtle, his touch smooth.

"Dance is energy. Connection is energy. It starts here. The first place you ever connect with your partner is here, in the hands. This is where we communicate, where all the signals are given and received. If this connection isn't strong," he made his hand limp, "there won't be a follow through. Connection needs grace and flexibility, but a healthy amount of tension— resistance. The goal is to keep your eyes locked on your partner while your hands do the talking and your feet follow."

His hands played with mine as he used them to make his points. I gulped at the softness in his voice and the sweetness in his touch.

"So, attention here, okay? Eyes on me, but this is where we connect."

I gulped again and nodded. This was a lot to pay attention to.

"Okay, 1, 2..." I stepped on his foot and we fumbled. "Oh, that's okay. So, the woman always steps back first. The man steps forward on one. Again. 1, 2, 3... 5, 6, 7." Success! He smiled.

"Easy, you got it! Another basic... the cross-body lead. This is just how I get you from one side to the other. Follow my hand movements and keep your basic step."

Stiffly, I followed and landed on the other side of him, only to hear him chuckle.

"Hey! What are you laughing at? I did it. I'm here!"

He stopped and looked me in the eyes. "You're not used to being led, are you?"

His question hit me like a brick wall I chose to run into. My eyes fell to the floor. Touching my chin gently, he pulled my eyes back up to his.

"That's the thing with partner dances. The woman has to be led, taken care of. Which means... she has to *let* herself be led and taken care of." His obvious gesturing and emphasis were nauseating. I couldn't stop my eyes from rolling.

Maybe if I met men who knew how to lead, I would know better.

"I get it. I need to relax."

He tried to hide his stupid smile but failed.

"One basic and then a cross-body lead, okay? 1, 2, 3... 5, 6, 7. 1, 2, 3... 5, 6, 7."

When he tried to sweep and I yanked, he broke out in laughter despite my obvious frustration.

"I have an idea..." He walked over to the mirror where my phone was plugged into the sound system. He took my phone off the chord and replaced it with his, scrolling until he was clearly satisfied with his song choice.

I knew the horns immediately. *Stand By Me* by Ben King. A high voice started singing the familiar lyrics, but it wasn't Ben King. This song had a funky hollow drum sound on the track.

"That's not salsa..." I stated the obvious.

"Oh, Love, salsa would not help you relax right now. I'm going to show you bachata." He laughed again. I furrowed my eyebrows and pulled back with confusion. He paused and tilted his head. "Trust me, okay?"

I sighed my tension out, shook a bit, and gave him my hands.

"Follow my lead. It's just a four step and a tap with your hip on the fourth and eight counts." He gently grabbed my wrists and counted me into a four step that went from the left to the right and back again. An easy basic. He counted the first few and then stopped and swept me from side to side with a slight tug.

I sank into Prince Royce's charming Spanish tune.

I was doing it! Side to side and back and forth. And side to side again. I couldn't quite hold his eye contact, but I focused on the lead in his hands, the energy that pushed me back and forth and side to side. This music was awfully... cozy.

He turned his hand in mine and lightly tossed it up his shoulder, extending his arm under mine to cradle my shoulder blade. He pulled me in closer.

Gulp. At least I didn't have to hold eye contact in this position. My forehead was right under his chin and the space between us was much less. I wasn't sure how we were moving together so fluidly, but we were, and those hollow drums were rattling my legs. I could feel them... inside me.

My core moaned at the sensation.

He let his grip go a bit on one of the back steps and gave me a quick eyebrow raise and a head nod for a turn. I followed the arch of his arm to an inside turn and won a sweet smile from him when I landed on the correct foot. He took me to the other side and signaled me again. I turned and turned. He pulled me back into his frame, this time much closer. Tucking my right hand into his chest, he cradled it.

Connection. Connection starts here, I reminded myself.

I rested my chin on his shoulder and settled into the lyrics, remembering the magenta mountains and the hazy skies surrounding us.

This had to be what being led felt like. I mean... he was definitely leading me. I knew because I had no actual idea what the hell I was doing or where I was going next. He started turning both of us together as we were holding each other. I was lost and couldn't care less.

His knees inched between mine. It was subtle and comfortable and gave my hips room to sway with the music. He was teaching me, silently. Little by little, he was showing my feet to follow, teaching my hips the rhythm, easing my frame into his. I could feel his breath on my neck as his chin rested against the side of my forehead.

Connection.

The song ended and we froze for a second. He pulled away and smiled probably the biggest I'd seen yet, and it flushed me red again.

"See! You're a natural! And… now that you're relaxed, you'll pick up salsa much faster."

"You're crazy." I laughed him off while he hustled back to his phone.

I knew that voice. Marc Anthony's *Flor Pálida*. I had no idea this was salsa. All I knew was that it always lit me up. I'd listen to it and sway to the strings of romance and adventure, ease and wonder.

Ramón hustled back over to me, clearly as smitten as I was by this whole thing. I looked over at the front desk phone he left on the floor and back at him.

"Shouldn't you be working or something?" I teased. He hid his guilty smile and ignored me, grabbing my right hand and throwing my left arm up into his frame.

The beginning of this song was… slow, intense. And he cradled me as such, holding my hand to his chest.

"And 1, 2, 3… 5, 6, 7."

He stopped counting pretty quickly. It was easy to tell he loved this song, too. As soon as he was sure my feet got the step, he pulled me closer and I could hear his hum echoing in his chest. He swept me from one side of the room to the other, stopping only to turn me.

The melody picked up and his feet couldn't contain their excitement. He pushed me back and threw me into a turn, then a double, then a triple. He grabbed my shoulders with his hands and pulled me backward, guiding my feet forward and then back. His hands dropped to my hips, clearly trying to show me how to twist them with the music as he sang along.

I laughed and gave it my best effort. His joy was contagious. I swear I felt it shoot through my rib cage and up my torso.

Connection. *How sweet it is.*

Flor Pálida bled into yet another salsa song and another and another. Time was lost between us.

We danced and we laughed and we danced some more, until we'd fallen in circles to the ground. Relentless laughter filled the air and our heads hit the wood.

"Is that finally the end of your playlist?" I teased.

"Hey! You liked my playlist!"

"I did. I did. What time is it?"

"You don't want to know. Come on." He chose another song and walked over to me, offering his arms to help me up. Sweaty and tired, I reached my arms up but made no effort to pull myself up. He smiled at my dead weight and shook his head. Bending down, he reached one arm under my back and the other under my legs and lifted my body off the ground.

Surprised, I reached my arms around his neck to sturdy myself. The song began and he spun me in slow circles while I threw my head back and enjoyed the bliss.

When I pulled it up, his eyes were on mine but he didn't mirror my excitement. He was calmer… steady, happy. I got lost in his eyes trying to figure them out and he slowly let my knees fall down his side to the ground.

No Hay Nadie Más by by Sebastián Yatra was another bachata, a much slower one with those same hollow drums laid over an acoustic track, complemented by a beautiful raspy voice.

The lyrics reminded me of that day with my first love and his sultry green eyes, of how then, I never believed there would be anyone else.

Ramón pulled me in closer this time, my face tucked beneath his jawbone. He placed my hand on his chest again, but left it. I was wondering where his other hand was until I felt it on the back of my head, slowly sliding down my hair and pausing at my neck. I felt him pull me in a little tighter.

The song carried us as we swayed four steps to the right and four steps to the left. Salsa was magic for sure, but there was something quite soothing about those congas in this track. His hum rose again, from his diaphragm and past his collar bones.

I was enjoying here, with Ramón. But I wondered if there would ever be anyone beyond Enzo.

His hand didn't leave the back of my neck until halfway through the song when he spun me out to an open position and taught me a few new easy moves. It wasn't long until he pulled me back in and led me back and forth with his knees again.

His arm braced my shoulder, and as the song came to a close, his hand came up over my shoulder and peeled me backward into a slight dip. I followed and arched myself backward, my toes lifting off the ground as the air inside me escaped.

He gently and ever-so-slowly pulled me up to face him. My toes dropped to the ground and my whole body felt limp, weightless… euphoric, like I was spiraling once more through the light in the trees. I couldn't tear my eyes from his.

The connection started in our hands, but now… it was everywhere.

We both jumped at the sound of the phone, and then shuddered as we realized we should probably let go of each other so he could go get it. His arms fell from around me and he squeezed my hands and smiled before he walked away.

I moved to gather my things as he answered the phone and proceeded to calm someone on the other line. I stuck my sweaty shirt and phone in my bag and threw it across my shoulders, simultaneously slipping my skirt over my shorts and putting my shoes on.

He hung up and turned to face me with a smile. "Can I walk you to your bungalow?"

"Oh, that's alright. It sounds like someone needs you," I insisted.

He tilted his head once more. "Can I please walk you to your room, Miss Scarlett?"

"Are you afraid the howlers are gonna' eat me?" I teased.

I shook my head at the little sabe-lo-todo head tilt that allowed him to get away with so much tonight.

We tip-toed in single file down the dimly lit path in silence so as not to make too much noise for the bungalows we passed. My head was down so I could focus on where I was stepping, but when I thought about how dark it was, I sprang my eyes toward the treetops. There they were! Those little spinning balls of fire! No wires to be seen, no bulbs. Just hanging, floating fire.

Sure, not strange at all.

"Ramón! How did you guys—" I bumped into his chest before I could finish. I didn't even realize we'd arrived. He was stopped, waiting for me, and I ran right into him. "Oh! I'm so sorry!" I pushed myself back off him a bit. "Well, goodnight."

"Miss Scarlett, with all the respect you deserve, I just want to tell you…"

My heart stopped at the look in his eyes.

Please, just let me go to my bungalow.

"You are so very beautiful."

Oh, I wasn't expecting that.

I tried to hide my surprise, as his compliment clearly flattered me pink. I paused, speechless. But only for a moment. Placing my hand on his shoulder, I stretched up to the tips of my toes so I could reach my lips to his cheek. I don't know what overcame me, but I left a light kiss.

I ducked my head and walked past him before I could see his face.

Hopping on the broken stones and between the tree roots soaked in mud, I stopped and turned back.

"Hey, Ramón!" I blurted quickly when I found him still facing me, not an inch from where I'd left him. "Gracias... por todo."

He smiled sweetly. "Buenas noches, Miss Scarlett."

"

What is to give light must
endure burning.

VIKTOR FRANKL

Eleven

"Coo Coo! Coo Coo!"

I stretched my tired eyelids open and, as I rolled over from my tummy, a sharp pain sling-shotted from my hip up through my diaphragm and into my shoulder.

I slowly tried to push myself off the mattress, but my arms and abdomen refused. I flopped back down.

"You have a long night, Roomie?" Jenna shot me a playful smile from her bed where she was reading and sipping her coffee.

"Mmmhm," I groaned and, with all the strength I could muster, managed to push myself up from the bed. Scooting back, I rested my head on the metal headboard. "Whew."

"Wow." Her face grew a bit more serious as she realized just how sore I really was. "It must've been one hell of a class last night!"

I nodded in agreement, as I gauged just how badly I'd hurt myself. I wiggled my toes, elongated my arches, bent my knees, turned my hands, and extended my fingers, then curled them back. Every single part of me hurt.

"Have you thought about working with one of the Awapa they have here? I think there is one who does massages. Everyone has said they really are magic!"

I shook my head at the word. "I hadn't planned on it."

"Well, if you are planning on going on any more excursions, you might want to consider it, girl."

"Hmm."

"What? What are you thinking?" she asked.

"I just… I don't really know how I feel about being touched like that."

"Oh, gotchya!"

I quivered at the thought of the last human whose hands touched me bare-skinned.

Yeah, no.

I twisted to lift my legs out of the bed. My hips throbbed and, as I pressed on my feet to stand up, my knees completely gave out and I fell back onto the bed.

Jenna gawked at me in disbelief.

But actually, what did I do to my body last night?

I wondered how I could be so stupid, doing that to my body on a trip where I needed to be able to move.

"Damn, I don't think I have a choice. I sign up at the front desk, right?"

Baffled, she nodded at me.

"Okay, I'll meet you up there." I hobbled to the bathroom with my toiletries, showered, and washed my face, grinding my teeth with every jolt of pain that accompanied my movement. It had never hurt so much to just lift my arms to drop soap over my head.

I dropped off my things in the bungalow and headed slowly toward the front desk where Jenna waited for me patiently.

I scanned the paper for a familiar name. "Do you remember the name of that one Awa? She had long, dark hair?"

"Oh! Aaina! Oh yes, she was the masseuse."

"Ah, yes, her! Thank you!"

I looked up and noticed a tuft of silver hair swaying in the wind amid the bushes. He was on his hands and knees again in the distance. Though his body was a bit lost in the shrub, I could swear his solemn eyes were fixed on me.

I shook my head and dropped my chin.

Turning my eyes back to the paper, I found her name on the list and scribbled mine next to it. There were no time slots, of course. Their organization made no sense here.

I wrote *as soon as possible, please,* knowing I couldn't do much else unless I worked through some of this.

Jenna slowed with me as I struggled to maintain an even pace on the path to the morning workshop. She was so attuned to my incompetence, she even grabbed me a yoga mat and blanket when she grabbed herself one. Laid it out for me and everything. It was a struggle trying to find a comfortable position, and I finally just settled on my bum and hugged my knees, knowing I wouldn't last too long in any position.

"Good morning, everyone." Rebecca's voice was soft this morning, very mellow. "How is everyone doing?" Her eyes wandered around the room and I got the feeling it wasn't one of those rhetorical questions speakers ask without expecting a response. She was genuinely waiting for one. Moments later, the silence was deafening and a bit awkward.

"Very relaxed here." Eyes shifted to the redhead at the front and I realized it was Aileen who spoke.

Rebecca smiled and nodded, and then waited some more. "Did anyone find any doors yesterday?"

The room looked a little puzzled until we collectively realized she was referring to the teaching in the workshop the night before. I didn't remember seeing her there.

My mind flashed to the Salsa music still vibrating through my muscles with such radiant intensity.

Feeling so inside my body, alive, connected.

"I wrote a poem last night!" Jake's arm shot into the air from the left side of the room. The excitement in his voice made everyone jump a bit. "Sorry, I just... I haven't written in years, and I felt so inspired last night after our ziplining trip through the forest and really..." He turned all the way around until his excited eyes landed on me. "After watching Scar face her fear with such... ferocity, and then inspire us all to do the same... I don't know. A poem just came through. It felt, you know, like a meditation."

My cheeks flushed with embarrassment, and I tried to tuck my head into my arms and away from the smiles everyone tossed me.

I guess I just hadn't realized the ripples those decisions had. I was a little lost in the whole thing.

Rebecca gave both Jake and me a very warm smile.

"Thank you for sharing."

I didn't like the attention. Didn't like it at all. It made me too nervous.

"Anyone else?" I felt her eyes on me as she scanned the room, almost as if she expected me to speak up, and part of me wondered if she'd somehow come to know about the dancing last night. I hoped she didn't see me with Ramón. I didn't see anyone there.

"Alrighty, well let's move on with our stillness this morning. Go ahead and close your eyes and follow my words." As soon as everyone's eyes shut, I laid back on my yoga mat, feeling the tension recoil in my core and release as I fell. I tried not to moan out loud.

"Shoulders back. Spine straight. Inhale and follow your breath from your mouth, down your throat and into your lungs, and down into your diaphragm. Let your belly rise. And let your belly fall. Follow your breath back up through your lungs and throat, and out your nose."

I was able to focus on what she was saying without my mind wandering too far this time.

Go, me.

"Now, this time, as you inhale deeply, imagine inhaling light. Pure white light. And, as you follow it down into your lungs and diaphragm, I want you to imagine it filling your body, entering your bloodstream. Watch it flow through your arteries and illuminate your capillaries. Feel it seep through your skin and out of your pores."

Light. Weightless.

She followed with more words, but I was clearly too busy in my self-talk to hear what she said.

Dark wooden beams lined the ceiling above me. I squinted closely, trying to make out the tiny crevices in the wood, the discolorations of the years, the layers of circles in the yonis. A few minutes into my concentration, I noticed I wasn't feeling my body so much anymore. I closed my eyes, realizing my freedom from the tension.

I was just… still. Unmoving, I tried to repeat how Rebecca started the meditation. I imagined myself inhaling light and watching it travel as air through my body, into my bloodstream, and to my skin. I watched it flow to every organ and limb.

Suddenly, I felt weightless again. I was floating, spiraling upside-down through the golden streaks of light that trickled through the trees. I was mid-air with my legs high as my hair spun around me in a tour jeté.

Someone's rustle broke through my vision and jolted my eyes open. I looked over and saw Nick rolling his mat. The room was empty except for him. Everyone was gone.

Confused, I moved swiftly to spring up and immediately felt my abdomen shriek in so much pain I almost vomited. Instead, I heaved to the side.

Clearly, the pain hadn't gone anywhere.

Nick rushed over when he saw my discomfort. "Scar, are you alright? Do you need help?" I shook my head and tried to thank him through my gasps for air. "Are you sure?"

I coughed to catch my breath until I heard a sweet sultry voice chime in.

"Hi Scar, we are all set for your session." I looked up but, with blurry eyes, I could only make out a robust beige shape draped in a dark curtain. "Oh, we need to get you there right away." I felt dainty hands catch me.

"Here, let me help." Nick's voice faded with the wrapping of his arms around my torso.

My world went dark.

"

Most battles,
we never want to fight.

JADE ALECTRA

Twelve

I woke to her fingertips grazing my skin, untying my shirt. My eyelids peeled back to a dimly lit room. From the high ceiling lined thick with vines, there hung those beautiful little balls of fire, tucked delicately between leaves and coffee beans. I watched through my hazy lens as they expanded and contracted. They seemed closer to me here than outside in the trees.

Lavender and orange peels filled the air. Delicious. Busty, colorful flowers scaped the walls and hung around me, swaying gently of their own accord.

Me... I was on a bed, but unaware of the trip here. Aaina moved around me so gracefully, I could feel her body without it touching me. Her energy. It was so smooth and easy. I looked down while she eased my arms out of my shirt for me. Every time I tried to assist her, I twitched with pain. Only half conscious, I knew the truth. I couldn't be any help right now. Nonetheless, with patience in her touch, she unraveled my skirt from around my waist and pulled my black panties down my legs.

Her skin was silk against mine, every move she made slow. I'd never gotten a professional massage before, let alone in another country. I had no idea what to expect here, but she had me so relaxed, I didn't really care what she did to me at this point.

I watched her eyes trace my body slowly, steadily, as she loosened my bra and finished undressing me. I was bare, naked, with no sheets. Totally exposed, and yet, all those self-conscious feelings I'd experienced in my bathing suit in front of the bathroom mirror vacated me now.

The room was neither cold nor hot. I was exceptionally comfortable lying there, in all my nakedness. She left behind me and I desperately wanted her to come back. My skin had never before ached with this intensity.

Her footsteps tapped lightly behind my head, as she reached for something high on a shelf somewhere. When she came back, the top of her uniform was gone and she wore only the bottom skirt with a loose black spaghetti strap tank top. It hung low down her chest, hugging the curvature of her breasts with grace. Her hair was pulled to the side the way it was on orientation day, elegant as ever.

She can't be a minute over twenty-eight.

Young with a deep beauty and captivating eyes, the class with which she carried herself emanated all the richness of a grown woman. Her lips, full and warm, rested in a sweet, natural smile.

The desire in my body was growing fiercely. I wanted her. She moved behind me and pulled all of my curls from under my neck to the back of the table. Digging her fingertips into the base of my neck, she began tugging at the roots of my hair and massaging my skull in circles.

She dipped her hands into a small steaming pail on the side of the bed and they were drenched in oil when she lifted them. I closed my eyes as she neared my body and, before they even touched me, I felt the oil drop to my chest. Hot. My whole body reacted with heat and moisture as she dripped it over my left breast and then my right and then rested her hands on my decollate. There, she kept them and my muscles froze despite the heat. Lavender filled the air.

"Breathe deeply, Scar."

The rasp in her voice was the only invitation I needed.

I inhaled the steam. Her hands stayed there until the desire in my body calmed and the air was so still, I could hear the blood coursing through my veins. I'm sure she could, too. We both waited in silence while it pulsed through my body and my breathing evened itself.

Her hands steamed as they pressed into my neck, digging deeply at my muscles. It hurt at first and I cringed at the years of pain her fingers dug at. It clearly wanted to get out and I bit down on my teeth to brace for it. She slowed again, bringing her hand to my jaw and drawing tiny circles down and around it until my bite released. I quickly eased into her growing pressure. She continued kneading the tension out and a peace trailed her hands as she held my jawbone to navigate my neck.

The ache was still there, but it was distant now. Numb almost. In fact, my entire body seemed dead, like it wouldn't even flinch if a car came plummeting through the room.

My neck loosened, her hands moved over my chest. Her movement was slow as she massaged into my breasts, lightly pushing her fingers around them and over them. She grazed my nipple with such ease, my body flushed with more heat. I opened my eyes to her black tank top hanging over my face. Her figure was arched over me and it made me want her more.

I'd never wanted a woman before. I hadn't even had a man yet.

I could smell her perfume, her scent, her sweet earthy oils as her hands dug into the muscles on my neck, my arms, my side. Her skin ignited sensation up and down the length of me and I let it, moaning and arching as her hands moved over me. My eyes rolled in and out of consciousness with every thrust of her weight into my body.

I felt the tense energy vibrate when she'd push into a new muscle. It shivered with frenzy and then fell as she continued, almost as if she released it. My physical body swung between sensations, desiring her from the inside of me and then feeling so limp, I couldn't even continue with the thought. I just hung there floating, in a stillness of space and time, feeling everything.

Maybe I was still on that studio floor meditating. I hadn't felt an ache like this in god knows how long and every time I tried to think about or contemplate for one second what was happening, I couldn't. Her fingers found the sides of my head and somehow massaged all the confused wonder out. I was lost. Lost from my mind, from my thoughts. Lost in sensation, in pleasure. I didn't want it to end.

I was dazed when I felt her move around the table and my head swung to the left to follow her hands as they traced my rib cage and the print which lined them: *Love Conquers All.*

I think I might've forgotten entirely about that tattoo until I watched her long natural nails carve over each one of the letters. Her figure was a growing blur as she moved down my body, her hands curving over my hip bones and massaging them at every angle.

Fear struck lightning through my body and my chest ached miserably. When I winced, she paused. I opened my eyes lightly, finding hers full with tears as she towered over me, knees now bent on the table beside me. She wore a look of apology as she moved her fist to the side of my right hip and drilled it directly into the tissue which housed that scarred dislocation.

Pain radiated through my pelvis and then reverberated in my tail bone, shooting up my back with fury. I threw my head back and muffled my shrieking as the tears streaked down the sides of my face. She pushed deeper and deeper, and then I was gone.

Opening my eyes as my fists slammed against the wooden floor, a streak of pain lit up the entire right side of my body and my skin broke out in a quick sweat.

This attempt was different, and I knew it as soon as I stepped. I jumped early, before my prep was settled and with too much momentum. The imbalance forced a faulty landing and my left knee gave out, forcing a collapse onto my right hip.

I'd been training all day. My mental exhaustion shattered my resistance quickly, and my entire being was overcome with shock. There was no bracing for what had just happened. One moment, I was in the air, twirling out of my fifth pirouette and leaping into a full split spread. The next, I was on the ground, writhing in pain.

My vision blurred with red on the wood before me. I pushed my fists against the ground as I tried to steady myself. I searched for air but found none. So, I waited... and waited.

Breathing deeply over and over again, I tried to tap into my limbs. I moved my torso, my chest, my neck, and arms. Then I moved down to my left leg and was able to wiggle my toes. I shifted my attention to my right leg as it grew numb. It didn't seem to matter how hard I focused; I couldn't quite feel my toes.

And so, I waited... and waited.

Eyes darting around the studio, my phone was at the other end, resting on the speaker while my playlist still serenaded me in the background. I couldn't move. This was the first time in my twelve years of training and eighteen years of life that I'd ever felt so helpless on a dance floor.

My training. My scholarship. My dream. My body.

The salt stained my cheeks and sunk into my perfect little ballerina bun as my body laid there, filleted by fate, and my vision fell dark.

I drifted in a blurry daze as I looked back to find Aiana's face, too, was dripping with streams and strangely warping. The hair draped over her shoulders was growing lighter and bouncing from its straight length into curls. The pain in her eyes morphed them green, and her lips looked like the ones I'd seen in the mirror my entire life.

I frowned as I tried to make sense of what was happening. The tank top, which had been tight at each of her full curves, was falling as her frame changed and her skin lightened from the deep native color to an olive Southern Californian tan.

I quickly tried to clear the water from my eyes to better my vision, but as I leaned forward, I felt her. I felt the aches in her body—the sensations. I felt the desperation pulsing from her chest, the grief pumping vigorously through her veins. I felt her confusion and her fear. I felt her rage grow hot with steam as she came closer and her lips met mine. They were soft and spoiled with years of fear unspoken. She moved calmly as she brushed the hair from my wet face and pressed her forehead to mine. I felt her loss, her depth, her brokenness.

Eyes closed, I slowly kissed her back, softly with tenderness. I felt her shattered pieces and desired only to cradle them—to love them.

Her now tiny frame fell into my arms, pushing me back to the table. She kissed me with force now and I felt her fury tornado through her. I could hardly see and my hands moved as if they didn't belong to me, pulling her straps down her arms as I kissed the weight she carried from her shoulders and licked the grief, still trailing from her eyes, down her neck. She moaned with release as I accepted all of her shattered pieces.

On top of me, her skirt was tugged around her thighs and hips. Heat rose from her skin weighted with years of emotion. My hands traced her curves with gentleness as I grabbed at the tension and frustration her body had become home to and dragged my fingers over the letters on her ribs.

My head fell back with the gravity of confusion, as I only partially realized what was happening through my blurry vision and the emotion roaring through me.

Her hair fell on my chest as her lips tugged on my oily skin— over me, down me. I could feel the water still falling from her face as it toppled to my chest, and I cradled her jaw while she continued to love on every part of me. My body rippled with desire as her mouth consumed my breasts.

I hadn't felt this much in years. I hadn't felt this much... ever. My head rolled as I finally let my body feel it all.

Her arms wrapped around my thighs, as her hands braced my hips. She kissed my protruding bones and the loss of appetite that carved them. She reached and grasped my breast with such tenderness, more tears rolled from my eyes. Her mouth met me, open and wet, warm with gentleness and hungry with acceptance.

The pain in my nerves rolled into a deep pleasure and I moaned at every transition as it coursed through each limb. Every stroke of her tongue took me further and deeper into my body, and my hips dropped in total release. I felt no tension in them now, no resistance. They rolled back and forth with each pull of her lips.

My hands searched for her skin but could only reach her hair. Her now gorgeous golden locks fell all over me and I admired them with nostalgia.

I peered down and marveled at her familiar curves. She was petite but filled in all the right places. Her legs were long and flawless, muscular from the years of training, of accomplishment. A humble pride swept through my soul as I remembered the stages and auditoriums, the competitions, the heights my body had reached. I grabbed at the surgical scars on her hip with remorse, with guilt, for how I'd punished my shortcomings with so much disgust... so much anger.

Her mouth pulled at me with ferocity and I combed through her hair as her eyes mirrored mine.

I feel you.

I was positive she could hear my thoughts as her tears had ceased and her bottom lip sent a pulsing vibration through my joints, up my torso, and down every inch of my skin. My head fell back as I moaned with every ounce of strength my body could allow at once.

She slowly pulled away and dragged her lips over my scar, tracing it with forgiveness while I twitched in every place. Crawling up to my face, she laid her shaking body on mine and rested her head in my neck.

I was overcome with sensation, unable to move in her embrace, with nothing… but gratitude.

"

Freedom begins when you loosen
the grip from your throat.

BROOKE SOLIS

Thirteen

A tapping on the roof top dragged me to consciousness and I rolled my neck to scan the empty room, still dimly lit with candles. I opened my eyes wider as I looked down to see a blanket covering me, rolled up over my chest and under my arms. My skin was moist with oil and the blanket stuck a bit as I lifted it.

No Aaina.

I realized quickly that I was sitting up—that I had just pushed myself up and felt no pain, not one ache. My abdomen, my shoulders—all relaxed. I moved them a bit, swinging my arms in circles but there was nothing to be found. Everything was loose.

Confusion taunted me as I recalled the last few moments I'd remembered.

Had I been dreaming? I reached down to run my hands over my legs and hips, down into my panties—warm with sensation.

I turned swiftly to the mirror behind me. The woman looking back at me was… pretty, and bright. She was light and her smile full. My curls bounced around my glow and when I peered a bit closer, I noticed the dark caves around my eyes had lightened… dramatically.

My clothes were gone. I stood to grab the beautifully white-laced dress with turquoise trim hanging on the mirror. Throwing it over my head, I tied it around my waist. And as it draped over my knees, I just couldn't help but look at myself, like really look at myself.

My bones felt so deeply rested, I figured I must have slept at least a few days in that room. I looked around and took a deep breath, wondering if all I remembered had actually occurred. My body shuddered at the thought.

I opened the door and stepped into the water pounding all around, toppling from the leaf canopies above. When I closed the door, I heard a thump and turned only to see a football-sized flock of majestic feathers laying at the foot of it. Its purple streaks were so gorgeous, I wasn't sure if this hummingbird was real or decor. Looking up and around, and finding no nest, I reached to poke it, assuming it was the latter.

Shock threw me backward when its eyes shot open, and its wings spun with the ferocity of helicopter propellers. The sound deafened and completely disoriented me as it spun in madness right before me, around me. Fear-stricken, I screamed and before I knew it, the damn thing had found its tarmac and flew straight at me. Ducking, I turned quickly to watch it fly past my head into the rolling fog of rain and thunder, vibrant and free in the face of a pending storm.

I couldn't help but smile at its wildness—its thoughtless bravery. A chuckle filled my chest and I grabbed at it to secure my breath, feeling at least a bit more confident in my reaction time than I did with the damn bat the night before. I made a mental note to share my triumph with Jenna later.

Everything looked a bit abandoned, making me wish I was still in that room with Aaina.

Bare-footed, I followed the broken, flooding brick path to my bungalow, but quickly stopped. I padded my non-existent pockets.

No map.

Cazzo.

I didn't even know where Aaina's room was in the village, so I had no idea where my bungalow was. Or, where I was, for that matter.

Consumed by the enormity of nature's doom, I focused on breathing.

I dropped my hands from above my head and let the rain topple my face as I wandered the opposite way down the path. Each time I touched my dress, I marveled at how the cloth somehow stayed dry. It actually felt warm. The air was dense with humidity, like nothing I'd ever known in California.

I spun as the thunder roared around me, louder now. It wasn't just a faint echo in the background anymore. It growled and vibrated the ground as if it were right under me.

The vibrations. Strangely, they felt more welcoming than frightening. My body was empty of tension and I didn't even feel fear rise with that roar. No ache. No crackle.

I kept walking until I ran into a lantern that hung high on a post with a little wooden sign under it: *La Piscina Sagrada, El Portal Del Presente.*

I hadn't realized there was a pool here. I trudged on down the path now narrowly carved through the trees and rounded a hedge where I saw a massive body of water, guarded on every edge by giant boulders and framed against a mountain shadowed in the distance.

Stepping closer, I found the water sparkling with diamond-like light. I couldn't tell if those were crystals formulated by the rain or deep stones penetrating the pool walls, but the optical illusion was enchanting. I looked further to see the pool floor, but it was extraordinarily deep and the gradience of darkness expanding from the center made it seem... endless, boundless. I shook my head at the impossibility. I looked up to see the edge of the pool that wasn't against the mountain appeared to flow right off the side of the cliff.

Everything was so still in the rainfall and gray fog. I stared closer into my very clear reflection, half-expecting some form of movement when suddenly, light flashed behind me through the mist, illuminating the water, the boulders, the mountain, and all of the surrounding trees.

It's closeness spun me but fear seemed to keep its distance. Through my squint, I marveled in awe of its danger—its evasive beauty.

I turned to look for the entrance where I had come in, but saw only those captivating little sparkles in the water.

The wind ruffled past my neck and through my curls.

"Vita…" I turned swiftly to find that faceless, formless voice, "Remember…"

My eyes drifted back to the silver dancing upon the water.

Hypnotized, I remembered. I remembered the calling. I remembered knowing. I remembered following. I stared deeply until I grew faint in the face of the glowing clusters beneath the surface.

Thunder roared once more, and I knew that was my sign.

I turned toward the exit pathway between the trees and stopped. As I stared at it, I felt a deep knowing that there was nowhere else I'd rather be. There was nowhere else to be.

I looked up to see yet another beam of light streak through the indigo clouds, breaking the sky into pieces and emanating an all-consuming glow. Rain toppled heavier now down my cheeks, over my lips, through my curls.

Magnificent.

Silence froze the force of nature cycloning me. I stood in awe while its rainbows of colored light traveled in the mist. I stretched my arms out to the side and let my spine collapse.

Suddenly and without warning, I was falling backward. Slowly first, and then all at once, my body plummeted through the water. Thunder roared with fury this time, shaking the ground with violence, as I fell into the belly of the Beast.

The vibrations of impact shook the body of water with vigor and I remained fixed on the rainbows dancing through the sky above me as they exploded once more into an array of light. Familiar red sparks flashed through the air.

"Scarrrr! Scarrrr!" My door slammed open against the wall as Mamma yelled for me to get up, a desperation in her voice I'd never heard before. Disoriented and barely able to find my way to the hallway, I stumbled to the sound of her short staccato breaths. I rounded the corner of my parent's bedroom only to see my mom straddling the floor next to my father's limp body.

"Gabriel! Stay with me, damn it!" She continued to pound on his chest with a ferocity I didn't know my tiny five-foot-three mother had. "Gabriel!"

"Scar! Go open the door!" I watched blankly as Papà's eyelids fluttered with every pounce on his chest.

"Scar!" Mamma's shriek pierced my paralysis, thrusting me backward into the wall. "Go get the door!" The fear pulsating in her tone sent me stumbling down the stairs, for what, I didn't know. Just as I managed to open the door, I made out the sirens screaming around the corner. Without thinking, I raced into the street, frantically stretching my arms around me as far as they would reach.

The fire truck and ambulance both screeched to a halt when they realized my shock-riddled body wasn't going to move out of their way.

"Miss? Miss, are you okay?" The fireman riding passenger hopped out of the truck and ran to stabilize my wobbling legs, guiding my confused self to the sidewalk. "Miss, we missed you by only a foot! Why didn't you move?"

Anger flared to my fists. My throat choked and I started coughing uncontrollably, "My... my... my papà ..." The dark night blurred around me as I lost my balance.

"Miss, I'm going to need you to sit here on the curb." Strong hands set my body down on the cold concrete. "Do you know where you are? Look at my eyes. My name is Mark. I'm going to breathe with you, okay? I want you to follow my breath."

My fury was building now.

"You don't understand... my..." All of my confused weight tried to push past him. I had to get back to Papà. As I looked over his shoulder, I caught a glimpse of three men, dressed in white, running a gurney across the lawn. Two men in black jackets followed.

"Guys, can I get some help over here?" Mark now had his hands wrapped around my wrists. But as he turned to get his crew's attention, I found my footing and took off for the house. I stumbled my way up the stairs, adrenaline sweating down my body.

Paramedics knelt at every corner of my papà's body. I watched in wide-eyed shock as these strangers in white pushed, prodded, and pumped the arms and hands that had cradled me my entire life, and to no avail.

"One, clear. Two, clear. Three, clear." Nothing more than a rhythm, a weak rhythm.

In only a few blurred moments, the white coat entered our waiting room with a hopelessly sullen look on his face, my shock dissolved into horror.

"Hi, Juliana? You are Gabriel's wife, correct?"

"Yes, and this is our daughter." My heart fell through my stomach as I watched my mamma clear her eyes and try to focus.

"Okay, so let me explain what's happening. The medics were able to pick up a rhythm and our team is rotating the compressions to sustain it, but we've been unable to get a pulse."

"A rhythm? What do you mean by a rhythm? A rhythm can turn into a pulse, right?" I interjected, having zero knowledge of his terminology. Mamma's face fell to her palms. I might not have known, but her thirty years of nursing experience knew exactly what this meant.

The doctor's face contorted, a clear hatred for this part of his job.

"So the rhythm could very well be due to some residual electricity still coursing through his body. As long as we can detect that, we will still work on him, but..." His eyes kept deviating to the floor as if he had dropped his words and couldn't locate them. "It doesn't look... this usually means..." He didn't have to finish. Now, I understood why my mamma's face was buried. "We will only stop working on him when we have your confirmation."

After a long pause, Mamma raised her head and through her sobs, muttered, "Okay, you can stop."

"Wait! What!" I screamed in disbelief, every nerve igniting with panic. "Mamma! You can't..."

"Scar, it's unlikely he will–"

"But there's a chance! You heard him! That's why they're still trying!"

"Scar, please–"

"Mom! We have to try! You can't just give up!" My panic was morphing into a shaky rage.

"Okay, Scar, then... then you'll make the call, okay?!"

Her words froze me and I gulped for air, for thoughts, for words.

The doctor's eyes shifted to me, clearly filled with doubt in my ability to think objectively and remorse for how the next moments in his emergency room would play out. I nodded to her and then to him.

Panic. Rage. Fear. It all spiraled into one giant cluster fuck of throbbing emotion as we made our way around the corner and through the curtains. My swollen eyes looked up to see seven white coats in a circle around the bed, one thrusting all 110 pounds of her body's force into my papà's chest and then rotating out as the man next to her took over.

My eyes fell to the table where my papà's bloated and quickly discoloring body laid. I watched with horror as every compression pumped his shoulders into the air.

"Can I... can I touch him?"

The doctor nodded and my mom brought her hand up to cover her mouth, as if she knew something I didn't.

I placed my hand on his hands...

The hands that first carried me into this world, the hands that taught me to walk, the hands that showed me how to hold my bicycle handles, the hands that still held mine in the parking lot.

They were ice cold. All trace of life had already disappeared from them. I slammed my eyelids and the tears splattered on the emergency room floor.

My mamma's cracked voice whimpered, "It's your call, Scar."

Without looking, I felt every eye in the room turn to me, as if my next words would decide everyone's fate for the night.

I traced my shaking fingers up to his face, around his bearded cheeks, and behind his big ears to his silver hair.

There would be no words for this. No words to understand. No words to explain. No words to say goodbye. No words to accept. No words to find life, to create meaning, after this. None.

"Papà, I…" My desperation tempted my sanity as I sought within myself for even just a little faith that my words weren't falling empty. "Papà, please…" I could hardly muster a whisper. "I love you."

Without looking up, I took the deepest breath my body could handle and nodded to the doctor, collapsing to my papà's shoulder.

There, in the crevice of his cold lifeless corpse, I wept more than I ever imagined possible. I wept into the darkness of the night and into the early hours of the morning. I wept as the nurse's hands attempted to comfort my heaving body. I wept as the words of family and friends fell deaf on my ears.

I wept as time stopped, and I wept as time refused to cease.

I had clearly failed to prepare for this fall with a gasp for air. Or, had I? The strain in my chest was now wondering if I needed it. I was sinking deeper, my body limp to the memory before me, to the screaming in my lungs.

I didn't fight it. I didn't want to.

And as I watched the bubbles float to the surface from my sinking mouth, the words I'd written the first time this happened danced across my vision.

The water filled my lungs.

I let my eyelids relax

as I inhaled this Beast called Death,

feeling the readiness in my bones

to ask my questions, to demand my answers.

I wouldn't say I tried to kill myself,

but I certainly didn't fight it.

I welcomed it.

I opened my lips like a normal twenty-one-year-old

would lay a welcome mat down in front of her first apartment.

But tonight.

Tonight, I let my toes slip from the faucet handle

as the bubbles climbed the stem of my empty wine glass,

ran over the edges of the bathtub,

and toppled to the tile floor.

My lover's screams fell to an echo.

His fists on the door faded

with the darkening eclipse of my vision.

And I exhaled the last of my will,

the last of my resistance.

I remember peace in the silence

of my asking Death to swallow me whole,

begging the blackness to devour me like it did him.

And right before the water seared the wires in my brain,

his voice pierced the darkness

as his fingers combed my hair,

"Sei la mia vita."

Perhaps this was it—this was acceptance.

My body, fatally relaxed, sunk further from the surface, deeper toward the shadowed center of the pool. A streak of light splintered the sky and pierced the water. As the charge dispersed around me, white shattered my vision. I closed my eyes, and let it come as the last of my air left my lungs.

I was alone.

I was gone.

I was free.

"

You are the trembling of time
that passes between
vertical light and darkened sky.

PABLO NERUDA

Fourteen

"Scarlett! Scarlett! Miss Scarlett, please! Stay with me!"

The compounding pressure on my chest sent water up through my esophagus until I coughed and sputtered, turning to my side instinctually. My throat burned while the water spewed from it.

I gasped deeply for air and Ramón's hands rolled over my sides, supporting the twist of my airway for the gushing water. I tried to steady my breathing when I noticed my hands shaking intensely.

His hands found my face and moved the hair from it to check my eyes. Dizzy, I stared back, confused as my vision refocused him. He sighed with relief and pulled me into his chest.

The distant tremors in my limbs would not cease. I could only see them, not feel them. My hands, my feet—everything was disconnected. I wondered desperately what had happened but couldn't seem to catch any of my thoughts out of the hurricane in my head.

We sat in silent chaos beneath the rain and thunder, Ramón's arms wrapped entirely around me. As my mind attempted to steady itself, I realized the warmth of his body penetrating through his soaked uniform, radiating to my skin. I relaxed into his heat and let my head fall deeper under his chin. His arms locked me in tighter and his hand cradled the back of my head.

Melting into the safety of his embrace, I dozed in and out but was awake enough when his lips pressed against my forehead.

"Scarlett, what were you thinking?"

He lifted us both from the ground and I drifted far from my skin.

I woke to white cloth draped high above me and braided around mahogany posts. Blinking, I discovered I was laying on a low bed wrapped in knitted blankets. Ramón was sitting on the ground next to me, cradling his chin with one hand and extending a stick into the small fire next to us with his other.

"An-uhuuum." I coughed as I tried to find my voice again.

He turned to me with all of his attention. "Heyyy, take it slow. Take it slow."

"Mmm, hi," I coughed but winced at the burn in my throat as I attempted to wet it. Slowly, I turned on my right side to face him as he re-tucked my blankets and moved the hair from my cheeks behind my ears, his hand a sun all its own.

"Hi, Miss Scarlett." His dark brown eyes, usually sweet and rich with playfulness, were filled with concern and an obvious loss for words. He dropped his head and covered his eyes. "I-I don't even… I don't want to know."

I located my hand under the sheets and reached it up to cradle the one that held my face.

"I'm okay. I promise." I kissed his hand and combed my fingers through his damp dark brown hair, attempting to recall the details of the last few hours.

Or, days… I wondered silently at the time lost, hoping I did not miss anything in all this time away from the group. I blinked my eyes while I fought to locate the memories.

Water. Light and water. I remembered colors everywhere. And release. I remembered release. I think I remembered his arms.

"How long was I out?"

"I don't know." He shook his head, "Too long." His eyes were red with upset. As I looked closer to see if the water in them was left or just starting to fill, I noticed the light imprints down his cheek bones.

Who was this man who cares so much for a stranger?

I eased his head to my chest in an effort to soothe his upset. Vacant of explanation, as I laid staring at the fire, I found myself wishing he hadn't jumped in after me. I remembered how my papà once told me we never die in our dreams because of our instinct to survive, that we will always wake up before. I wondered what this meant for my will, if my longing for that freedom had forfeited it. Answers not yet accessible, I looked past the fire and saw the floor scattered with books and a couple empty coffee mugs.

"Where are we?"

"This is my place. It is the closest to where I found you. I can take you back to your–"

"You like to read... a lot!"

"I mean, I don't get out much, no. This is sort of how I see the world."

There was a book propped open and resting on top of the others.

"What's that book?" I interrupted him.

He wiped the wetness from his face and reached past the crackling fire to grab the one my eyes were locked on. The bright orange and yellow of the cover shouted to me, *"El Alchemista."*

"I've heard of that one." I found the opportunity to redirect the mood a bit. I had to. I didn't have any answers that would suffice for what had happened. "How do you like it?"

"Uhm..." He cleared his throat and tried to focus on my question. "It's, it's pretty magnificent. Paulo is a Master."

Oh joy, another Master.

"Tell me about it," I coaxed.

"Well..." He took his time recalling. "It's about a boy who devotes his life to searching for his treasure."

"Mhmm..."

"He doesn't know where it is or how to find it, or even really *what* it is for that matter, but just continues to follow each next step as it comes. Then, when he asks for directions, everyone tells him he needs to find the Alchemist." He paused and looked at me.

"So, does he find it?"

"Well, you'll just have to read it to find out." He teased a good eye roll out of me.

"Mhmm." I kinked my neck and stared at him for a moment, grateful to see his light.

Magic. I remembered his story of his grandfather's land.

"I've been meaning to ask you." I thought of the fireballs that hung from the trees, the rainbows in the misty light, the golden dancing specs, the crystals from the pool... the Shapeshifters and the Guardians. "That magic that your grandfather spoke of, did you ever find it?"

Ramón smiled. "I did." I shot him a curious look and he chuckled in response. "Would you like some?"

His snarky smile clued me into his tease, and I pushed his shoulder as I laughed along. "Whatever."

"Whatever? I just saved your life, and you are going to 'whatever' me?"

"Well, are you going to give me some of this magic you found?" I mocked, ignoring the other part of his comment.

He shook his head and smiled.

"Miss Scarlett, you have enough magic for this entire village."

His sweetness caught me entirely off-guard and flushed me red.

"Are you this charming to everyone who stays here?"

He rolled his eyes and shook his head. "Hay dios mío contigo." The phone rang and he grabbed it quickly. "Si, nos vamos pronto." He hung up and pushed himself off the ground, using the side of the bed to stand up.

"Where are you going?" I asked.

"It's almost time for the waterfall excursion. I have to get everyone on the bus. Gitana is busy today. That is, if everyone still wants to come now that the lightning has finally subsided."

"What? That's now?" I shook my head. "I literally cannot keep track of the days here." I said as I pushed myself off the bed. Standing too quickly, I struggled to find my equilibrium.

He put one hand on my elbow and one on my waist to steady me.

"Whoa, whoa. ¿Que estás haciendo?"

"I'm going on the excursion."

"Miss Scarlett..." His expression grew serious, and he held his hands up to gesture an *absolutely not*. "You're not coming on this one."

I frowned and tilted my head in confusion.

"Seriously? Do I need to explain why? You literally almost died in the water with all that lightning."

He had a point. I took a few deep breaths and stretched my body in a few different directions to try to check in with it a little bit. My throat and my chest were quite tender, my arms a bit sore. Mostly, I just felt weak. But, in contrast to earlier, I felt pretty incredible. Plus, there was no way I was going to miss the only excursion to the waterfalls.

As I stretched, I made sure to control my face so I didn't give him any cues I was anything other than fine. He watched me carefully and I just stared back at him.

"Ramón, you just said the lightning is gone. I'm okay."

He was getting agitated—an emotion I'd not seen on him yet.

"Scarlett, you are *not* fine. I don't know what is going on with you, but I don't think you should be anywhere around water—at all—right now." He stuttered a bit through that. "I– I really think you should stay here and rest."

His care was really sweet, but it wasn't going to deter my decision. I stared back at him and resolved to try a different strategy.

"Ramón, I... Look, I really appreciate you and your concern, but it's not every day that I get to go swim in waterfalls in an exotic Costa Rican jungle." I tilted my head and looked up at him to reinforce my point.

He ran his hands over his face and through his hair as he realized he didn't really have a say. I respected him and honestly appreciated everything, but he wasn't in any position to decide for me.

Or so I thought. Perhaps he could refuse me a seat on the bus.

"Alright, just. Look, just… be careful around the water. Okay? No funny business."

I smiled and stood, wobbling as I tried to find my footing. Of course, he grabbed my hips and steadied me—shooting me yet another questionable glance, to which I responded with a small *thank you*. I reached my hand out and pointed subtly to the opening in the tent.

"After you…" I smiled.

He let out another deep sigh, put out the small fire, and then led the way through the large white tent and into the trees. When we walked past the hedges that guarded the pool, Ramón shot a glare back at me.

"Shhh…" I teased some more.

Despite the light heartedness I was aiming for, questions wrestled within, and I wondered how the hell I'd even found this area earlier.

"You want to see somethin'?" He stopped and turned to me with bright eyes. "You can't tell anyone though."

I crooked my neck with curiosity and waited for him to reveal his secret.

He backtracked a few steps and then brushed some bamboo and fallen trees to the side. Quieting his movements, he placed a finger over his lips and silently invited me to follow him. I mimicked his quiet approach as he led me to a small cave in the trees where a large, gray creature with leathery thick skin slept, cuddling its young one in the crevice of its tummy. As I inched closer, I made out its long snout and stout ears. Eyes sunken, the round belly and short tail on this large fella reminded me of a hippo.

We backed away slowly before I whisper-screamed, "What in the world is that thing!?"

"She's a tapir. They are very rare here in Costa Rica. In fact, the only place anyone ever really sees them is in Corcovado, but that beautiful beast has been here for quite some time. I found her and her babe bathing in the pool one day and followed them to their cave. I just haven't told anyone."

A mischievous smile crossed his face.

"She doesn't need anyone bothering her. A few generations back, some of the other tribes used to hunt tapirs. No one really does anymore, but I guess I haven't been able to shake it. That actually used to be a tradition, you know? It's crazy! They're such sweet, gentle creatures. And... they love that water! Spend hours in it. It's a wonder no one else has seen them yet." He shook his head at the thought.

We walked quite a bit of distance and it was refreshing not having to keep track of where I was coming from or going with him in the lead. We finally approached the front canopy with the little wooden desk where Nick, Aileen, Sybil, and the strange man I'd noticed before waited.

"Alright, we have some brave troops," he joked. "I promise the lightning has subsided now. There won't be anything to worry about out there. This is a truly magnificent excursion and I'm so happy you've decided to join us."

I shot my hand out toward the tall, lanky, dark-eyed older gentleman.

"My name is Scar."

"Caleb." He didn't even try to force a smile when he shook my hand.

"Are we all ready?" Ramón prompted.

"Oh, I'm um. I'm just going to run back to my place really quickly," I said, realizing that I needed a few things for this excursion.

"Alright, we're going to load onto the bus."

I hurried back to my bungalow in what seemed to be afternoon sun, though everything around me was still dewy from the rain and fog. I unzipped the door quickly and saw Jenna napping. I wondered if I should wake her like she did me—to see if she wanted to go just in case she'd forgotten about it—while I changed into my bathing suit and shoved my journal, camera, and towel into my bag. Nudging her shoulder lightly, I spoke in a low whisper. She was clearly in a deep sleep and couldn't hear me.

I zipped the door and hurried to the small bus where I stole the seat next to Ramón.

"Estamos listo," he told the bus driver and we pulled forward around a couple bends and right by that magnificent tree arch I couldn't find for the life of me the other day.

"Where is Caleb?" I thought he was joining us.

He shrugged his shoulders. "No sé. He decided not to come."

I hoped I hadn't scared him off.

Through the window, the jungle captivated me and suddenly, I was filled with energy and awe of this precious land. Ramón shot a glance back to me and it didn't feel like the most endearing one. Without saying it, I understood his concern and offered a gentle smile. I tucked my arm under and around his and rested my head on his shoulder to say thank you again.

We drove even further into the jungle for at least an hour. As we winded through the mountains, Ramón delighted in orienting us to the areas we passed, the locals who occupied them, and the exotic flowers, plants, and herbs which were most famous for growing there due to the richness of the surrounding volcanoes. He explained that while the village is a decent distance from the volcanoes, it still reaps the benefits of fertile earth.

The volcanic soot is considered by the villagers to release an atmosphere-warping chemical, one that apparently contorts certain elements of reality. I couldn't help but notice the familiarity in his excitement as the corners of his lips and eyes pulled back while he shared these details.

Disappointment displaced his joy when he explained how the land around Irazu had not been cared for by tourists. Trash and cigarettes were strewn everywhere, and it was a big sign of disrespect to the land. He advocated sharing its beauty, but not at the cost of destroying it and the wildlife that lived there. The communities were now working to fix this issue with park regulations. While he pointed in the direction of Irazu Volcano and spoke of its beauty, he said that the hot springs and waterfalls tumbling down Arenal were truly unfathomable.

Arenal Volcano had been dormant for over six years and was considered one of the top ten most active volcanoes in the world, and the most beautiful at that. He shared about the last eruption and how many of the villagers feared it would be as bad as the past ones, but it wasn't.

My chest warmed with admiration for the animation with which he spoke about his land.

I longed to see Arenal very badly, but he explained that we didn't have an excursion there in the agenda and that it was too far—that no one would leave that early in the morning. I was saddened, but considered it an excuse to make another trip here someday.

Someday.

The more Ramón spoke, the louder he became, welcoming Nick and Dorene to chime in with questions. I could tell that because this was a small group, he was really enjoying sharing so much more than he could with a bus full of people.

He had the driver stop several times in between the onion fields so that we could try some local strawberries and fresh white cheese. It was such a lovely experience.

For the first time since I'd arrived—it had to be months now—I actually felt a sinking into *normal*, contentment. It was nice to just be *here,* and with others in this moment. Laughing, enjoying, and forgetting the tragedies and struggles that weaved each of our paths here.

Finally, we arrived at the entrance to La Paz Waterfalls. While we unloaded from the bus, Ramón explained that we would hike a few trails around the mountain to get up to the peak of the waterfalls. We all walked together, chatting and enjoying the sweetness of company and the fucsia onagráceas blossoming over the path and tumbling with the reddish-brown cortaline leaves down the sides. Ramón stopped to point out the same little orange fungus I'd seen growing on the trees around the village.

"Hongo copas o copa de vino, we call them!" We chuckled at the similarity the mushroom took to a wine glass as he showed us how to feel its hairy, rubbery body.

As we neared the curve at the top, winded and a bit tired, there was a flutter in my hair. Large white wings quivered into my vision and I startled, recalling instantly the white-coated men flying in my nightmare. I settled and filled my lungs with air again as I stared at the wings and my eyes took in the full butterfly before me, colored with more palette than I first made out and glowing faintly in the pools of light streaming around me.

It flew between us and then another, almost three times the size, joined. The panic subsided as they appeared. And then, before we knew it, we were surrounded, tunneled in a flurry of turquoise and violet, radiating a pure ivory aura. Either their rabble ambushed us, or we'd unknowingly entered their home. As they swarmed, we all giggled. A pearly vibrance filled the sky, and I reached my hands out and stretched my eyelids amid all the fluttering wings around me.

Magic.

Then, that second giant one, practically translucent in its holographic glow, settled calmly in all its elegance right into my palm. Her wings didn't flicker with panic like the others. Instead they opened and blanketed the outline of my hand.

She was still, and she was stunning. Her presence was profound, practically intentional. Moving her wings as if in slow motion, her strength exuded from her with a gust of airflow all of her own creation. I stared at her, my eyes wide with wonder.

She was *here* and *now,* and she gleamed with all the glory of a million lightning strikes.

I gazed with awe as a couple smaller butterflies settled near her. She didn't even flinch at their presence.

She knew her power. She knew her presence.

Hearing Ramón's footsteps, I shook my head ever so slightly to signal him to slow down and not come near. He got my hint and slowed, but continued toward me. Reaching his hand to this grand saint, he stole her to his finger.

My heart sank a little. I really wanted to enjoy her longer.

I could see his smile in my periphery and his finger, with her on it, slowly lifting toward my face. "Don't move, Scarlett."

I froze as he placed this incredible little being, still as ever, right onto my nose. I hardly breathed for fear of scaring her.

Who was I kidding? Thunder and lightning wouldn't scare this one.

She was a warrior.

She stayed there about a minute and I couldn't hold my breath any longer. When I broke out in laughter—genuine, joyful laughter—she took off and fluttered around me a bit while Ramón watched me get my giggles out. He grabbed my hand and guided me around the curve of the trees, where we stood over a massive cliff shadowing the largest waterfall in the garden. It was a long way down... a very long way. And the water roared wildly, echoing in the canyon while the breeze shook the bridges tangled through it.

What dream had I just walked into...

I felt Ramón's palm on my tummy as I leaned closer. He was preoccupied instructing the group to follow us, but keeping a hand on me.

Jaw-dropped, I marveled at the view.

He guided us up a small path where the main pool of water seeped from the earth. It was clear blue and reflected the tropical lush that hung over it. I looked closer, mesmerized by how it sparkled the way the pool at the village did, lined with those same stunning crystals.

"Miss Scarlett." Ramón shot me a very firm look and I continued to follow the group along the inside of the cave where we left our things on the ledge and stripped to our suits.

Everyone took their time easing in, but Sybil already had her feet in and was sitting along the ridge, her oddly intense gaze on me. Her eyes bouncing to me and around me curiously, she always looked a bit dazed and it made me wonder just what she was thinking.

The water had an icy chill to it, but the sun was determined and strong at this elevation and I was going to take advantage. I held my breath and dove in, opening my eyes under the water as I swam to the bottom, at least ten feet at this end.

Yep, crystals.

I dove deeper and dragged my hands along them. Gorgeous and glowing. Yellow, red, blue... they reflected the colors of everything, of the fish, the lily pads, the flowers. In the blackness of the sand around them, I sifted a flattened cream-white shell out.

It was delicate, so very thin, and stamped with an almost completely symmetrical flower pattern. These were the same sand dollars I used to hunt for along the LA beaches with my grandmother. I swam to the surface quickly and gasped for air in the sun's embrace.

Ramón's eyes, fierce and focused, grew soft and filled with joy when he saw my smile. "You guys, come in! This is extraordinary!" I laid on my back and floated while some fish nibbled on my toes. The Caribbean sun was strong, and I bathed in its warmth.

Heaven.

I closed my eyes and disappeared in the moment. I wanted for nothing.

I felt him before I saw him. Two large hands curved around my spine and I opened my eyes to Ramón standing over me.

"Shhh..." He smiled. "Relax." I let my arms fall to the side and couldn't help but show a full-teethed smile. His gentleness coerced a blush in all the right places, and I squinted out the right side of my eye when I realized this was the first time I'd seen him without his shirt. His arms, his shoulders, his chest were just as muscular as I had felt them to be when I'd crashed into him on the zip line. Heat blazed down my chest and straight through my abdomen.

He was turning me in circles now, beneath the swirling sun rays. Joy crept up on me again and I let out a little chuckle. He shook his head and stared at me with those deep brown eyes.

"¿Que me haces, mujer?"

I stared at him, perplexed. I did not find him. I did not seek this out. I did not ask for any special treatment. I was not *doing* anything to him.

But... I was about to. I looked up and around and noticed a stream behind the two big boulders in the water.

Gesturing with my gaze, I invited him to follow. I took a deep breath and dove under water toward the stream, quickly discovering an opening in the rocks under the water just big enough to fit through. I wasn't sure he'd be able to fit, but I wiggled my body through the blurry hole and swam to the surface.

When I surfaced, I was in a secluded little cave covered by rocks toppled upon one another with a hole just big enough for the sunlight to peek through.

He was taking a while and I wondered if I should return, but I waited when I thought I saw his head come through.

As I wiped the water from my eyes, I was tugged under. Surprised and struggling, I reached for the surface and laughed as I pushed with all my weight upon his shoulders to sink him further. Both at the surface, we laughed and wiped the water from our faces. I reached for his chin and brushed the side of his face with my hand, cradling the steadiness of his jaw as I pulled him close. So close I could taste his breath. He remained still, waiting.

My nerves lit with anticipation and my heart thudded. I pulled away and looked at him. His energy was dense with tension and he was not making any moves, just staring intently at my lips. I took a deep breath and started to push myself off.

"I…"

His palms curved over my jaw to my cheeks, and wrapped their fingers behind my ears and in my hair. For a quick second, my eyes closed and I mistook them for Julian's.

I couldn't make out the confusion in his face, but the conflict within him pulsed hot through his hands and snatched my body from its memory. His lips hovered right between mine. I thought I'd faint with anticipation.

He wrapped his arms around me and my legs found their way up the side of his. We stayed there in the dimly lit cave breathing each other in. His arms were so warm, so familiar, I could practically feel Enzo in them—his tenderness, his chivalry, his genuine care for my well-being.

What else was I to do? My heart raced with excitement and disbelief, with the awe of connection so fierce and strong... so beautiful. I missed this connection and while my lips were so close to his, Enzo's sweet smile flashed before me, and I quickly fought to dissolve that memory too.

"Ramón?" Aileen's voice echoed somewhere in the distance and bounced within the cave walls around us.

"Ah, Miss Scarlett." We dropped our heads into each other.

All that transpired between us hovered—the fuming between our bodies, between our souls. I'd forgotten this. My eyes began to water at the thought and just as he noticed, I threw my arms around his neck and pulled myself up to my toes to hug him. He held me close. So tight in his arms, I could hardly feel air move through me.

One hand combed through my hair and held my neck.

"Come on, Love, we should go before they wonder where we are."

I pulled him in closer. I didn't want to breathe. I didn't want to leave this moment. I slid my hands to his neck and he grabbed my wrists.

"Mujer. What am I going to do with you?"

"Alright," I smiled. "Vamos." I dove underwater in search of that little opening again, squeezed my way through, and Ramón followed. He swam out in the open and I regained my floating posture as if nothing had transpired. But inside, my heart was vibrating with all the fervor of the cosmos.

As I floated around the boulders, I listened to the group chatting, still exchanging stories of their sessions with the Awapa as if they'd never noticed our absence. I smiled to myself and laid atop the water on my back, staring into the sky's fire, absorbing all it had to give with gratitude.

And for a moment, all the tragedy and devastation which brought me here was gone. For a moment, the pain strangling my thoughts, my joints, and the functions of my basic systems was finally quieted. For a moment, the euphoria I felt by escaping my body in that lightning storm had vanished. I was just *here* and *now,* breathing in the sky through the treetops spinning above me.

Watching the leaves sway, I caught sight of a rope-like swing hanging in the distance. It was positioned over the bigger pool below us.

"Vita…" a breeze called to me, whistling through my hair in a tornado around me.

Again.

Awe consumed me as I tried to figure out how I could get to that rope. I wanted to fly through the trees again, to revive that bliss, once more.

"Scar, come hang out with us." Aileen's voice welcomed me over. I stared at the rope and thought it better not to run to it anyway. In addition to giving Ramón a heart attack, my clumsy self would probably just belly flop. So, I swam back to the group.

The afternoon was magnificent and rather than spending it in meditation or study or the unraveling of our past, we spent it in the light, in the earth, in conversation, immersed in effortless connection.

I looked around at the people I was with and was overcome by comfort. Nostalgia sparked within me as I remembered my small circle of close friends back home, Raya and Enzo. I hadn't seen them since the memorial, and before that, I hadn't seen them in months... *years* actually.

I was so consumed in the daily antics of caring for Papà that I hadn't reached out to them or spent time with them in so long. Yet, they continued to be faithful—checking in on me, sending me gifts, showing up when I did call. It was more than I could do for them. I was grateful, very grateful. But as I sat there, soaking in the pleasure of this company, I couldn't ignore the guilt that gnawed at me for letting them slip away.

The sky began to dim and Ramón encouraged us to wrap things up so we could make dinner at the village. How he could tell time in this timelessness was beyond me.

I was throwing my clothes over my suit and packing my bag when I felt Sybil's soft touch on my elbow.

"Miss Scarlett, do you think we could find some time to chat later? I'd like to talk to you."

"Of course, Sybil. Anytime!" I smiled, but felt uneasy at the offbeat seriousness in her tone. I even wondered if I might be in trouble.

She smiled a sweet *thank you*.

"Would you mind handing me my water bottle, Dear?"

I grabbed her bottle and helped her down the rocky stairs. Ramón led us out and I made my way around the others to swing my arm under his.

I still wasn't quite sure about all the magic talk, but if anything was going to make me reconsider the thought... it was this place.

"Will there be time to come back?"

He clearly didn't want to tell me no, so he just smiled and shook his head a bit. My head on his shoulder, we all drove home, weary with delight.

"

Every explicit duality is an implicit unity.

ALAN WATTS

Fifteen

I must've fallen asleep. The tires on the rocky road shook me awake in Ramón's arms, out of a deep sleep that left me seriously groggy. My tummy ached. I couldn't recall the last I'd eaten, and I was glad when we pulled up and the aroma from *El Placer* wafted toward us on the breeze. The five of us wandered in the light drizzle toward the fragrance. When we entered and the rich mixture of Central American aromas overwhelmed the air, I grabbed a plate and got to work.

"¡Buenas tardes, pequeña bailarina!"

I turned with excitement at the sound of Sol's voice.

"¡Buenas tardes, Sol! ¿Cómo estás?"

"¡Estoy muy contenta, Señorita! ¿Estás bailando esta noche?"

I raised my eyebrows and sighed with exhaustion as I quickly evaluated whether my body could even fathom the thought right now. "Ayyyye no seee. Estoy muy cansada. No sé cómo lo haces."

Sol laughed loudly and swayed her hips left to right with pride, as she pursed her lips and walked around me and through the kitchen door where that gorgeous, loud music followed the light, pulsating through the cracks and into the hall.

Her stride dripped with solidarity and confidence. I hoped that someday, I would walk like her, trailing light in my wake everywhere I go.

Our little group was clearly not ready to part. We all nestled in next to each other and kept the laughter going. The only one missing was Ramón.

I was mid-grilled-pineapple bite when a tall ghost drifted over my left side. I looked up just as Caleb squatted to his knees, his energy solemn and serious. The deep carvings that housed his crystal blue eyes were much more haunting up close. His wrinkled skin hung around his cheekbones and as I studied it closer, it almost looked as if carved into his skin, were streaks from his eyes to his jaw. He stared at me and then dropped his chin to search for his words.

"Hi Scar, I um, so I just had a…" He stuttered his way through what was clearly some difficult emotion. His English was very good, but I struggled to understand him through what sounded like an accent of Hebrew origin. Swallowing my bite, I tried to shift my posture toward him to give him my full attention. "I just did a session with Rebecca and she told me to um, to come find you and talk with you."

"Me?" There was no hiding my confusion.

He looked back at me intently.

"Yes." This clearly made him a bit uncomfortable, but he was pushing through.

"Oh, alright. Um, well, we're just finishing dinner. I don't think we have a ton of time before the workshop tonight."

"Oh no, I know." His shyness intensified as he turned his head. "We don't have to talk tonight. Anytime is fine."

"Okay well, let's find each other after the workshop. We can make time tonight!" I tried to ease his discomfort with my willingness. It couldn't have been easy to ask. I'm not sure what Rebecca had in mind but if I could help, I wanted to.

He nodded a thank you and rose to his feet. While I watched him walk away, realizing he had not stayed for dinner, I felt a familiar ache—a gnawing at my insides, remembering my not-too-distant lack of appetite over the last few years. Even with no clue about what was torturing him, I could empathize. I looked down at my plate, three-quarters finished now, and then at my waistline which had grown at least two inches since I'd been here.

Dio Santo!

After we finished eating, we hustled through the jungle and under the dark sky to *La Encarnada* until Nick suddenly stopped and the rest of us domino-ed into him. He reached his arms out on each side and bent slightly to shush the group's chatty whispers. I followed his eyes to a line of at least thirty white-faced capuchin monkeys, only twenty feet from where we stood.

We tried desperately to quiet our awe and slip to our knees so we wouldn't interrupt as we watched them crawl from one palm across the grassy sand to another, climb it, and then jump from the top to another. With tiny limber bodies, they swung from the palms easily, carrying their young upon their shoulders and squeaking signals to one another. They kept their eyes steady between them, checking in as they made each move, ensuring one another's safe journey, turning back when a straggler needed help.

This sight was worth the tardiness we apologized for as we filed into *La Encarnada.*

Once more, candles were lit. But this time, there were fewer and they were pushed to the edges of the room. Sage and palo santo filled the air. There were no chairs in a circle tonight, only yoga mats and blankets waiting at the door.

Standing in the far corner, staring out the glass wall, was a large lean gentleman with skin dark as coal. Arms locked together behind his back, his stance was strong—immovable.

There was no welcome to the group or ushering of us in. Rather, the room began throbbing with a solemn weight. Carefully and hesitantly, we filed in one at a time and laid down our mats. There was no need to hush everyone tonight. An intimidated silence fell upon us and we waited awkwardly.

After several minutes of looking to one another in hope of a sign, we collectively began breathing in unison. The large man was still staring out the glass into the darkness. He hadn't moved even an inch, and I wondered if his statue-like form was real as we continued breathing and waiting.

"Delusional." A deep, haunted voice, wrapped in a thick Rican accent, vibrated from the corner of the room. "Delusional. Delusional. Delusional." The air immediately thickened with tension as everyone turned their necks slowly and with caution. "Only fools search outside of themselves for the answers they possess within."

Hushed and afraid to flinch, we all remained still and squeezed by the unexpected hostility in the man's words. He shook his head slowly and skulked to the back of the room.

"I will not be teaching you the way the others do. Nor will I sugarcoat our subject tonight, but I do intend to keep this lesson brief." He kept his chin down as he circled the yoga mats. The room remained stiff, waiting.

"I'm positive you have heard the term 'paradox.' Hopefully, by the end of tonight, you will understand it like you never have before." I gulped as his premonition gripped me. A sickly fear enveloped the space and suddenly pulsed through me.

"Paradox: two opposing statements, both equally true." Chin still down, he paced another circle in silence.

"Time." He circled.

"Free will." He slinked.

"Oneness." He prowled.

"All paradoxes." I found myself waiting for a truck with blazing headlights to storm the room.

"It was the best of times; it was the worst of times. It was the age of wisdom; it was the age of foolishness. It was the epoch of belief; it was the epoch of incredulity. It was the season of Light; it was the season of Darkness. It was the spring of hope; it was the winter of despair. We had everything before us; we had nothing before us. We were all going directly to Heaven; we were all going directly the other way."

I struggled to understand his direction as he quoted Charles Dickens.

"Both perspectives will always have a defense. Time is a social construct. Time is a constant. Free will is a lie. Free will is all we have. We are separate. We are one. Death is an illusion." The large man stopped directly across from me and, as he lifted his chin, his emerald eyes pierced through my solar plexus. "Death is real."

I was tempted to look at the floor while he circled us again.

"The truth is this. You will not heal. You will not grow. You will not find peace. Until you develop the capacity to hold both worlds as truth within you." The darkness weighted in his words stabbed a dagger through my rib cage, tearing right through the remainder of my armor.

"Tonight, you begin this work. It is time to stop gathering information from outside yourself and start gathering it from within."

The room's energy collectively plummeted into a pit of confusion. I was two seconds from rolling my mat up and heading for the door, but something kept me glued.

What exactly had we signed up for here—in the middle of a village lost to civilization somewhere in the vast Costa Rican jungle?

He instructed us to lay down.

"Do not be mistaken. This is not meditation. This is training." Skeptical and a bit frightened, we obeyed and listened as he guided us.

"Inhale. Feel the breath travel down through your torso to your diaphragm. Exhale. Feel your breath travel back up through your body and out your nose. Inhale. Imagine your body filling with light. The light is flowing through every vein, every artery, every limb. Easy, breathing easy. Exhale. Exhale the darkness. The darkness is leaving your bloodstream. Chased by the light, it is exiting your body. Easy, full breath in. Inhaling light. Watch the light flow through your body. Exhaling time. There is no past. There is no future. There is no time."

Oxygen soothed my insides. My limbs grew light as I watched my linear construct of time crumble to darkness from my mind.

I'm… growing.

"Inhaling light, follow it as it courses with more force now through your blood and swirls in each organ. Exhaling objects. There are no more objects. There is no house waiting for you. There is no car, no laptop, no phone. There is no comfort of things. There are no objects. There is nothing to have."

Each object fell, a sack of sand in the ether, and I watched it fade to black in the hollows of my mind.

Lighter.

"Inhaling light, watch the light filling your pores, seeping into your wounds—your aches. Exhaling relationships. There is no boss. There are no loved ones. There are no friends. There is no family. There is no one here. There is no one to have. You are alone."

My hands and shoulders twitched as grief, fresh and stinging, coursed through and out of me.

"Inhaling light, watch the light settle around your bones, in your joints. Watch it rest in your cells. Exhaling action. You are made only of light now. Your body is made of wood. It cannot move. There is no action to take."

I searched for my limbs at the sound of his words and met a rush of fear when I could no longer feel them. I tried to open my eyes but couldn't, and my throat filled with panic.

"Inhaling light, watch the light travel up your brain stem and through your skull. Watch it seep through and fall around the rolling hills of your brain. Exhaling emotion. You no longer feel. There is nothing to feel. There are no more emotions."

My panic quickly dissipated, and I was floating… expanding.

"Inhaling light, watch the light travel through your nasal cavity and down to your tongue, flowing back over your eardrums. Watch it peel over your eyeballs and encapsulate your skin. Exhaling senses. There is no smelling. There is no tasting. There is no hearing. There is no seeing. There is no touching. There is no sensation. There is nothing left to sense. You have no senses. You have no body. You have no self. There is no separateness."

I... am... no more.

"The world goes on. Without you. You are not breathing. You are just observing."

In a suspended darkness so complete, there were no cracks, I watched the last strings attaching me to this body snap with the force of a thousand rubber bands from the edges of my being. Dust perforated the air in their wake.

"The breath continues alone. Notice it's fluidity. There is no start to the inhalation. There is no end. There is no start to the exhalation. There is no end. You are floating. You are expanding. You are one. You are all."

Light pulsated around me, dissolving the darkness. There was only oneness as I drifted in the vastness, as the fabric of the atmosphere, of the universe, ushered me back and absorbed my essence.

The source from which I came beckoned me to return.

And suddenly, this was all there was.

My being had no want, no desire, no regret, no sadness, no thoughts.

I moved on with ease into the warm unknown, and suddenly the only known, welcoming me home.

There was stillness. There was peace.

There was forever.

"

I was wild and tame
and pulled into shreds and
crushed into being
all at once.

MAGGIE STIEFVATER

Sixteen

"Scar! Scar!" Darkness flashed through the light. Once, then twice. "Scar!" The vastness began to shake, and wonder pierced me. "Scar! Scar! Wake up!" I fell backward, quickly. Too quickly. My senses returned. My inner vision began to take form once more. All the weight of the universe plunged me into the earth.

"She's alright. She's coming back. Just whisper. You will scare her," a distant sound echoed. Behind the skin now heavy on my eyeballs, adrenaline flooded back through limbs that were now mine and weight swept through the stone of my frame.

"Scar!" Panic roared around me as everything shook, and I slowly began to recall Mamma's face... Trix, Bella, Alex, Raya, Enzo... my everyone.

They were home, at my home in Los Angeles. Where I live, where I have lived. But I wasn't there.

"Scar, it's time to wake up." The sound bellowed again in my eardrums. Time encompassed me as memories of my birthdays, of holidays, of tragedies, of celebrations, of Enzo's deep loving eyes... as each of them flashed through my mind's eye.

Tremoring from my core, my eyes slammed open, and my vision struggled to steady itself as air filled my lungs and my body seethed with sensation.

There were several shapes above me. I followed the blur of Sybil's fragile arms to her hands now cradling my neck, but I still couldn't quite feel them.

"Shhh. It's alright. You are back now. Look at me." A blur of Ramón was closer than the others. But as my vision steadied, all

I could see were the large dark man's emerald eyes in front of me just over Ramón's shoulder. His chin was still high, his face grim.

Ramón continued, "Follow me. Breathe in, nice and deep. And breathe out. Alright, again. Breathe in. Whew… doesn't that air feel good? And breathe out."

A few moments passed and I let my eyes travel to the nervously shuffling figures over me: Nick, Aileen, Jake, Jenna, Caleb.

Concern was palpable and, at one point, I thought I heard Jake trying to argue with the strikingly silent leader.

I stared down at my legs, my knees. They looked so, so strange. *Those are mine.*

"Scar, keep focusing on breathing, okay? That's all that matters right now." Sybil's voice soothed my confusion and I let my vision roll out as I melted into the charcoal skin of the only silent and still soul who stood before me. The emerald portals became one as they consumed me.

"Let's get her to her bed."

I woke to the tapping of raindrops, confused and a little on edge. I turned over to see Jenna fast asleep with her flashlight on and a book open on her chest. As I tried to reach for the window, I centered my attention on my hand, now heavy as a paperweight. Focusing on my breath, I sent signals to all my limbs, calling to them. When I finally collected myself, I pushed my heavy body up to the edge of the bed and just breathed for a few minutes.

"The truth is this. You will not heal. You will not grow. You will not find peace. Until. You develop the capacity to hold both worlds as truth within you." His voice reverberated somewhere in the cave of my cranium.

I am not sure how, but I managed to get sweatpants up my legs, a sweater around my shoulders, and my feet into my shoes. Everything was arduous. I didn't quite hurt though. I was more relaxed actually, so I grabbed my bag, which was hanging from the edge of my bed, and realized I had no recollection of placing it there.

I threw it around my shoulder, pulled out the map, then zipped the bungalow. It was the middle of the night. A night. Which night it was evaded me. Hours eluded me. Days escaped me. There was only darkness. I stared at the map but couldn't make anything out. No path appeared before me.

A sweet breeze came with the thought and, without resistance, I followed.

As I trudged forward under the trees, a pearly glow tangled my toes. And when I looked up, the moon was pendulous and free, entirely full and blooming with a beautiful ring expanding around it. I turned to face it while its light scaled a translucent pattern in the dirt beyond me.

I changed trajectories and followed it off the stone path as the hefty Guanacaste trunks made way for me. I almost questioned their movement, but for some reason, it felt too natural to second-guess. Their roots curled and vacated from the glowing path before me. I pressed forward and slowed as their branches opened and shared with me their boundless view.

"Whoa!!!" I gasped as a gust of wind rushed through me. I was standing right over the mountain's edge. The wind whirled through my curls and then quickly ceased.

"Vita…"

I fell to my knees at the sound of Its whisper.

I'm dreaming this. I have to be.

I looked up for it—the voice who knew my name, who was calling to me in the wind. When there was no appearance, I caught my hands shining in the moonlight and recalled the last few hours.

Tears waterfalled down my cheeks and I wept myself of all my residual strength.

I wept at the thought of losing my family, my loved ones, of losing all that the generations before me had worked to achieve in my country, in their country.

I wept for our careers, for our home.

I wept at the thought of losing my senses, my ability to move, to speak, to feel.

I wept because they came back.

I wept for time. That it ceased. That it continued.

I wept because, for the first time, Death's breath desired me. Because I wanted more.

I wept with gratitude for this humanity of mine. With grief for it.

I wept that I woke up tonight, that I couldn't stay in that tremendous, dangling detachment—that connection to everything in existence, that elusive separateness and yet, oneness with all in existence.

I slid down the trunk behind me and collapsed to the ground as my fingers clamored for my pen.

Part of me

died with you that night.

A big part.

Perhaps, the biggest.

My palms pulled the skin down over your eyes

and I collapsed on your body,

while the minutes turned into hours

that I wept over you,

to feel your beard scrape my cheek

in exchange for the last I love you's

I would ever whisper into your ear.

Part of me died with you that night,

and all my other parts know they will never be the same.

Just then, a twig snapped to my right and, in the nightfall, a silhouette of four legs, stout ears, and a steely jaw glared back at me with beaming emeralds. Stillness filled my being and fear vacated the forest as the elusive creature before me held the duality of the world upon his bulging charcoal shoulders.

I stared back and filled my chest with air, dropping my chin to his nobility.

Eyes steady on mine, he slowly, silently bowed his head.

If a moment could last a life time, this one—honoring the virtue, the purpose, the destiny in this creature, and him honoring mine—would be it.

The black panther turned and moonlight glimmered on his coat as he disappeared into the darkness, leaving a peace pulsing in his wake.

"

I am learning the only difference
between a tragedy and a miracle is
where you decide the story ends.

DAKOTA ADAN

Seventeen

My eyes sprung open and my lungs moaned for air. I peered around the dark room and strained for the outline of the shapes around me. When I saw Jenna still fast asleep, I knew I'd woken before the parrots too. Shifting my attention to my body, I tried to find my fingers. They twitched violently as I begged them to wake up. My focus traveled throughout my limbs, as I noticed it was strangely difficult to move this morning. I was heavy, and my thoughts were dragging, like someone had turned the lights off inside.

Slowly lifting and stretching, I tried to collect the events of the day before. I remembered crystal blue water. I remembered Ramón's eyes on me, his hands on my jaw. I remembered those stunning butterflies twirling me in circles, my head in Sybil's lap, that yummy dinner and all the laughter we shared. Then, Caleb. His sulky eyes and heavy demeanor.

Cazzo!

I'd forgotten. We were supposed to meet the night before. A quiet stillness stopped me.

"Scarlett! Scarlett!" Different voices filled my ears and I recalled my back flat on the studio floor.

"Scar?" Jenna must have heard my thoughts. She turned to face me, rubbing her eyes and clearing her throat. "How you feelin' today, Roomie?"

"Hey, Jenna," I whispered. "Sorry if I woke you. Trying to keep quiet."

"Oh no no no, don't worry about it. You feelin' better today?" She moved her silky blonde hair from her face.

"Uh, yeah. I feel okay. I vaguely remember last night. What did you think of that... meditation?"

"What did *I* think of it? What did *you* think of it?" Her eyes widened with curiosity as she appeared to wake quickly.

I crooked my neck and turned my body to face her.

"What do you mean?"

"Scar." She chuckled and raised her eyebrows. "You're kinda concerning me. Screaming nightmares and then totally disappearing during the death training."

"Disappearing?" An immediate wave of vertigo washed over me.

"Girl, we couldn't wake you up! We tried for a good twenty minutes. It was like you weren't there, like you didn't... like you didn't wanna' come back."

Her words settled as I remembered waking to the faces above me. I couldn't see much prior to that.

"Inhaling light. Exhaling time."

"I... I remember the large man, the teacher, but..." I paused. "I think I might've just knocked out?"

Jenna just stared back at me, clearly unconvinced.

"Well, I'm here, Hun, if you need support with anythin'. Just want you to know."

I smiled a *thank you.*

"Hey! I wanted to ask you! Do you know what the symbolism is behind hummingbirds?"

She shot me a contemplative glance. "I believe they're symbolic of joy, but lemme' check!" I rearranged my clothes as she dug through the bag of books by her bed and found her treasure in the flipped pages.

"Oh okay, yea! Darnit, look at me! That was it. Mainly joy and healing... but actually, in some regions, they're revered as messengers from spirits. Like, they carry messages from spirits to the living."

Spirits.

"Interesting."

"So… what's up with you and Ramón?" Her eyes lit with excitement as she waited for the chisme.

I blushed. We laid there facing each other while tucked under our sheets, turning back the hands of time and embracing our inner schoolgirls. Interacting with her filled me with the joy of friendship again. The face of Raya flashed as we chatted and giggled, and I promised myself I'd reach back out to her when I got home.

Jenna and I exchanged stories and excitements, wishes and wonders until the red-lored parrots begged us to join them. On we went to complete our bathroom runs in preparation for the day. Drying my hair in the mirror, I recalled Caleb's hollow eyes looking back at me.

I have to find him.

I pulled my gray cardigan over my head and slipped into my comfy white shorts. The weather was perfect—the air dewy and the sun just warm enough to complement the cool of the ground. I took a deep breath outside the bungalow and smiled at Jenna, letting her know I was ready.

We made our way through the floating pollen to meditation. This morning seemed brighter than the others and I found myself searching through the jungle for that marvelous green-eyed feline, wondering if he'd ever grace me with his mystery again.

As we passed the front desk where Ramón had his head down, clearly buried in some paperwork, I smiled.

"Buenos días, Ramón."

"Oh, buenos días, mujeres." Hardly smiling, he dropped his chin and continued with what he was doing.

I couldn't help but wonder where his morning cheer had gone. And, the coffee, which I had been sure would be waiting.

"Was that weird?" Jenna inquired. "Do you think it's because I was there?"

I shrugged.

"Uh, I think it was… a bit, right? I have no idea. Maybe he was just busy."

We grabbed our mats and huddled to the right side of the class by the mirrors. I felt a soft hand on my shoulder and turned to see Aileen.

"Hey honey, how are you feeling?"

"Good morning, Aileen. I feel good!" I smiled as I noticed Nick's curious eyes peeking at me from around her.

"Oh, that's great! Morning, Jenna!" She smiled and moved to sit next to Nick. I sat, a bit hypnotized by the vines wrapping around the glass walls. They reminded me of the ones I swung through in Bosque Nuboso while I twirled through the air.

Dio Santo, calm down, Tarzan.

I tightened my eyes closed and listened to the group file in. I couldn't help but feel their eyes scanning me as they passed. If Jenna hadn't filled me in earlier, I would have felt a little uncomfortable.

I kept my eyes peeled for Caleb, but I didn't find him before Rebecca appeared and walked slowly to the front of the room where she sat crossed leg and began to lead us in meditation. I followed her voice with much more ease today. I actually sunk in pretty quickly this time.

Maybe there was something to this meditation thing. I rolled my eyes. I didn't care, as long as I could feel the air pumping through me again.

After we concluded, we rolled up our mats and I slowed as I followed the group outside, trailing in the back. Separation sounded a lovely refuge from the curious stares.

I didn't flinch this time when his soft hand touched my shoulder. I turned to see Sibú's sweet smile and indigo treasures settled on me. "Ciao, Scarlett. Buongiorno."

Ah, a language I actually know.

"Sibú. Ciao. Buenos días."

"You are different today, Traveler." His eyes seemed to travel more around my head and torso than at them. "You are lighter. How do you feel?"

I smiled back. "Lighter is a good word. Definitely lighter."

His cheeks pulled back to his ears and we began walking together.

"So, how did it feel?"

I looked at him blankly.

"How did what feel?"

The evening's training flashed through my memory and I recalled floating into the darkness. "Oh um, it felt... I'm not sure. It was definitely... different. That was definitely one way to try to understand death... by experiencing it?" I think I turned my response into a question to see if I was on the right track, or at least, the expected one.

When he didn't respond, I continued, "It's been difficult for me these last few months to... get through the whole acceptance thing. I think mostly because I don't really know *how* to understand it. Death, you know? I was raised to think of it one way, but that doesn't quite resonate with me anymore. Last night was the first time it felt... natural... okay." He listened to me think out loud as I reminisced on how good it felt to fade away from everything I know—to fade into that darkness, completely.

"It felt... like bliss." I glanced back at him, "Do I sound crazy?"

He chuckled. "Scarlett..." He stopped before the path narrowed and, when he turned to face me, the warmth in his expression radiated. "I think that's the first time I've heard you sound sane since you got here." He winked and held his hand out, motioning for me to pass in front of him. I smiled easily as we approached the big wooden doors and I swore I could hear that music from all the way outside.

I filed in and grabbed two plates, turning back to give him one. But he was gone.

Quite the disappearing act, that man.

Filling my plate with mountains of voluptuous fruit, almond butter, and banana bread muffins, I practically drooled through the entire line. My mouth watered as the echo of the music filled the hall. I watched Sol float between the serving counter and through the kitchen door where the light trailed as usual at her heels, even brighter today.

Breakfast was colorful as ever and while a few more people stopped me to kindly ask if I was alright, no one pried. While they talked among each other, I wondered what had transpired on that floor while I floated away. The more I thought of it, the more the lightning from the afternoon before flashed through my memory, pushing me away from the breakfast table and back into the moments before I woke to Ramón pounding on my chest.

I could still see streaks of it shooting across the sky, flickering through the raindrops with enough power to light Times Square on New Year's. Standing on the edge of that pool again, the energy that whirled around me made my knees feel safe enough to give out with no concern for how the rest of my body would land safely. I fell back, back into the earth.

His voice rose through the house, calling my name. I don't know why I didn't respond. I could hear him, but I had no reaction, no thoughts, no words to let out. His large fist tapped on the door.

"Scar, you need to eat."

I stayed curled on my side while he came and sat in the curve of my tummy and followed my eyes to the wall full of sticky notes next to my father's bedside. He sighed all the air from his lungs.

"Alex, what do you think happens to us after we die?" He sat still, staring blankly with me.

My brother, second oldest, had been the first of generations to part from our very Christian home and his position as the church's worship leader to pursue an academic career in the sciences, and to much success. Although it was not dinner table conversation in our family, everyone knew he'd left his faith and all its warring doctrine.

And until I'd done the same, I'd resonated with the consensus of judgment toward his choices and his growing distaste for our home religion.

It wasn't long until my passion for studying societies, their cultures and traditions—faiths all over the world—quickly led me down a similar path, along which I too grew to question everything I knew to be true.

That year had been, until this one, the hardest of my young life by far. It was the same year my papà's health began to disintegrate and I quickly learned that leaving my faith meant surrendering all its coping mechanisms.

I'd lost that first ten pounds off my tiny frame trying to keep up with life after it had been stripped of the only purpose I knew, pleasing a god I swore to love—a god I swore loved me.

"Everyone keeps saying he's with the angels now, that Jesus wanted him up there with him early, that it's all part of some divinely orchestrated plan." I paused as the water refused to moisten my dry, blood-stained eyes. "I can't go back, Alex. Those comforts. They're just… momentary. Merda. I know that now… I can't."

His head dropped and water rolled down his cheeks. Perhaps my brilliant brother was wrestling with the same conversation inside.

"But … what do you think happens after death? I don't mean heaven or hell. But, to our souls, you know? Or is that just it? Do we disappear?"

His breath was short and his rib cage fought the words that fell from his lips, "I wish I had an answer for you, Kid…"

Suddenly back at the breakfast table, I shook my head. There was so much madness happening in this place I couldn't wrap my mind around. The more I tried to figure it out, the further I fell from reality. I was psyching myself out and I knew it.

I knew why I didn't fight back, why I didn't paddle my legs and try to swim up, why I just watched the last bubbles of my air float from my mouth to the surface. I knew why I didn't leave the room when the large man said death training.

The truth is, part of me wants it.

The pain of living without my papà's presence the last few months had been so unbearable, I just wanted to escape. I didn't want to feel anymore. I didn't want responsibilities or obligations. I didn't want to be angry or confused. I didn't want answers. I just wanted to disappear.

Perhaps, my falling into that cave was a sort of surrender, a sort of acceptance. Maybe I didn't need to understand death. Maybe I just needed to stop fearing it. Maybe… it wasn't the big scary beast I thought it was.

"¡Buenos días!" Gitana's perky energy vibrated in her voice. "¡Espero que tengan un buen día! Our next excursion will be to the coffee fields in a few days. We will be taking it easy until then."

I cleared my plate and swallowed my taunting thoughts, deciding to replace them.

Deciding some coffee would be good right about now, I thought of Ramón and his aloof demeanor earlier. Maybe I could catch him at the front desk on the way to my bungalow. I hustled down the path but rounded the corner to find an empty front desk.

"Oh Scar, I'm so glad I found you!" I turned at the sound of Sybil's honey-sweet voice. She smiled and focused on getting her wobbly cane to pick up speed so she could get to me faster.

"Are you free right now? I've been meaning to chat with you." Again, her eyes seemed to bounce more around me than actually at me and I couldn't quite pin down her gaze through her glasses.

"Uh, yes, I'm free." I looked around, "Would you like to walk a little?" I motioned for her to lead the way.

We walked around the pond and enjoyed some small talk. She mentioned she'd come from Oregon—Portland, to be specific—and the beads in her white braided hair suddenly made sense. She was such a sweetheart, but something in me knew she'd been around a few blocks. Following her cane off the main path through the bushes, I laughed at her stories and walked just behind her until I looked up to see a familiar gazebo with a couple of hammocks on either side of it, a well between them.

I thought I'd dreamed of this place. I tried to help her into the hammock, but her feisty independence wasn't having it. Resigned, I settled into the opposite one and faced her.

"So, Sweetie, I've been meaning to ask you... have you lost someone recently? A man, maybe?"

And I thought I was direct.

I shuddered a bit at her brash. I'd been managing to weasel around this conversation with everyone here. No one knew my grief brought me here, not even the roomie I'd spent hours chatting with. Not even Ramón.

Not even Sibú knew.

"Uhm..." I shifted in the hammock a bit. "I have, yes." My awkwardness became apparent, and I couldn't really figure how to hide it.

"I'm sorry if I've overstepped, but I have been putting this off for quite some time now, and I simply can't anymore."

She had my curiosity piqued.

"So, I am a medium. Do you know what that is?" she asked.

"Uhm," I recalled the old witch cartoons Mamma never let me watch growing up. "Like, you talk to dead people?" I managed through my perplexity. My palms were beginning to sweat.

"Well, sort of, yes. Not always talk. Sometimes, I feel or see or hear someone who has passed *on*, but they're usually people who haven't really passed *through*."

I was following as much as I could. After all, it was only a few years ago that I started to even consider that maybe people who claimed to have these gifts weren't actually devil-worshippers.

"You see, there has been a man hanging around you and he has been... well, persistent."

My focus quickly narrowed, and I could tell she was wary, scanning my body language to see if I was ready.

"I... I usually don't go up to people and tell them these things unless they ask to know, but this man has literally been poking me."

My brows furrowed as I remembered my papà periodically walking over to Mamma in the kitchen and poking her shoulder when he wanted attention. She'd get so annoyed every time.

"Can... can I just describe him to you and you can tell me if the description resonates with you at all?"

I cleared my throat, reassured myself this was probably a hoax, and nodded.

She kept her eyes wide open as her gaze lifted around me and to the right. "He is about five feet eight. Dark skin, very brown. He has a very big jaw and..." I gulped as she continued describing my father in explicit detail, "...very foxy gray hair. It's almost silver on the sides, but still black on top. He has small brown eyes and coffee-stained teeth. A shadowed, very short prickly beard. He is wearing black gloves on his hands."

Goosebumps shuddered across my skin as I recalled the black golf gloves he wore everywhere. He swore they helped with the neuropathic pain in his hands. A whimpering seized my chest. The pressure was building now against the dam behind my eyes.

She looked at me curiously, as if for approval to keep going. I didn't move.

"It's a bit strange. He hasn't actually said much. Mostly, he just laughs. And like, really laughs. Very, very loudly!"

My hands grew clammy, and the pace of my heartbeat picked up. I dropped my chin and fought the tears while Sybil waited. I wanted her to keep going, but I didn't know how to process this strange woman telling me that my papà, in some form other than human, was revealing himself to her.

I took a deep breath.

"Yes," I stuttered. "He was kind of… known for that."

"Oh, it's beautiful! It's just *really* loud sometimes!"

"So, you said he has been visiting you today?"

"No, our entire time here actually. Well, I first saw him hanging around you at breakfast when I met you. Really, he was just sort of following you, watching you. Then, yesterday, he woke me up and told me that I needed to tell you something and that it was extremely urgent. But when I saw you, you seemed fine and you were so happy and busy that I just wanted to talk when the time was right, you know? I didn't know how… receptive you'd be to this."

She was making me a bit anxious and I struggled to pay attention through my watery eyes.

"And then around dinner time last night, well that was when he started poking me! And let me tell you, I've had spirits be persistent before, but your dad literally shoots his little finger right into my shoulder."

"Spirit? My papà is a… spirit?"

She crooked her neck. "It's a bit difficult to explain, Dear, and I don't want to impede on any beliefs you might have, but…"

Beliefs?

I didn't even know what beliefs were anymore. I had no idea what was real and what wasn't. I'd left behind the only system I had for understanding this stuff even a little bit.

And now, all of this…

"What did he want you to tell me?" I stammered, interrupting her and choking on the tightness in my throat.

Her eyes shifted from me to the right side of my hammock, a little beyond, and I glanced back and forth.

Is this happening?

"He wants me to tell you that… It's not your time yet. He seems… a bit… worried about you. He knows you miss him, but…"

"Is he saying this to you? Like, those are his words?" Cognitively, I struggled to find a way to comprehend this.

She took a deep breath. "It's a bit difficult to explain this part because he's not exactly saying it. But Dear, his heart energy is so swollen, it's surrounding him. This man loves you so very much, it's difficult to put into words. And from what I gather, he always has."

I couldn't believe what I was hearing. I hadn't seen Papà in months. I hadn't heard his voice. I was here trying to make peace with that.

I'd been aching and aching to just be with him and now… this crazy hippie lady was telling me he was standing behind me because he was worried about me? My chest was caving in. I closed my eyes and focused on a bizarre whirlpool of Rebecca's and Sibú's voices.

"Inhale. Exhale." I seemed to hold off the crackle for a second and create space for an idea to strike. If this woman could see and talk to my papà, what if… this was the only chance I got?

I never did get to say goodbye.

I opened my eyes to her waiting patiently. I understood, if by some miracle this was real, that she was acting as a messenger. "I'm sorry, I just… are you able to tell him something for me?"

She nodded. "He can hear you, Sweetie."

Awkwardly, I looked to the right of me and imagined his outline, his shape, his skin and eyes. I couldn't help but puddle with tears.

"I– I…" I looked back at Sybil. Embarrassment washed over me and doubt swelled within. "I can't do this."

"It's okay, Dear. I don't think he is going anywhere."

I closed my eyes while the tears poured through my lashes.

Mio dio.

I missed him so much. And… I wanted him here, even if it was in *spirit.* I couldn't understand any of this, and I melted into a blubbering mess. Somewhere in my heap, Sybil made her way over and plopped in my hammock and wrapped me in her arms.

"

Magic is alive in the world, Traveler.
I intend to share with you the secrets of Alchemy.

DAN MILLMAN

Eighteen

The interaction with Sybil sent me down quite the rabbit hole after we parted ways. The questions heaved through my psyche in hurricane-sized waves and none of the answers I explored seemed to calm them.

"It's not your time yet…" repeated in my head while I packed my bag for the coffee fields until Jenna marched into the bungalow with an undeniable frown.

"Hey Jenna, how are you?"

"Ehhh."

"Uh oh? Everything okay?"

"I'm not sure to be honest. I just had the craziest damn experience with the masseuse."

That got my attention. "Really?"

We both grabbed the last of our things and headed to the bus as Jenna shared her superstitions about this place. She couldn't tell whether her experience with Aaina was a dream or not.

"I don't know. At one point, her hands just… they felt exactly like my husband's. They even looked like them! They were big and strong and… they were… full of pain. It's difficult to explain."

"I am all ears, Girl…"

I figured hearing about her experience with Aaina might help me make some sense of mine.

"I just, I swear I saw him and his eyes. I saw his tears. I felt his… betrayal. I remembered making love with him and feeling like… he was hiding something from me or maybe I was the one hiding. It just… Uggh. It felt like secrets. Like big, nasty, disgusting secrets. And I just wanted a friggin' massage."

I sighed and stayed quiet, trying to give her some space to process.

"My grandpa used to call them Shapeshifters." Hearing Ramón's voice, I turned to look for him.

Excitement coursed through me at the thought of him coming to the fields with us, but I didn't see him anywhere. In fact, I hadn't seen him in days.

As we filed onto the bus, I wondered where Caleb had disappeared to as well. I needed to speak with him.

We drove for at least an hour and a half along the windy mountain road, and I watched the sun shudder through the treetops. There were at least ten people who came on this excursion, but everyone was unusually quiet today. Jenna, aloof and a bit lost in deciphering her puzzle of experiences, stared out the window. I decided to close my eyes and try to process mine, especially my time with Sybil. I couldn't quite shake it.

There was no way, absolutely no way, Sybil could've known so much about him.

But, a *spirit?*

"He has passed on, but not exactly through." What did that even mean?!

I played an internal movie reel of the last few confusing weeks and wondered if he saw me fall in the water during the thunderstorm or, the training. Could that be his worry?

"It's not your time yet." Perhaps, somehow, he knew how I felt.

The driver turned us very sharply off the main road where we drove down such a steep rocky street, I thought the bus was going to flip right over itself. We made a few more rights and then a left outside a rusty gate. Clouds started to roll over a bit darker and I wrapped my coat around my waist while Gitana gathered everyone in a circle.

"¡Entonces, una sorpresa! The big reveal… ¿estan listos? This coffee field is actually a labyrinth. We will each enter at different points." She pulled out a map with writing in Spanish so faint, I could hardly make out the enormous scribbled lines.

"Here, here, and here. We will go one by one, and you will need to wait until I say when you can enter."

Confusion swirled as I looked up to see the hedges of these coffee bushes, much taller than the last. This looked more like a corn maze than a labyrinth.

Aileen raised her hand and communicated our collective confusion ever-so-politely.

"Señorita, what exactly is the point of a labyrinth? I have only ever heard of them. I don't think I've ever actually completed one."

"I'm so glad you asked! The labyrinth is an ancient practice in our culture, and many others. You begin by asking yourself a question or thinking about something you really need support with. Think of it as a map, designed to help you find your answer. But... the treasure lies within. It's representative of a journey within yourself, and then back out into the world."

Cazzo.

I was already lost.

I looked around and while everyone else seemed pretty trusting of the exercise, Aileen's resistance mirrored mine. I followed Gitana's instruction and stood behind Nick. Waiting to follow him after he stepped about ten feet in, I looked over at Jenna who was clearly still grumpy and unsure if she really wanted to do this.

Gitana smiled and nodded for me to proceed. I followed Nick, but after I passed the entrance and looked up, I could not see him. Frowning, I picked up my speed a bit and looked for him around a few bends.

"Nick? Nick?" No response. I looked back toward the entrance but saw only a wall of green.

A vanishing entrance. Fucking wonderful.

Frustrated, I pushed on, trying to think of what I needed to ask.

How about... why the actual fuck did I come here? To Costa Rica? What am I doing? What is any of this nonsense good for?

I continued rounding corners for what felt like at least a half hour. There was no sun to set, but it was certainly getting darker. The clouds were starting to roar and, as soon as I looked up, water splashed on my face.

This certainly wasn't the beautiful day in the coffee fields I'd hoped for. I unwrapped my sweatshirt from my waist and tucked my arms in. The wind picked up and it started getting a bit stormy, so I put my head down and trudged on. The further I walked, the worse it got and I wondered if I should just turn back.

There wasn't even a back to turn to! I crossed my arms over my chest in an effort to keep warm—and calm. Mostly calm. It's not like I was getting lost completely alone in some coffee maze in a foreign country or anything.

What the hell am I doing here!

I thought of Ramón and remembered all his help during the ziplining. He was so sweet and he was just there, supporting me, holding me, catching me at every turn. The frustration quivered up my arms and neck.

Why wasn't he here today? Why was he being so distant with me?

I remembered Julian and a red-hot flare of anger shot down my back. He had to fuck it up. What a beautiful soul he has. So sweet. He was always there too... catching me, saving me. And he just had to...

The thunder grew louder and let out a giant bang against the clouds. I tucked my head in my hoodie and tried to stay calm, but I just felt like I was getting more lost.

I couldn't shake Julian, or the ways I had pushed him away. I wanted him to save me from this, from my grief, from my confusion and my anger. I wanted him to make it all go away. That's what love is supposed to do, right? We'd spent three years doing that for each other. Why couldn't he help me with this?

My inner chatter halted when I noticed a flutter of white in the hedge to my left. Wiping the rain from my face, I moved toward it. It was faint and not yet fully formed, like a blurry bundle of luminescence in the shape of two clouds. Knowing she wouldn't survive this storm if she stayed there, I stuck out my finger and this brave little creature crawled to it.

Steady, Scar.

I attempted to calm my cold shakes to carry it in front of me.

My footsteps turned into giant marching thumps through the mud as I continued rounding hedges only to sink further. I held my hand up for my little friend but couldn't keep my thoughts from wandering back to Julian. My frustration was growing to rage, and I just wanted to scream.

Why would he do that to me? How could he cheat? That wasn't love! Did I make him do it? Was I too lost in all my pain for him to reach me, to keep loving me?

I could feel the red pump hot to my face and swell my eyes with anger. My head was surely on its way to an explosion. Sound thundered through the sky, and light emanated from the gray haze.

I swear my papà was the only one who could ever really love me—all of me.

He was always there, caring for me, saving me. He would have been so upset with me here, in some lost land, about to get struck by lightning. But I knew he would have found a way if I needed it.

My anger burst through my eyeballs and the waterfalls poured forth.

"How could I seriously have any more god damn tears left! Agggggggggh!"

I refocused my eyes on this fluorescent light on my finger. It almost felt as if she was leading me, further and further into the rain, into the darkness. But as we pushed on, this little beauty's wings began to take form. They grew larger as we rounded more corners in the dark of the night together. Rays of purple and blue glowed from her center to the tips of her wings.

I knew it. This was the butterfly from the falls.

I was aggressively fighting the sticky, watery mud now. I felt like such a damsel, so weak and tired.

I am so fucking over needing to be saved.

I was angry, so angry. Angry that I didn't know what to believe. Angry at the mentors who made my faith look like bullshit. Angry at the church leaders for refusing to answer my questions, refusing to support me while the pillars of my world crumbled. Angry at the man I loved, the man I relied on, for betraying me. Angry at the one person who always knew me and loved me... for leaving me. Angry at death for robbing me, for stealing the meaning from my existence, for taking my desire, my ability to feel!

I am so god-forsakenly angry.

With my next step, I fell deep through a hole in the ground and faced the clouds as the rain splashed on my face. Rage exploded through my body in waves of blood coursing beneath my skin. Taking what felt like the deepest breath of my life, until my lungs were completely full, I screamed. I shrieked so loud my ear drums started throbbing before I'd even stopped and no line could be drawn between my roar and the thunder.

I was waist deep in the mud now, body heaving, pulsing with waves of emotion as I sunk. I looked up and wiped my eyes through the rain, realizing my sweet little butterfly guide had vanished. Aching to surrender, I tried to make out the hedges in the fog when I realized they all looked the same. They curved round me in a circle.

Quiet started crawling through my shaking body, and I became still as I searched for my breath. I looked up and around the hedges. A slight glow beamed around the hedge on the far side of the circle. I looked down at the watery darkness that consumed the lower half of my body and focused on Sibú's voice.

"It's all we really have."

I kept my breath steady as the mud disintegrated around me. I pushed my waist from the sunken pit, and then stomped forth, one foot after the other. My skin was still pulsing hot and I fought the water running down my face as I trudged toward the light.

Could it be?

They looked an awful lot like the others.

As I turned around the corner of the hedge, I found a white wooden door, splintered and cracked, aged elegantly and tucked into the massive, at least twenty-foot-high, roots of two overarching ceiba trees. Entangled at the trunks, the two trees intertwined in a beautiful twist that seemed to dance with the settling wind.

They were even more majestic than before—massive, wrinkled with timeless strength, and sprouting from the earth with confidence. I marveled, remembering the bodily transcendence that lightning and thunderstorm shook up in me upon my arrival. I stared at the door tucked deep in the curve of their roots, vines and seeds draped all over it. I looked closely and quickly picked up a pattern in the scars on the door that reflected more red than brown. Etched in the wood, I traced a circular shape with my fingers. As they curved down to a rectangular shape at the bottom, my head fell to the side with wonder.

"No."

The word trickled from my tongue as the full picture deepened before my eyes, etched further into the wood and appearing as gently against the background as the illustrations on the map. I jumped back as the terror that rang through my nightmare filled my chest once more. It was a balloon, a hot-air balloon above a basket. The top cracks began dripping a thick blood and the balloon was soon drenched in red.

I rubbed my eyes.

It's just my imagination.

I blinked again.

It has to be.

Nope. Unless I am sleeping right now, this is real.

My heart pounded so loudly, I couldn't differentiate it from the distant thunder.

Moving the vines away from the door, I pulled and pulled on the door until I fell back on my butt. When I looked up, the door slid open slightly. The light, white and strong now, glowed so brightly, it reflected off the world around me, disintegrating it. The blazing ivory butterfly reappeared and led the way. Cautiously pushing the door wider, I squeezed my eyes shut as I followed her into the blinding light.

Before I could see anything, my ears were my only guide. A Spanish guitar, some Latin drums, a trumpet. The instruments, so many of them, clanged back and forth.

The music from the dining hall, from the class.

"

Be the woman you shiver to be
and be the woman that scares the absolute
shit out of you and for the sake of the sun,
be the woman that makes you feel so
fucking alive that your coffee hits like
ecstasy and you become the kind of magic,
we were taught not to believe in.

BROOKE SOLIS

Nineteen

My hips itched to move with the sound of the music. I continued forward, squinting as I tried to identify where I was.

"¡Señorita! ¡Que buena para verte!"

"Sol? Are you there?" I peeked between my fingers and, as the light began to fade, shapes started taking form before me. To my right, I saw the silver of a giant refrigerator shine into view as teal and fuchsia-colored tiles shuffled up the wall behind it. The light faded more and, to my left, a flank of wood was piled from left to right with fruits and veggies so plump and vibrant—a full rainbow.

As I looked forward and around, steam filled the kitchen from the boiling pots on the far stove. The light was tamed now and I let my arms drop from over my eyes.

"Puesss, no puedes cocinar con esa ropa!" Sol scanned me up and down, refusing to hide her strong disapproval of my clothes. I looked down to see the filth I was covered in and dropped my chin in confusion as I looked at my drenched body, white shorts, and long bare legs stained with mud. I turned to search for the door I'd come through. It too had vanished.

I was dreaming again.

I have to be.

"Mmm un momento." She hustled past me, dropping the pot in her hands on the stove and opening a nearby closet.

"¡Aquí tienes, ponte esto!" She handed me a beige uniform that looked similar to hers and then walked over to the sink where she ran hot water over a towel she'd grabbed off the shelf.

"Sol, uhm estoy… confundida. Un poco." I silently begged my Spanish not to fail me now. She was my only hope for understanding what was happening.

"No te preocupes, mi bailarina. Nosotros vamos a cocinar."

She wanted me to cook?

"¿Yo? ¿Cocinar?"

She chuckled as she scuttled over and bent down before me with the warm towel. She wiped my legs up and down, scrubbing every last bit of mud from my skin and eventually slipped my shoes off. Then, she wiped my feet too and assisted me in changing.

I dug my nails into my arm to see if I could pull myself out of this.

Nope, still here.

She folded the towel, rinsed again, and then wiped the dirt from my face.

"¿Entonces, ok? Estamos listo." She flashed an accomplished smile and bounced her hands on her hips in a ready position.

"¿Uh, Sol, cocinar? No sé cómo cocinar."

She chuckled as she grabbed an apron off the wall, draped it over my head, and tied it around my waist. "¡Clarooo! ¡Por supuesto que sí!"

"Uhhh…" I laughed nervously at her blind confidence. She had no idea how wrong she was.

She stopped and stared at me.

"Señorita, en esto momento, nosotras cocinamos. Vamos." I realized I was not getting out of this. When I nodded, she tossed me a chopstick and I pulled my long, wet locks up into a bun atop my head and secured it.

Focusing, I followed each instruction Sol gave me—well, the ones I could understand. When she wasn't singing, she shouted the next step over the music and with much candor. I don't think she stopped dancing for even a moment. Her hips swayed across the kitchen with so much ease and grace, it was hard not to get distracted.

Every time I became concerned about how this dinner was going to turn out, Sol danced over and bounced her hip against mine or sang right in my ear as she walked by. Her joy was contagious, and I couldn't help but laugh.

Something about her reminded me of Mamma, of the days I'd follow her around the kitchen, watching her dance to Barry White or Lionel Richie, swinging her hips back and forth. A wave of nostalgia washed over me and then another of guilt as I thought of her alone in our home. I missed her with my whole being and I felt terrible for leaving her. It pained me to think of her being there alone. We were supposed to be looking for a new home together, consolidating things, making decisions for our future.

My vision blurred white with the powder in the dough I was rolling...

"You are not my caretaker, Scarlett!" Mamma snapped back at me as she paced from her closet to her bedroom, throwing old paperwork, clothes, and junk into a trash bag, her hair toppled in a flurry above her head.

"Papà may not have been healthy, but I am perfectly fine and I don't need you to take care of me."

This explosion happened when I'd tried with too much force to help organize the accounts, passwords, and paperwork for her.

"Dio Santo! I am only sixty years old for god sakes! I can do this."

I watched with awe as my mother furiously stomped around the room to emphasize her point. She hadn't lived alone once.

Before her forty-year marriage, she lived with a roommate briefly in Milano, who'd been a childhood friend. She'd admitted to me that she had no idea how to manage bills on her own, track down accounts or paperwork, or fill her car tires with air. I knew I could help.

There were so many things I'd watched her figure out on her own in the last few months. And apparently, my efforts to assist were not being received the way they were intended. She felt smothered and was desperately trying to navigate her newfound, albeit abruptly forced, independence.

She sighed and walked over to me.

"Scar." She moved the hair away from my watering eyes as she realized this was about much more than helping her. I didn't even know who I was without caring for Papà.

"You have to live your life. I want you out of this pattern of taking care of all the things you did before. I need to learn this stuff on my own. And you have a life that needs you. Remember, Vita." She shook my face with her hands.

"Remember who you are."

Hands still stuck in the dough, I saw Mamma's face again, this time on the ground, pushing me away, telling me to go, to leave, to save myself as the men in white hurried toward her.

Sol interrupted. "¿Sabes que hace que la comida sepa tan bien?"

A secret ingredient?

"¿Uhhh, Amor?"

She smiled wryly and shook her head as if she was about to pop a myth. Shuffling over and moving my curls from my ear, she whispered, "La sonrisa... la sonrisa del momento."

The smile of the moment.

I chuckled and swung my arms around her waist. She pulled me close with a nice tight squeeze. And for a second, I felt every piece of her. Her light, her ease, her beauty and grace, her freedom and joy. Her energy vibrated with all the power in the wings of that gorgeous little hummingbird. I wanted her to be around me forever.

Someday, I hoped to be like her.

I relaxed even more into the music. I let it whirl through me and around me, widening my hips and stretching my shoulders.

I was so lost in taste-testing all of the delectable sauces and dancing to more Marc Anthony, that I hadn't even realized just how close we were to being finished. We started organizing the tamales, rice, and beans on the serving trays and pouring the guacamole and salsas into their own serving bowls.

I looked around at the assortment of goodies before me, baffled the two of us had just accomplished so much. I looked down at my powdered white hands and wiped them on my apron.

"Okay, ¡Vamos!" Her eyebrows bounced up as she strong-armed the serving tray full of tamales and I followed her with the rice. We spent a few minutes setting everything up for everyone in *El Placer*. After all the food was out, Sol popped two straws in a couple of coconuts and we celebrated our achievement.

"¡Salud!"

The door cracked and Jenna and Aileen were the first two to enter.

"Scar!" They gasped simultaneously, rushing over to me.

"Where did you...? How did you–" Jenna started as her eyes dropped to my uniform. "I'm so confused!"

I laughed. "Me too, Hun. Me too."

Aileen chimed in, "I'm so glad you're okay! You took so long in the labyrinth. We waited at least a half hour until Gitana made the decision to head back to the center of the village. We thought she was crazy and something had to be wrong! But she just brushed it off like it would be fine. She said you might have taken another route, that sometimes that happens, but it's been days since we've seen you!"

Days?

I sobered up at that one. I couldn't have been gone that long.

"We were so confused. Like, what other route would you take? You were in the middle of a labyrinth at least an hour outside of town!"

"Con permiso, mujeres…" Sol squeezed my shoulder and excused herself back to the kitchen.

Chatting a bit more with them about their experiences with the labyrinth, I struggled to focus—stuck trying to make sense of mine.

"It is designed as a journey within yourself, and then back out into the world."

But I'd ended up in the kitchen with Sol.

I'd sampled so much while we were cooking that I actually didn't feel hungry. Unraveling Sol's apron from my waist, I leaned through that silver swinging door to hang it on the hook just inside it. I stopped and peered around the kitchen, remembering the light that brought me here—the storm, the rage, the confusion.

I blinked a few times, pondering the magic of this place, before I headed out the dining hall door.

Night had collapsed around me. The air was damp and dewy. After I stopped to breathe it in, fully, I headed to the front desk in hope of catching Ramón.

Nowhere to be found again. I walked on through the trees and marveled once more at the fireballs dancing in the branches above me—no wires, no strings. And finally, I didn't care. They hung independently and free in all their beauty. A breeze blew through, carrying some faint slow music from the east side of the village.

"Vita…."

I stepped off the path and through the trees, searching for *La Encarnada*. As I leaned around the door frame to peek in, I found Ramón sweeping the floor, whistling with melancholy to what I supposed was some awfully sappy bachata music.

"Ramón?" My voice strained at the sight of him. I was so excited to tell him about my adventure. There was so much I couldn't understand or explain, and I wanted desperately to share all of it with him.

Startled, he looked up at me and stopped sweeping.

"Hello, Miss Scarlett."

"¿Hey, cómo estás?" I playfully nudged him, but he remained unexpressive. "Is everything okay, Ramón?"

"Yeah, everything is fine. I just... I'm just finishing up here. Going to move onto *La Transparencia* next." Everything about his demeanor was different from the man with whom I'd spent my first magical weeks.

"You seem... different—bothered or something?"

He frowned and shook his head as he continued to sweep the floor.

"Mmm nope, todo bien."

Shifting awkwardly, I tried to lighten the mood. "Oh, well good. I haven't uh, I haven't seen you in a while. You're usually everywhere!" I smiled, hoping to get one in return.

"Yes, I've been busy."

This was feeling like a put off. One more try.

"Too busy to bring me that delicious coffee?" I playfully teased.

He stopped abruptly and picked up the dustpan and the phone in the corner before he walked over to me and met my gaze.

"Not everything is about you, Miss Scarlett." He brushed past me quickly, leaving his dagger in my stomach.

I stared at the studio floor he had just swept, the floor we once danced on and rolled on in laughter.

I left the building and turned to find him, but he was gone. Insecurity flooded me and I fought the crackle creeping to my chest cavity.

I turned again, feeling like there were... eyes on me. Like someone else was there. I looked around but the darkness was too dense. A bit spooked, I headed back to my bungalow, replaying the roughness in his tone as I combed through my memories for some clue.

The last thing I remembered was his face when I started to wake from the meditation. I stared down, past this beige uniform at the ground, and a feeling of shame washed through my cheeks.

What was I thinking? Getting romantic with some guy in Costa Rica... Thinking he liked me. I ruffled my clothes and stomped through the trees back on the path to my bungalow. I was so tired of feeling confused about everything!

"Scar, how are you?"

I jumped back with surprise. I couldn't help my rapid breathing as I tried to zoom my vision onto the tall figure in the trees. As I peered closer, I could make out the hollow eyes and rigid nose looking back at me.

"Caleb?"

"I'm sorry. I didn't mean to frighten you!"

"Oh." I paused to reclaim some of the air that had escaped. "No, no, that's okay. It's just really dark around here. How are you? I've been looking for you, so we could talk. You wouldn't believe the..."

"Actually, yes. I was hoping we could? I promise I don't think it will take too long."

"Oh, sure. Yeah, of course." I looked around for a place we might be able to sit and remembered a familiar walkway just around the corner. "Uhm, let's go over here. I think there is somewhere we can sit."

Caleb followed me through the trees to the well I'd visited with Sybil. After all this time, I was finally finding my bearings in this village. Or at least my body apparently knew the way. As we approached, I noticed it was lit with candles all around. The hammocks were gone, replaced by two cushions on the ground right next to it and, oddly, two steaming cups of melted cocoa beans.

I looked around, wondering if we might be stealing someone's spot, but I figured we could just leave if anyone came.

"So, you had a session with Rebecca?" I started.

"Yes, yes, I did. Look, I'm not exactly sure why she said I should come talk to you, but I figure I will just tell you my story and we can go from there."

He'd clearly been trying to articulate the best approach to this, so I nodded, sensing the weight of what was coming. I watched as he drew some air in, between his barely-opened lips, as if his lungs were reaching for just enough. His eyebrows furrowed as he focused on his words.

"My daughter Elizabeth is, uhm…" He cleared his throat, "… was twenty-one."

I gulped at the familiar dissonance of tenses.

"She was an artist, a painter. Oh, she was so talented. Like, it all came so naturally to her, you know?" He lost himself in memory. "She was perfect. She had light brown hair and deep blue eyes like her mother. We, uhm, we lost her mother to breast cancer when Elizabeth was just a young girl. So, it was just her and I for many years. It was… very difficult, you know? But, we had each other and we were close… very close. And… that felt like enough."

He was holding back the tears as he cleared his throat again.

"School was rough for her. I knew that. Lots of things were just hard growing up without a mom. But after she left for college, we kept in touch. I kept encouraging her to… keep painting. Said I'd pay for her classes, whatever she needed. But I just felt like she wasn't quite as… open with me. Then, one day, I got a call from one of her friends saying that she was in the hospital. She'd passed out after she'd done, uhm, heroin, and, they thought she overdosed."

My whole chest cavity sank to my stomach.

"Turns out, she'd been doing this for a while, a few years actually. And I had no idea."

He looked up at me, eyes glazed over as he shook his head, as if to assure me that if he'd known, he would have done more.

"After that, she was in and out of rehab for a couple years. I tried to support her. I found her a sponsor and begged her to keep up with her meetings."

His hands trembled.

I looked at my hands while he spoke, and felt them warm with gratitude for their stillness, for how far they'd come since I'd arrived. Gratitude… for the ten pounds I'd regained, for the air that easily flowed in and out of me, for the connectedness I'd restored within—with others, with nature, with divinity somewhere in the darkness.

My hands—they hadn't trembled in weeks.

"Then about a year ago, I got a call. She overdosed."

His chest hardly heaved as the tears fell, as if his body had completely abandoned its most basic function. I dropped my chin to the ground and watched my own tears plop into the steaming mug as I listened.

"She uhm, she was twenty-one when she died."

He wiped his face and looked up and around with confusion.

"I just, I can't fathom the fact that she's gone. She… she was all I had, you know?"

I do know.

I gulped as I listened to Caleb find words for the very same grief-stricken thoughts that had coursed through my body the last few months. He'd been grieving almost a year and still hadn't found any answers, any closure, any acceptance.

I was reminded of my own pain, of its inescapable depth, and my hands began to shake too. I'd almost managed to forget all that heartache these last few weeks. For the first time in what felt like a century, I was just beginning to really feel again. I'd almost completely forgotten about the ghost of a girl who showed up here in that little blue Volkswagen.

Life was… inescapable here, even for a ghost.

I didn't just know or feel this man's pain. I was him.

"I, I'm sorry. I don't know why I'm telling you this. You seem really young and I know you might not have any idea about this stuff. I'm really sorry to just unload all of this on you…" He continued rambling apologies that didn't make any sense and I let him for a little while until my trembling hand, remembering this pain, reached for his. He stopped and looked at me.

Suddenly, it all made sense.

"I'm twenty-one."

He crooked his neck.

"You're what?"

"I am twenty-one, the same age your daughter was. And, I lost my papà this year. And while heroin wasn't the cause, the opioid medications played a huge part in his decline, too—a massive part, actually. And, he was… my everything, too."

He stared at me with eyes that looked as if they'd finally found a puzzle piece—some inkling of something that could help him make sense of his reality. I squeezed his hand and wrapped my other around the ring hanging from my neck. Taking a deep breath, I noticed our hands together begin to calm and saw his mouth open a bit more through the snot and tears.

"I came here, desperate. I came in hope of finding some sort of acceptance, too."

His breathing was following mine now.

We sat exchanging stories and memories, aches, and pains. He shared with me, through blubbering tears, how awful her funeral had been and how sick he was of every pitiful phrase that was offered to soften the pain.

I shared how weary I'd become of all the things I watched the people around me tell themselves to cope, how there had to be something more out there than these false proverbs people drip from their lips when they didn't know what else to say. He agreed with relief that he wasn't alone, his eyes lighting up as we sarcastically mocked the clichés.

He told me in detail about every one of his favorite paintings Elizabeth had done and how he'd stacked them in his garage with no clue what do with them. I told him of the golf course I grew up on with my papà, how we couldn't afford summer camp, and how I'd spent all my time out there, reading my books in the golf cart while he worked.

He told me about how stubborn Elizabeth was as a young child and how she didn't have many friends because she was so close to her mom. They were inseparable. I shared all the stories my papà would tell me about his younger days, how they were ravished with adventure and abandon, aching with rebellion for something beyond the known of his world.

Hours passed as we basked in every emotion and memory our loved ones left us with... the loss, the anger, the connection, the rage, the friendship, the sadness, the joy, the confusion, the love.

By the time we were finished, the mist that hovered in the darkness had thawed and our laughter was all we could hear.

"

Humanity is the intersection
of glory and dirt.

DAKOTA ADAN

Twenty

I woke before the parrots, before Jenna, before the sun.

I woke and laid there, still and breathing, still and thinking. I recalled slowly these last few months. This land, so full of mystery, these people whose paths had so divinely crossed mine.

I thought about how many of my memories here didn't make any sense, how some of them didn't even have an end, or a beginning for that matter. How I couldn't, for the life of me, piece them together.

I wanted so very badly to ask Ramón about these things, and I couldn't understand what had happened with us. One minute, we were holding one another and the next, he seemed incredibly upset with me. The thought made me sad, but I'd resolved to give him the space it appeared he wanted. I decided I wouldn't chase him down anymore.

I wasn't sure how much longer I'd stay, but I didn't want to leave. Everything about this world, irrational and contradictory as it was to the laws of my normal reality, was just what I needed.

My thoughts tumbled over each other again and again.

When I heard Jenna rustling awake, I rolled out quickly and grabbed my toiletries. Stepping into the shower, I let the water burn my skin. Above me, palm leaves hung over the tile walls and bamboo door. A nice misty drizzle fell past them.

I took some deep breaths and leaned against the wall while I soaped myself. My skin felt incredible, soft and sultry. I looked down at my body with wonder, and compassion rolled through me.

I'd truly abandoned it. Years I neglected it by forgetting to eat, by not listening to it when it needed to move, by failing to manage my stress, by getting angry when it was too tired to keep up. This tiny little frail body had been through so much with me and, in this moment, I finally understood. I wrapped my arms around my shoulders and squeezed.

"Grazie," I whispered. "Grazie mille." I stood under the water, bathing in gratitude for quite some time enjoying the air, enjoying the earth, enjoying my body. Feeling for the first time in so long, like I was the center of all that was interconnected, and that I, this body and I, mattered.

As I started my post-shower routine, I caught sight of myself in the mirror.

I looked fine—more than fine. I looked full and awake. My skin a bit more tinted with Caribbean color. The caves under my eyes much lighter, much plumper. My hair even felt thicker and longer.

Incredible what a little basic nutrition and sleep could do. It'd been a hot minute since I'd actually let my eyes linger in the mirror. My hips were fuller. My posture straightened. Confident, I smiled. *Grazie, Costa Rica.*

It was early and everything was very still. I thought, perhaps, I could sneak into the studio before the group arrived for meditation and get some stretching in, maybe even some dancing. Slipping my sweatpants, socks, and a comfy sweater on, I grabbed my bag and hustled over to *La Transparencia*.

The door was open, but all the windows were covered with curtains. I put my bag down and pushed the curtains to the edge to find the sun waking, lighting the room just enough for me to see myself in the reflection of the windows.

I opened my music app and scrolled to Allman Brown's *Ancient Light.*

I took several deep breaths and threw my arms over my head. A few more and I rolled my shoulders out, bent my knees, and dropped my torso deep between my hips. Slowly, I rolled my hips out, straightened my knees, and dropped my chest forward.

While my joints were tense, they were noticeably freer of the fiery burn that had lit them before. I inhaled deeply and closed my eyes to follow the air as it traveled through my body. Every time a thought came to mind, I tried to exhale it.

I just want to be here. Alone with the music and my body.

I focused on my hips and quickly felt Aiana's fists pressing into them, puncturing the core memory that locked them up.

"Why did you stop dancing?" Ramón's words haunted me. *"Why did you start?"*

I pulled my shoulders up and threw my arms to the far side, and then the other. Slowly, I worked my way down to a straddle. When I caught a glimpse of hair in the reflection, I looked up. Scanning my body in the translucence of the window, I marveled at the years I'd been away.

Disappointed with its slow recovery after the injury and the surgeries that followed, stressed with the weight of caretaking and balancing work and school, devastated with the loss of a future at Juilliard, drenched in shame after being cheated on by someone I thought loved and accepted it. A pitiful sadness rushed to my eyes.

"How do I heal you?" I whispered, inviting the ghosts in my bones to answer me.

Death took it.

I closed my eyes and let my head fall to the wooden floor between my legs where I marveled at the ways Death had stalked me, without my slightest notice. My dreams, my relationship, my body… it's no wonder I crumbled so quickly after the Beast had taken Papà, too.

Focusing on this gift, this tool that I had within me, I pondered the beauty of this precious life force, this source of my existence, this ancient light.

"You should take it back."

Opening my eyes, I raised my chin and stared deeper into myself. Slowly and carefully, I started rolling my hips forward from a straddle into the splits. My breath quickened as I fought the adrenaline wetting my palms and forehead.

I can do this.

I repeated it again and again until I was sturdy enough sitting in my splits to lean forward and grab the strap of my bag. I pulled it close and fumbled for my pen and paper.

Every child has tasted Divinity.

Every child has heard It

shouting in the darkness,

calling through the storm,

recorded in centuries of broken records

bleeding the same six words

over endless melodies,

"Come dance with me, my Love.

Come dance."

I pushed my journal forward and locked my palms to the ground. Carefully, I guided my weight forward and lifted my hips to the ceiling. Tension shot down the sides of my thighs and into my calves. I pushed on until I was steadily balanced on my feet. Huffing and puffing air in and out of me, I attempted some of my old tricks. High kicks and arabesques.

I played with my newfound energy, my momentum, and guided it into the axels and pirouettes I'd always loved so much. Delicious... to be here, connected, and present.

I was just finishing my turns from the back of the room to the front when I noticed a white head peek in through the door. I turned to see Sibú's wide and smiling eyes.

"Well, good morning, Traveler."

"Ah, good morning, Sibú." Surprised, I looked over at my things and then instinctively started searching for a clock. No one had shown up so I didn't think I was taking anyone's space in here.

"Those are some very elegant chaînés you have there."

I blushed, silently wondering what this foreigner might know about ballet.

"Oh, thank you... very much. They're a bit rusty."

"Didn't look rusty to me at all." He smiled. "Do you feel like taking a break?"

I wiped the sweat from my forehead and realized just how heated my body actually was. Some of these things might feel like riding a bike to my muscles, but my cardiovascular system was surely out of shape.

"Oh, yes, a break sounds... just perfect. Rebecca will be guiding meditation in here soon, right?"

"No, today's meditation will be a bit different for everyone. I was wondering if you would like to take a walk actually."

"Oh, sure." I agreed and reached for my bag. Tossing it over my shoulder and walking through the open door, we exchanged a bit of small talk as we passed the front desk under the canopy.

Beyond the empty front desk, I noticed Ramón on his way out of the log-style building a few feet back. I noticed his shoulders first, arms crossed over his chest, as he nodded his head. The firmness in his posture piqued my curiosity.

As Sibú and I rounded the corner and headed toward the large wooden gates, I looked over again and saw, beyond Ramón's shoulders, the silver-haired man with dark skin and furrowed eyebrows who'd stared me down from the garden. His frame was small and yet somehow, its particular sense of authority filled the whole door.

Although Ramón seemed to be talking to him, the man looked directly at me and held my gaze. His eyes were set, and I gulped. After a few seconds, Ramón realized his focus and dropped his chin to look away, but the older man kept a steady gaze.

I turned and continued alongside Sibú. The day was brightening and the sky was clear and blue, and I took several deep breaths of the crisp air.

"Your breath work sounds like it has been coming along great, huh?" The approval in his voice tickled my high-achiever.

"Uh, yes, I hope so. I've been working on it. It is our life force… after all." I shot him a little smirk and we treaded on mostly in silence. After we'd been walking for some time, he put a hand on my arm to slow me down and introduce me to a tent-making bat, tucked deep under the giant umbrella-like leaves.

That must be the guy who slapped me in the face the other night.

He stopped me again and pointed at a rock about ten feet away from us, "Jesus Christ Lizards, we call them! Have you seen one yet?" I shook my head as I tried to decode his metaphor.

"They quite literally walk on water!"

"Oh my!"

"And these!" He walked past me, eyes steady on a tree grown with all the same might as the ceiba trees I'd walked through the day before. "Ufff. These." He placed his right hand on the gigantic root and closed his eyes, radiating a sincere and tangible gratitude as he exchanged energy with the beauty.

"Ceibo Barrigón. These beacons are charged with bringing souls to the next realm after they finish their time here." He took a deep breath, filling his chest cavity with air and exhaling before offering a final pat on the tree root.

We continued on.

His love for this land emanated as he spoke of its healing properties, explaining that the people who tended to it were deeply connected to it.

"We have had to keep this land very... restricted, if you will, but not because we do not want to share our resources and knowledge. We have a long history and seek only to protect it, to preserve its integrity."

I nodded. This story sounded like one I'd heard a few months earlier in that clunky little Volkswagen.

"What kind of healing properties, if you don't mind my asking?"

"Well, I'm not sure if you've noticed or not, but time has a remarkable way of slowing down here, Traveler." He let out a bellowing laugh. "That alone is a healing property! You, my Dear, have actually only been here for five days."

My feet stopped, and I looked at Sibú, shock hardening my jaw.

He turned and crooked his neck at me.

"Ah, I forget. You're so connected, I forget you don't know these things."

I stared at him, absent of expression. "I've been here for months, Sibú. I... I don't know how many exactly, but it has been a long time! I think... I think two at least!" I stuttered in protest.

"Mmm no, Scarlett, you haven't. You have only been here for five days and you have two left."

A shake crawled into my palms as my pulse quickened, and I tried to recall the dates on the plane tickets I cached in. I shook my head, intent on clearing my apparent amnesia.

"My apologies," he chuckled. "I should have let you enjoy it for a bit longer. Come on." He nodded his head in the direction we were headed. "We still have lots of work to do."

I stared at my feet as I tried to force them to move. Confusion washed over me with every step. Hushing my denial, I struggled to comprehend the time machine I'd walked into. I wondered if anyone else knew.

And despite my body's resistance, I reminded myself of my faith in this man. His energy reminded me of my grandfather back in Milano—soft, wise, comforting. Perhaps, in addition to our intimate conversations, that energy drew me to a sense of trust in him. After all, he was my only compass when I'd arrived.

Hesitantly, I followed him as he led us on our unfolding path.

"Sibú, what did you mean *connected*?" That is the last word I would have used to describe any part of my emotional or physical state.

"Death has visited you recently, hasn't it?" he asked calmly, resolutely.

It's obvious, apparently. Perhaps he'd spoken to Sybil, or Caleb.

"Yes," I gulped.

"By the looks of how that training meditation went for you the other night, I would guess that it was someone very close to you. And... your first time, right? First time experiencing death?"

His words made me quietly search for air as I tried to recall his face among the others in the room but failed to.

I nodded. There was no hiding my melancholy with this conversation.

"And if I'm wrong, please tell me, but it seemed an awful lot like you didn't want to come back."

I recalled the bliss of catapulting from the strings which held me to everything I knew, and nodded once more.

"How do you know all of this?"

We continued to hike and it seemed nature was on our side today, parting left and right in an almost respectful manner as

Sibú's presence carved a path for us into the jungle. The trees and bushes peeled aside to make way for him... for us.

"Well, Traveler, our bodies are magnificent. They allow us to experience and feel this plane, but they can also become traps—prisons practically. We hold all sorts of stories in our bodies. Stories that become pains that, often, we can't figure out how to free ourselves from. Sometimes, when you actually get a taste of death yourself, you realize, it's a form of freedom from those stories and pains."

I wrapped my fingers around the ring hanging from my neck, remembering Papà—his body, his pain, his prison.

I wiped the silent tear from my face as we continued to walk in silence for a bit.

"Sibú, what *is* that place? That state I experienced the other night? I mean, we are calling it death, but it didn't feel like what I've thought death to be. It felt like... life, like another form of it, like you said—another state."

He didn't respond quickly this time. Instead, he leaned forward and pulled a curtain of vines to the side, motioning for me to walk through. I stumbled forward over a tree root and found myself in the middle of a natural, but almost ceremonial-looking circle imprinted in the jungle, surrounded by boulders under yet another darkening sky. The mist rolled past the hills and over into the clearing, and I desperately hoped this would not be another thunder storm. I thought I saw a blast of light inside of them, but there was no sound. It was quiet. The fog rolled in quickly and I could barely see the tree line.

"Sibú?" I couldn't see him behind me. I turned again and realized I couldn't find the hanging vine door I'd just come through.

"I'm here."

"I can't see you." My palms grew clammy and my heart quickened.

"It's alright. You don't have to. Remember to breathe. If you have your breath, you have all the control you need."

Confusion clouded my vision as my eyes darted back and forth. I closed them and inhaled, trying to focus on the air traveling through my body. My knees grew weak and I fell to the ground. I searched for my breath and gathered my legs into a criss-cross beneath me.

"Sibú? What, what are we doing?"

"You don't need me to tell you what that place is, Traveler. You've touched it. You've tasted it. You've been there. All the sensation, the euphoria, the bliss you felt falling from the things that keep you inside your humanity..."

I opened my eyes as I felt his voice close in. I thought I saw his legs under the fog in front of me, but then he echoed from behind me.

"It's always there, waiting for you. You can call it heaven. You can call it the afterlife. You can call it whatever you'd like. When I say you are connected, Scarlett, I mean you have a gift—an ability not everyone has. You can travel there whenever you'd like to."

My breath started regulating finally, my arms and legs falling into a deep relaxation beneath me. I tucked my toes into the dirt and the sweat in my palms evaporated into the mist around me.

Sibú continued talking, but I couldn't tell whether his words were coming from outside of my body or from within. I followed his lead as the entirety of my being filled with light, with power, with force. I tried to open my eyes, tried to move my hands, tried to wiggle my toes, to no avail.

"Remember your training, Traveler. Remember who you are."

"Be still."

His silver-bearded whispers

echoed off the trees which held me

as he circled.

"Do you feel it?"

I tucked my toes

deeper in the soil,

uncurled my fingers

of the last tension

binding me to this body.

"You are the earth which roots you.

You are the sky which frees you."

Senses engaged,

I expanded, exploded to

the outermost boundaries of existence.

Nothing separate remained.

"You are the light

Physicists equate with all matter,

that Poets define as love.

You are boundless.

You are infinite.

You are one.

You are all."

My DNA whipped through the elements as it raveled back under my skin in what felt like a cosmic tornado. My spirit plummeted back into my body and I inhaled more air than I ever had before, my eyes shooting open until I could see everything.

Unable to tell if I was going to throw up or fall weeping, I heaved forward with anticipation and looked up to see Sibú, sitting legs crossed in front of me. The sweet indigo of his eyes dripped an aura all of their own, full and wide, with arms that held me without even touching me.

For a few moments, time waited and we spoke without words as I struggled to digest the profundity of what just transpired. As I rested back into my body, I felt flattened, like the gravity of the universe suddenly cared to park solely upon my shoulders.

He spoke with gentleness.

"You can master this gift, control it, explore it, and determine how you use it on your terms. And... with this gift comes great responsibility, Scarlett. You cannot stay there until it is your time to. You have so much to do here. Your papà knows that. He wants you there with him, but not yet."

Somehow, my brain was no longer scrambling for sense. The depth within me knew and, for a moment, all questions finally subsided.

We waited in the fog. I looked up and around, inhaling and exhaling, as I surrendered, as I let this new reality steep.

What would this change? What wouldn't this change?

"

And, when you want something,
all the universe conspires to help you achieve it.

PAULO COELHO

Twenty-One

Some time passed before Sibú helped me to my feet and led us back to the village. We walked in silence. No words were needed. I'd stumbled into an entirely new realm, one of magic and mystery, of wonder and freedom.

And somehow, two perfect strangers had shown up to guide me into it.

I shook my head at the memory of Gelena handing me that ticket. *"Come visit me in Costa Rica. There is a special place you need to visit."*

"You can call me Sibú." I glanced his way as we walked, wondering who was really beneath his skin.

Once back in the village, Sibú said he had to go tend to some things and gave my hand a warm squeeze before he went his own way.

Figuring a soak in the pool would help me process this insanity, I managed to find the hedges and the entry sign. There were a couple villagers at the other edge of the pool and I heard some muffled words about the eclipse.

Apparently, it was a big deal around here.

Sticking to the empty corner, I slipped my shoes off and rolled up my sweats, now covered in dark dirt. I sat on one of the rocks at the brim of the pool and dangled my feet in, immediately getting lost in those beautiful little crystals.

"And... with this gift comes great responsibility, Scarlett."

Completely dark at the center, my reflection on the surface quite eerily called me back.

I waited as Alex, still in the crescent of my paralyzed body, thought carefully about his next words.

"There is one thing that gives me comfort, one thing I can know for certain, Scar. He's inside of us. And, not just in our memories, but our... our mannerisms and our features, our expressions, you know?"

He cracked a weak smile in my direction that proved his point.

"His DNA literally runs through our blood. He is part of us, intrinsically. And, that part lives on. We live on. And when we give the way he did and we laugh the way he did, and... when we love the way he did... he lives on. When I need it, that's what gives me comfort."

He moved the hair from my face and rested his hand on my head.

"So, when you wonder those things, just look at yourself. Look at your eyes and your skin and your hands and your nose," He pressed his thumb up against the tip of my nose, "And know... know that he's here. He lives because you live."

I stared back at him and our tears fell together.

Finally. Something of substance.

We walked downstairs to eat with the family.

I'd been sick with a cold the weeks prior to his passing and lost weight I didn't have to lose, so Papà had stocked the kitchen with all the makings of my favorite dish. Grated parmesan, shredded mozzarella, freshly chopped basil, and baked dough filled the air as we got closer to the dining room. Mamma's classic lasagna was stuffed deep in my grandmother's China serving dish in the middle of the table.

We took our seats and I couldn't help but notice Trix, her eyes sweet and brown, quiet and heavy with wisdom—just like his, despite her other features taking after Mamma's Russian side.

And Bella, her long dark hair fell to her hips, and her spirit was lively with his deep Portuguese storytelling blood.

And Alex, the familiar veins at the temples of his head protruding as he wrestled the emotion of being home again.

Then there was Mamma, her gray teardrop eyes cradled in tired lines, like those used to count the years on tree trunks.

This night would be the first of many I'd learn the ways in which Papà's heart, his legacy, would live on.

"Your name is Scar, right?" Startled, my reflection rippled and I bounced a little at the perky young voice that came from behind me. "Would you mind if I sat with you?"

"Hi, sure, not at all. Yes, I'm Scar."

I stuck my hand out and she shook it.

"Shawna, so nice to meet you."

She rolled up her pants and dropped her feet in next to mine. We chatted for a bit, getting to know each other.

At twenty-seven years old, she was an aspiring neuroscientist. After studying at Berkley, she too was taking time off before her PhD program began and enjoying being a semi-permanent resident here at the village.

Apparently, her deepest passion hid in her secret study of astrology, something she kept quiet from her peers in the academic community. She said she'd been training intensely for about four years, and I struggled to calculate the years as she spoke. Her eyes shone with the life of a twenty-three-year-old. She was clearly very passionate about it all, but I could see the glimpses of defeat in the transitions between her sentences. It sounded like a humbling experience, straddling two totally different worlds.

The light conversation was refreshing. I shared a little bit about my experience working with new small business owners and entrepreneurs and she said she might reach out for some website work as she was trying to get a side astrology gig off the ground.

"Astrology has just made so much of the universe make sense to me that science can't quite yet, you know? I just hate feeling guilty for it." She rolled her eyes. "But, I would love to help others with everything I've learned."

Her energy was delightful. We exchanged our experiences here at the village and, it turned out, I wasn't the only one out of sorts with time. We laughed as we mocked those stunning little balls of fire that hung in the trees and joked about how the maps they gave us were utter rubbish.

"I don't think I ever actually believed in magic until this place." I chuckled and raised my brows in surrender. "Now, there's no denying it."

"Have you noticed they don't have clocks anywhere either?" she asked. "To be honest, I am not even sure what month we're in now."

I opened and then quickly shut my mouth, resolved not to peep a word or break the news the way Sibú had just done with me. I didn't want to risk interference with her process. Who knows what this place was doing to her…

"Yes, it's madness," I answered.

"Hey, have you ever had someone read your chart?"

My right eyebrow perked at the word.

"My chart?"

"Yea, your astrology chart."

Another indoctrinated "no no" from the church.

"Oh, no. I haven't."

"Do you want to?" Her smile spread deep into her cheeks with excitement.

"Um, sure! That would be great!"

"Awesome. Yea, I love your aura and it has me really curious. When's your birthday?"

"It's December 21, 1995."

"The solstice! Wow! Do you know the city and the time you were born?"

"San Bernardino, annnd I believe 8:58 a.m."

"Mmm perfect. I am going to go do a little research with your chart and we can touch base about it later, okay?" She bubbled with excitement as she pulled her feet from the water and slipped her shoes on.

"Alright, that sounds great. Thanks, Shawna!"

"Yea, my pleasure! See ya later!"

Despite the weight of everything I'd learned in the last few hours, I felt light—extremely light. I stared into the water, at the crystals shining in the hollows and remembered the exhilaration of sinking into them.

Would it really be possible to control this? To master it?

Suddenly, I remembered that Ramón's bungalow was near this pool and decided to look for it. I rounded a few bushes until I saw a tall white tent. That was it! Since there was no door, I didn't knock.

"Ramón?"

No answer.

"Ramón, are you here?"

I heard shuffling as he stood and brushed the curtains aside. He looked at me and then down at the ground.

"Hi, Miss Scarlett, how can I help you?"

"Well, you can help me understand what is happening between us."

He stared back at me blankly and the fright in his posture told me something significant restrained him.

"Does it have to do with that older man? The one who's always scowling at me?" I probed.

He stayed silent, but his shifting body language made it clear I was on the right track.

"Ramón, what possible problem could that man have with you talking to me? I don't understand. Things were fine between us. Actually, they were lovely. What could he have against me?"

"Scarlett, he doesn't have anything against you. He wants the best for you."

I didn't hide my frown. His words were only frustrating me.

"What does that even mean? I don't even know the guy." Ramón urged me and my growing frustration inside his bungalow.

"Scarlett." Ramón dropped his chin in what appeared to be defeat.

I kept my eyes on him, intent on getting an answer, but wondering how much room I had to push.

"Scarlett, he's my father."

I crooked my neck at the dynamic emerging.

"Okay, what's his problem with me?"

He shook his head. "He doesn't have a problem with you. His problem is with this place." He scoffed at what appeared to be a much bigger story.

"I don't understand."

His eyes rolled back as he lifted his arms over his head and dragged his hands down his face.

"I can leave, you know, if this is too much of a bother."

When his eyes found mine, he stepped forward and reached to cradle my face. I tucked my chin into the warmth of his palms and held them. Pulling me closer, he leaned forward and placed his lips on my forehead.

The air moved through his body in one big inhalation. Then quickly, he pulled away from me and retreated back to grab his jacket and clunky work phone. When he returned, he lifted his hand to my cheek once more and then walked past me.

Frustration flushed hot under my skin and I paced for a bit, resolving to head to *El Placer*.

Food was probably a good idea, and perhaps Sol was there.

On arrival, it seemed I hadn't missed a thing.

The hall was full. I noticed Nick and Aileen sitting at a table on the far end with Sybil, as I grabbed a plate and filled it with cinnamon bread and fresh almond butter, eggs, mangos, and strawberries.

The lively music poured through the large silver door as Sol rounded the corner. "¡Buenos días, mi bailarina, pequeña! ¿Cómo estás?"

"¡Buenos días, Sol! ¡Qué bueno para verte!" She smiled back and handed me a coconut. "Gracias, Sol."

"Pura vida, mi amor."

I eased into the far chair at my friends' table and said good morning to everyone. Jenna mingled at another table with some friends she'd made and Aileen seemed strangely quieter than usual. She felt almost recoiled from the group. Nick was making a clear effort to compensate and keep the conversation going.

Usually, those roles were reversed. I hoped she was okay and wondered briefly if I'd had the same impact on these sweet people as they'd had on me the last few days.

Apparently, Sybil had heard my music in the studio this morning and popped her head in too. She said she didn't want to interrupt my flow, but was curious about my dance background. We talked a bit and I learned about her past life as a dancer, a ballerina in Russia, where she was born and raised. She trained in the Bolshoi Ballet for what seemed her entire life, but was actually about fifteen years from what I gathered. She too had put her dreams on hold because of an injury to her ankle. Then, she got pregnant and devoted her life to her son instead of going back to dance.

Incredible, the stories we carry.

I shared with her a bit of my history, how my grandfather was a Russian Ashkenazi Jew whose family had fled the Bolshevik Revolution as a child. They escaped to China where his family continued to suffer persecution, and he went to Italy where he met my grandmother. There, they had my mother. And there in Milano, my mother had met my father where he sought work after he left the Azores.

All I knew about my Kolesnikoff history was that it was dense. Sybil's eyes sparkled with curiosity and lit quite the flame inside me as well.

"Scar!" I turned to see Shawna bouncing through the big wooden doors with two books in her arms. "Scar! Oh boy, do we need to talk!" Her excitement caught me off-guard, but as I looked closer, I saw a very deep urgency in her eyes. I was awfully curious what she'd discovered.

"Uh, okay. Have you eaten? I should finish mine first. I'm pretty hungry."

"Oh, yes! I need to, too! Great thinking." She dropped her books to the table and hustled to the food bar.

"Have you all met Shawna?"

"Oh yes, she's a sweetheart!" Sybil said. "She has quite a gift with navigating the stars, too! You know she's trained in multiple types of astrology, right? She's incredible!"

As everyone finished eating and cleaned their plates, the room began to clear out. This seemed to be Shawna's cue. Her energy buzzed as she opened her books, slipped her glasses on, and dove right in between bites!

"So, Scar! Are you familiar with the houses in astrology?"

"Mmm, let's just assume I don't know anything about astrology and start there." I chuckled.

"Okay, no problem. So, there are twelve... Oh shoot! I'll be right back!" She hustled out of the hall and returned with a strangely-familiar pair of pointed, red-framed glasses and two more books, which she placed on the table.

She flipped open the one with the word *Location* in the title and combed through pages covered with grids and lined with constellations. Another, she opened to show me diagrams of the body, of pyramids, and patterned lines with the titles of *Auric Fields* and *The Tree of Life*. My mind scrambled quickly in an effort to keep up.

"Okay, okay. My goodness. Where do I even start?" She paused with one hand on her hips and a finger on her lip. "You were raised in a religion, yes?"

I nodded in response.

"Okay, I'm guessing Christianity?"

I frowned at the accuracy of her guess and nodded once more.

"So, you know how at the end of the Lord's Prayer... Thine is the kingdom and the power and the glory forever and ever, amen?" She paused to ensure I was still following. "Well, the power is Mars and Saturn and the glory is Jupiter and Venus..."

Annnd, lost.

She continued and I kept my ears peeled, filtering for something I could comprehend.

"...But don't worry! You don't really need to know any of this. It just shows the intersection of the divine realms with the physical one we know."

Well, that's good because my head is spinning.

She took me to the maps and attempted to explain an array of acronyms that flew right over my head.

"So Vedic Astrology is actually called Jyotish which translates to: the science of the light of the soul." She dropped her glasses and relied more on her hands to facilitate her words. "What I love about this type of astrology is that it has several branches..."

Whoa. Whoa. Whoa. Her terms spun me.

She slipped her glasses back on and continued educating me on the various types of astrology. I hoped she'd say something I could understand soon.

"All to say, in terms of location, I actually really love San Diego for you because of this Venus ascending line which crosses right through it. Now, Venus…" She flipped to another diagram in one of the other books. "As you see, Venus is the embodiment of love and passions, desires, and wealth. Over Los Angeles, you have a Uranus line right south of it. So, Los Angeles. to San Diego, really great area for you. You're about thirty miles from these lines—super intense energy. Highly recommend San Diego for you."

I nodded and mentally noted to remember that part.

"But, check these out!" She opened another bookmarked page to a global map and explained which places held which potentials for me. I wondered if I should express just how little of this information I could actually digest.

"And that line actually drops all the way down here through South America… Tons of energies here for you that are really good. Colombia, look! Bogotá, Medellin, Cali… all of these would be like… like a catalyst for you. The best signs to live in are the sun, Jupiter, and Venus. Jupiter is like… like God's glory. Life is like bliss on it." She shook her head as if totally impressed by her discoveries.

Wide-eyed, I marveled at her expertise and the way she navigated this other language so eloquently.

"Okay, enough on location for now." She set that book aside and crossed her arms on the table, leaning into me and setting her glasses down. "So, pardon my French, but what the actual fuck happened to you a few months ago?"

Her direct inquiry froze me and I stared back blankly.

She took out some loose papers and showed me another table with the same tiny little icons scattered across it. Laying them out, she began to point out the shifts in timeline.

"You totally don't have to share if you don't want to. I don't mean to pry, but this tragedy looks pretty epic for you."

I sighed and nodded, and Shawna sweetly placed her palm on my forearm, "I'm sorry." I smiled a small *thank you* and she flipped backward to point out the beginning of this unraveling back in 2014—the year his health began declining.

"Uhm, yes. That makes sense." I gulped.

"Well, good news. That moon will never hit your Mars again. And... did you recently have a relationship end?"

I nodded.

"Yes. Okay." She nodded as she read through one of the papers. "Okay, I see that right here. So fortunately, good news. You are on your way out of this three-year season. Check this out..." She pointed to a few other movements of the icons over the table lines and her tone ascended cheerfully. "This is really good news. This year, this year, is looking so much more simple for you."

The glee was short lived when she got to the year after and predicted yet another difficult time. She couldn't tell me exactly what was going to happen but used the planets to explain the principles I was bound to wrestle with: love and intimacy, manipulation and independence, control and freedom.

Perplexed, my stomach spun at her words.

Is it possible to opt out those parts?

"Fortunately, girl, everything about your chart literally screams that it's like... impossible to control you! Like... you're untamable."

"Okayyy, well, that's good news." I dropped a sigh of bewilderment as I tried to remember a time when anyone had ever tried. I didn't think I'd ever quite experienced that. Well, aside from the church I left and the leaders I turned away from.

"Hm, tragedy. Why so much–" I was hanging in there while I noticed the pattern in her predictions through the years, tragedy... triumph... more tragedy. Confusion flooded my vision as I noticed her trying to veer away from the dark spots that even she seemed stuck on. I tried to comfort myself by tempering the gravity I gave this foreign sorcery.

"Alright so, Vedic Astrology is really awesome because of the cycles it maps out, and see," she pointed, "you're about to enter, after about this time right here, a cycle that really favors travel and creation." She opened to a few more charts to show me some interesting time periods called dashas and walked me through some transits and upcoming phases. "Literally! This energy right here… phoenix rising from the ashes, all the way! Pluto crosses your ascendent. This is huge! People are lucky if they experience this once in a lifetime. This is like… like a grand makeover worth a hundred grand in psychotherapy! You'll be having a massive transformation at this time!"

I shuddered at the thought of the stars really being home to an entire map of my life—every season and transition. Baffled, I stared at her papers as I tried to process the drama in her enthusiasm.

"I am so curious though! While I was researching your chart, I noticed that it's literally drenched in literature."

"Oh, well, yeah that's interesting. I uhm, well…" I decided not to babble on about the work I do supporting other authors and entrepreneurs and instead, at the sound of that positive omen, decided to explore my own little dreams I'd never shared before. "I'm a writer, a poet actually. But… you know, I don't… I don't do it full-time or anything. It's not really my career."

"Oh!?" She jumped back. "Wow. Well, there you go. Okay, that makes an insane amount of sense." Her hands flung in the air with her realization. "You have no clue." She dove back into the papers and then glanced through her books. "You literally have so much Creator energy in your stars. Let me show you…"

Her fingers scanned through a circular chart with the icons scattered all over it, lines weaving between them all. She showed me the separation of houses, the movement of my secondary progressed moon and my retrograded mercury, and the conjunctions of my Neptune and Mars.

All gibberish. I wished I had a way to record this.

"Basically... keep writing, Lady. Don't ever stop, okay! It looks like mystery and psychology, lots of philosophy, yep! That's your sweet spot. Ooo what a beautiful, *spiritual* mixture!"

I flinched at the word and her emphasis on it.

"Novels are really, really great for you, too. And don't overlook screenplays."

It is an understatement to say she'd lost me. No way in hell I could do either of those. She continued rambling about fire trines and crossing ascendants.

"You've never had a dull moment in your adult life, have you?" She tilted her head and smiled mischievously.

"What do you mean?"

My adult life seemed to be just beginning. It had certainly been a roller coaster thus far, but the last few years, it felt, had really kept me on hold.

"You're just... you're... I'm baffled. It's like..." She removed her glasses and swayed. "You were born for the grand, the dramatic, the extraordinary." She started guiding me to the supposed signs in my chart of adventure and romance, of exploration and collaboration, of expansion and novelty. "It's like... you really came here for the fullness of human experience. The good... and the bad."

She paused, marveling in her own revelations.

"I do want to point out though, Scar. See here, you were born in the seventh degree of satirical Capricorn. This is known as the degree of jeopardy. It's like... it's like a harp with these beautiful strings that people will... get jealous of, you know? So, you have to note. You must always covet and protect yourself, keep an eye out that no one tries to come in and destroy what you're creating out of jealousy or fear or anything. It's REALLY important that you stay autonomous, especially in your relationships. My biggest advice, looking at this sort of karmic energy in your chart, is that you really have to let your soul music play out. You absolutely have to keep out anyone who tries to quiet you or drown it out."

I was gone. Zoned out, eyes glazed across the tables, the diagrams, the words before me and the words she'd shared. Until her hand touched my shoulder.

"Scar."

I lifted my eyes to her.

"I know this can all be a lot to process, especially with the doctrine you came from."

Her eyes dripped with a very sincere empathy.

"Think of all of this as... a map. A map that was made just for you. By god, by the universe, by destiny, or whoever you want to believe in. But in all of this..." She circled her palm over the table. "These stars mean *nothing* without you. You have a choice. You have agency in all of it, okay?"

I breathed deeply and nodded, appreciating her sensitivity. This *was* a lot to digest. And I certainly wasn't sure how much of it I really believed or understood or was okay with.

Certainly not the Shakespearean-sized tragedies.

"Hi, Scar." I turned at the sound of a refreshing raspy voice. It was Rebecca, standing by the doors with a smile. "It's time for your session."

"Oh. That's tonight?" I glanced back at Shawna.

I know she could have talked all night about this stuff, and part of me was grateful to take a breath from my sudden overwhelm.

"Oh shoot!" Shawna exclaimed as she bounced up from the table and began gathering her books. "I almost forgot about the eclipse tonight. Can't miss that! It's gonna be a powerful one!" I smiled as I collected my things and she placed her hand on my shoulder. "Hope you have a good session, Scar! We'll talk more later."

As I followed Rebecca, my eyebrows raised in anticipation and then surprise. I hadn't realized how dark it'd gotten outside, but there was mist tunneling in the air and fog trailing at our heels.

I could barely keep my eyes on Rebecca only a few feet in front of me as I followed her down the broken stones, which appeared to float through the mud and assemble into a pathway as she stepped.

Water trickled in the distance. This path dripped of eeriness, almost… danger. I looked for the moon in hopes of seeing some silver scales appear beneath me, some sort of guidance, but it was covered. Remembering the eclipse, I realized I wasn't going to find it.

No golden dancers at the foot of the trees either. Goosebumps flickered down my skin. I pulled the sweater from around my waist and wrapped it around my shoulders as we walked under some taller trees and came to a small lanky bridge suspended over a creek.

I wasn't sure I'd been to this side of the village.

Trusting Rebecca's graceful movement, I watched carefully and followed her every step across the bridge. We walked up a hill and rounded a corner to a small cabin with several hanging porch lanterns. She held the door open for me, and I was grateful to step into a warm room, its wooden floor lined with candles. There was a square carpet-looking mat with two cushions on either side of it. If it didn't feel so comfy, I might have thought I'd walked into some type of cult ritual. Rebecca smiled, disarming me as she offered a seat and invited me to join her in her in breath.

A very subtle crackle stung behind my breastbone.

"Go ahead and close your eyes, Scar. Get comfortable. Breathe some light in and through. Tell me, Scar, for which intentions have you come here tonight?"

Her question was strange and I tried to recall why I'd put my name down for this.

She wasn't rushing me, but I felt the pressure of trying to find the right answer. I gulped and racked my brain for something that would sound intelligible.

"Um, well, I came to Costa Rica hoping to find my next step, hoping to… I guess… heal... move on. I'm not sure." I choked on my next words, "This um, this is my first time ever... ever experiencing death and I just... can't. I've been spiraling. I can't... understand it. I can't... accept it. I've walked away from the only belief system that made sense of death and I can't even go back to that because it just doesn't work anymore."

"What's hindering your healing process?" Her tone was soft and genuinely curious.

I didn't have to breathe for that one. It toppled off my tongue, "Acceptance."

"What are you *un*willing to accept?" she probed.

I trusted there was a method to this tear-inducing madness and responded with the answer that immediately choked my throat.

"That he's gone. That I'll never see him again. That I'll never hear him laugh again. That I don't have him here with me." My eyes still closed, the tears poured forth.

After a few moments of silence, she tried to transition me into some sort of acceptance meditation. I tried to follow her but felt like I was forcing something completely unnatural. My palms were growing hot and trembles started rattling at my elbows.

"This isn't working. I can't do this." Immediately, the environment changed and I sensed a storm picking up outside the paper-thin walls.

Unmoved, she offered another strategy.

"Have you ever used cards before?"

"Like oracle cards?"

She nodded.

"No, I was always told not to mess with them, that they were... dark."

She smiled softly.

"Nope, no darkness. They can just assist, offer a sort of intuitive insight into situations where we feel blocked. We aren't talking with any spirits, I promise."

She winked and I brushed off my lack of knowledge. I was still learning to say yes to actually learning about everything I'd been taught to say no to—everything that was still so unknown to me.

Turns out Costa Rica is a fucking crash course.

I shook my head in *almost* amusement.

She pulled a few cards and organized them in a diamond pattern on the floor between us. Then, one at a time, she flipped them over.

The first showed a heart with three swords piercing it and I gulped, immediately seeing faces on those swords: God, Papà, Julian.

The next—the death card flashed a scene of war, white and black and dripping of blood, recalling the night terror I'd been haunted with since his passing. The ache in my chest started to expand.

The next—the Knight card flashed a man on his horse in sprint, eager to fight. Somehow, all I could see in his were Julian's sweet blue eyes, tucked in the knight's soft bone structure.

"Don't forget to breathe, okay?" Rebecca reminded me.

Had I stopped?

I nodded and she flipped over the third card—the Cup of Truth. A woman, seated cross-legged under a tree with a cloud appearing to visit her. Upon the cloud, there was a cup and the woman reached out for it.

"Mmm." Rebecca's eyes fluttered shut and she smiled as if a warm breeze had washed over her. She opened them and looked through me. "Are you ready to connect again?"

I looked up at her and back at the card with furrowed eyebrows.

"Connect again? Connect with who?"

Her eyes relaxed on me as she inhaled once more.

"With *God*!? Have you completely lost it!?" My shoulders cinched up to my ears, fear bleeding from my chest and through my body in what felt like an internal quake of anxious mockery. A roar of thunder beyond the windows echoed the terror bubbling in my blood at the mere idea. My hands were fuming, hot and steamy, as I realized the seriousness of her proposal. I shook my head.

"I don't think you understand."

She tilted her head and with a sigh, her eyes glazed a bit.

"Humans have really done some work on that word over the centuries." I almost saw the trajectory of her point but was distracted by the dangerously-intense rise of my body's temperature. She reached her hand over the cards and placed it on top of mine.

"Think of this as... reconnecting with *yourself*, Scar. Let's start there. Everything starts there."

But, we had one more card.

"Whoa, you *are* quite hot." Her eyes searched mine with concern. "Are you normally a kinesthetic person?"

"I'm never sensitive like this." I shook my head.

Lightning shot outside the window and the dim lights in the room flashed rapidly. She shifted, a new awareness crossing her countenance. She quickly recoiled back into her breathing, eyes closed.

"It's... it's your father," she stuttered. I paused and the fear began to drain itself. "He is ready to help you—to connect with you for this."

"With me? *You're* the medium!" I realized the aggression in my tone as I practically yelled at her.

Eyes closed, Rebecca stifled a chuckle.

"Oh, Sweetheart, you are more powerful than you know."

"

No matter how calm the seas may seem,
I cannot help but feel
there is a storm in the distance
with her eyes on me.

JENNIFER GORDON

Twenty-Two

I didn't understand what has happening and I racked my brain to make sense of it.

Connect with god? No thank you. Connect with my papà? I'd give anything.

My heart pounded.

Next thing I knew, Rebecca's hand was behind my head, guiding me down to the floor and moving my stiff body from its paralyzed, meditative state.

"I want you to tell me what you see, alright? Tell me what you feel."

My head rolled from side to side until a full-fledged spin consumed my vision. Somewhere far away, I saw a piece of paper placed on my solar plexus and a shiny gold trapped door morph from the blackness behind my eyelids. It began melting into my warped vision, but I couldn't tell if my mouth was delivering the message to Rebecca or not. Her being faded as I watched the gold spill into a black hole.

"Papà! Papà! Papà!" a young voice shouted. Then an older, then a younger. Every pitch. Every tone. Every emotion. I seemed to be walking, running, searching.

Moments. Memories. Grocery stores. Parking lots. Golf carts. Performances. Dentist offices. My childhood home.Opening doors. Rounding corners. The gold still brimming my vision now morphed into a gate.

"What is beyond the gate?"

Rebecca's still here? The thought drifted away as quickly as it came.

I stood up on the tips of my toes to peek through the golden gate bars. Green. Lots of green. Rolling mounds of green. Hills.

Through my clogged sniffles, I inhaled again and again, breathing fiercely until the sweet aroma of freshly cut morning grass overwhelmed my sinuses.

No, this can't be.

"Where does the path lead you, Scar? Keep following it."

I looked down to see a broken path at my feet, under and past the gate. I grabbed the bars and pulled myself up to see more. There it was—a ball of fire smeared flares across the clouds, like the Maker itself had dipped Its fingers in a palette of oil paint and dragged them through the sky. An explosion of orange and yellow swirled in shades of violet and magenta. The hills moved and skin flashed in the air between them.

Hands waving high above his head—just the way they used to when I lost him in the grocery store—I saw his bearded jaw and brown eyes, wide and bright, grow very clear. His mouth was moving. He was yelling to me. I strained closer, bending my body into the metal of this gate.

"I'm here, Doll! I'm right here! I'm okay! I'm okay! Look, I'm free!" He continued to jump and throw his arms around him in ways I'd not seen since the few years I saw him healthy. "I'm okay. I promise!" He wiggled his hips and screamed, "Yahahahooooo! I got my golf course and my sunset, Vita! I'm okay! I promise."

Speechless, my entire being begged for his laughter. And as quickly as my cells had wished for it, there it was. Louder and wilder, more untamed than ever, his laughter roared through the hills and danced throughout the sun-kissed sky.

I couldn't pull my eyes from his face—a sight I thought I'd never see again. Words failed me as my mouth turned to mush. Through my heaving sobs, I somehow exhaled a very broken "Ti… ti voglio… ti voglio bene, Papà."

"Sei la mia vita, Scarlett!"

I began to feel a stretch, a tug backward, but I pushed my body with more intensity into the golden bars.

"It's okay, Scar. I'm okay. They need you! I'll be right here. Do your best work, Doll."

My vision began a slow spiral as he turned and leaned on his club. My body fell, catapulted backward with the same rapid speed I'd experienced in the forest.

A chaotic vibration of frequencies rattled my skull and radiated from it around my being, as if rebounding after penetrating my body. I felt as though I'd been slammed against a wall. Still spinning, with little to no reference of time or space. A rush of air punched through my chest and up through my throat.

"Tell me, what's happening? Are you alright? What's he saying?"

With all the intention I could muster, I shifted my tongue and opened my eyes. Rebecca hung over me, stunned but determined.

"Shhh. It's okay! You're back now. It's okay."

I panted as her words settled and I relaxed into the blood weighing down my humanity, cognitively tracing it through my arteries and to my limbs so I could feel them again. I continued to breathe as I recalled my papà's face, clear as day. As I replayed his bellowing laugh, salty tears streamed down the sides of my face. I finally found my lips, shuddering in shock, and moistened them.

"I'm just… I'm back." I gazed around the room and then down at this very detached lump of meat. The knees. The toes. The hands. None of it looked familiar to me. None of it felt familiar to me. Everything was so heavy.

As I calmed, I noticed Rebecca slip her hands from my body and retreat to the corner under the window. She leaned her head against the wall and hollowed her lips as she steadied her own breath. Her shoulders were shaking. She was clearly trying to calm herself, too. Her mouth looked strong, but her eyes were full of shock. I let mine fall. All I could focus on was getting oxygen to these lungs.

I slowly gained control over my tongue and cleared the dryness in my throat, searching for my motor memory.

"Wha–" I coughed, "What… just? Did you?"

"Scar, I didn't do a thing." She continued to stare blankly at the opposite wall. "That… that was *all* you."

Dizziness dripped from my skull and my vision spun as I rolled my eyes back. Every limb felt weak, very weak.

It seemed hours had passed as we walked back to my bungalow, Rebecca's arm around my limp torso. Still struggling to be present in this realm, all I noticed was that the rain had settled in the darkness. All had settled, and I wondered if that sneaky eclipse had anything to do with tonight's events.

But something had also stirred when she asked a few questions about me, about where I was from, and then murmured—mostly to herself.

"I thought Shapeshifters were just from our land."

I hobbled into the bungalow and sunk into my cot, Jenna sound asleep next to me.

Despite my haze of contemplation, it actually felt quite good to be so lost in time, so lost in space.

I thought about Ramón as I drifted, about his grandfather and his stories. I wondered, hypothetically of course, which path I'd choose. Would I stay to protect the magic of my home or would I venture off into the unknown to create my own?

Perhaps… I'd already made my decision.

"

There are no maps;
no more creeds or philosophies.
From here on in, the directions come
straight from the Universe.

AKSHARA NOOR

Twenty-Three

I rolled over into fingernails tracing my scalp and my eyelids fluttered open. Panic arrested me until the blur of brown skin morphed into a familiar shape, and I settled into those big brown eyes. His finger was on my lip.

"Shhh." He put his hand on my chest and waited until my breathing calmed. "Come on." He motioned to some clothes he placed at the foot of my bed right next to my sneakers and then he quietly made his way out the bungalow.

Frantic, assuming something was wrong, I scrambled to dress as quickly as I could. I stumbled into the rocking chair, shoving it against the coat rack with enough force to tip it over, and jumped to catch it before it hit the ground.

I looked back at Jenna, head under her pillow, still just as asleep as I'd found her the night before.

Grabbing my sneakers, I carefully zipped up the bungalow and stepped into the pitch darkness.

"¿Todo bien?"

"Si, sí. Todo bien," he assured.

"¿Qué hora es?" I whispered as I slipped my sneakers on.

He chuckled. "Are you really asking me that?"

"Touché." I nodded.

Grabbing my elbow to stabilize my half-asleep and totally-dysfunctional self, he guided me in the dark.

"What are we doing?"

"There's something I want to show you." He grabbed my hand and we hurried quietly toward the front canopy, rounding the backside to the same little blue Volkswagen we'd arrived in. He opened the metal door for me before speaking with one of the men at the front gate who quickly opened it for us. I turned back to watch it close as we left, overwhelmed by the darkness around us.

"Should I be concerned?"

"You're the only thing to be feared around here, Miss Scarlett." The heat from his smile warmed my whole body.

He was back. My sweet Ramón was back. I was much too tired to decipher his metaphors, so I scooted closer to wrap my arms around his and drop my head on his shoulder. Dozing in and out as we bumped along the unpaved dirt, I finally fell back to sleep when we hit the smooth highway.

A sudden fear gripped my shoulders as I woke and he must've felt it.

"Shhh, shhh. We're here." He pulled out of the main strip of dirt onto the side of a mountain. And when my ears popped, I wondered what altitude could have achieved that. We were clearly on an incline as the hood was up and gravity pressed me back into the seat. As I climbed out of the car, I immediately became even more disoriented.

Ramón made his way over to me and I probed, "Hun, where are we?"

"Patience isn't really your thing, is it, Love?"

If only I had a dollar for every time I'd been told that. I rolled my eyes. We hiked for a bit through some forest and my sleepy calves struggled to make their way up the stark incline. As we cleared the trees, all that was left was the sky above and the clouds below. Ramón took my hand and guided me to the edge of a cliff, and I gasped as we neared it.

"Oh my god!" Adrenaline pumped hot to my legs as I looked over and realized just how high we were. My brain worked overtime to make sense of what I was seeing. Not only was I leaning over a cliff, but over a ginormous pool of thick white milky mist hovered above the water it encircled.

It was the inside of a volcano.

"Meet Arenal." He waved his hand to showcase her.

"Is it active?!"

"She's just sleeping."

I couldn't peel my eyes from this magnificent hole carved into the mountain, the blackness of the sand at our feet.

Stunning.

"No one is allowed here by regulation though."

I mocked a gasp, "What! Are you telling me Ramón is breaking the rules?"

He shook his head and pulled me close. "Only the locals know how to get up here." He tucked his lips into my hair. "You want to see something even more beautiful?" His fingers slipped under my chin as he lifted it to the horizon. The sun was rising in the east. As I stared, a flash of light, almost green, shot across the line dividing the sky and the earth. I could see water in the distance.

The Caribbean.

I opened my mouth but fell speechless. Ramón wrapped his arms underneath mine and around my belly, and I felt his forehead lean against the side of my head as he curled in like a child.

After several minutes, I found my words.

"This is… magnificent."

He took a deep breath.

"Isn't it?" I followed, recalling no crisper, fresher air having passed through my lungs in all my years. The world was frozen here. It was tangible—the almost resonant respect emanating from all the elements for the energetic power this beauty held.

"I wish I could stay here forever." I sighed and snuggled in closer.

"No, Scarlett, you don't." His tone dropped a few octaves and his sudden seriousness surprised me.

I turned inside the circle of his arms to face him.

"Why do you say that? Of course I do. This place is beautiful. It's been extraordinary. I feel like I've finally found somewhere that feels… safe—like a home I didn't know I needed. And… and you."

He smiled and brought the back of his hand to my cheek.

"You are too big for this place, Scarlett. I don't want you to want to be anywhere but... where you are."

I squinted my eyes and shook my head, hoping he'd explain this twisted rejection.

"Come with me!" I said matter-of-factly.

A big smile slipped out and his beautiful, perfectly-crafted white teeth shone for a quick second. I saw a pain in his eyes shudder as he dropped his chin.

"I can't."

"Why not?"

"It's not that easy, Miss Scarlett." He could barely hold my gaze.

"You chose to be a Guardian, didn't you?"

He looked up at me, half-impressed and half-expectant, but there was no hint of surprise in his expression—like he knew I'd figure it out.

He pulled both hands up to cradle my face, and our breath steamed in the cold morning air between us.

"I would travel the world with you if I could, Scarlett." His words tunneled through my chest and I welled with tears as he leaned down to meet my lips. The tension in his mouth matched the ferocity in his grip, and I felt my whole being surrender to this desire—to this connection. I could taste his spirit. And for the first time in so long, I let another taste mine.

When we were both finally out of breath and on the verge of panting, he pulled his lips back and rested his forehead on mine. We both waited. In silence so sweet, I fell into his chest, into this moment, spiraling deeper and deeper as I savored it.

This wasn't the first time I'd loved and been forced to let go.

"Come on." His hands slid down my arms and grabbed my hands. "There's more!" His face brightened with adventure as he led me around the edge of the volcano. We hiked down the mountain a ways. By the time we arrived, I'd thrown my curls atop my head and stripped my sweatshirt to my waist.

We neared a plateau and Ramón threw his hand in the air.

"Shhh!"

I stopped quickly, thinking he'd run into a snake or something. He turned back to me.

"Do you hear that?"

My focus drifted out to the land. Water—trickling in the distance. I couldn't keep my smile in. I was excited to see what was waiting and ran forward through the draping vines.

"Cuidado, cuidado! It gets slippery toward the rocks!"

We rounded a bend to a few layered pools with water heaving over the edges, steam swirling through the air.

I looked back at Ramón and smiled as I untied my sweatshirt and let it fall to the ground. Slowly, I peeled my shirt from my skin and pulled it over my head. I watched with pleasure as his bottom lip fell and he tilted his head as if to ask me what I was doing. Unzipping my jeans and pushing them to the ground, I left my skin bare and covered by nothing but black lace.

Who am I?

A few days before, I couldn't even look at myself in the mirror and now I was standing almost naked in front of this man I hardly knew.

He took a deep breath, looked around quickly as he walked over and lifted me from the ground, wrapping my legs around his waist and thrusting his lips into mine. He didn't even bother to take his jacket off before he stepped into the water and walked deeper with me wrapped around him. I was so lost in his embrace, I hadn't even realized my shoulders were under water. Looking at his clothes, now drenched in water, I bellowed in laughter as he continued to kiss me.

He dug his cheeks into my neck and wrapped his arms around my body. I let my head fall back and when I opened my eyes, something caught my attention.

I peered at the object hanging from one of the taller trees on the side of one of the higher pools. It was so covered in moss, I could barely tell if it was part of the tree or not. I smiled at him mischievously, released my grip, and swam to the edge of this spring to make sure I was seeing it accurately.

Yep. That was a rope!

"Is that safe?"

"Not safe enough, Scarlett."

"Mmm…"

"Scarlett."

"It looks safe to me." I shrugged.

I found a couple of rocks and pulled myself up to look into the pool and assess its depth. It looked at least twenty feet deep.

I figured that was enough and hopped from rock to rock and tight-roped the ledge of a mossy ridge where the water fell over.

Looking back at him with play in my eyes, I saw him shake his head in surrender.

"Just… just let me pull on it first, okay?" Ramón's eyes were fastened tightly on me as he went up the more predictable way. He walked in the dirt to where the rope was and grabbed it with two hands, tugging on it softly and then harder. His sigh of disappointment told me it was secure enough.

I focused and made it to the other side where I hopped in the dirt and bolted for the tree. He clearly wasn't thrilled about this but he helped prop me up onto the tree where I could get a better grasp on the rope.

"Focus on the center, alright? That is the safest place. I'm going to go down there just in case."

I hadn't anticipated all the scrapes from the chipped bark and branches. It'd been years since I climbed a tree and I laughed at myself as I made a brief amateur assessment of my distance—the rocks, the water, and the length of the rope.

I should be good. I had to be at least twenty-five feet up. And if not, well, Volcán Arenal didn't seem such a bad place to make my own peace with the Beast.

I strapped the loop around my foot so I could stand, but then had a better idea. I slid the loop under my butt, so I would be in a sitting position but with enough looseness that I could slip out at the right moment.

Nerves ricocheted through my chest and arms—the good kind. And the best part was: I could feel them.

With a nice back swing for momentum, I threw myself forward. Right as I neared the center of the pool, I fell backward and flipped from my makeshift chair, slipping my feet right through the hole and falling like a cannonball into the water and down to the bottom. Perhaps my measurements had been off. I figured with the depth of the pool, I'd have plenty of room to fall before hitting the bottom; but as I spiraled through the tropical water, my feet tapped the floor.

I opened my eyes on contact, in time to see the silky something that slithered past my arm. There were rainbow of fish all around me, circling me as they danced in and out of my hair. My lungs grew faint and I darted for the surface, smiling with the thrill of this adventure.

Gasping for air as I surfaced, I immediately met his eyes. He was leaning from a rock mostly outside of the pool where he could watch. Now stripped to his shorts, I could see how tense he was with anticipation… or was that terror?

Once he made out my face, he took a deep breath, shook his head, and smiled with relief. Letting out a nervous laugh, he gazed back from me to the rope. I saw something in his eyes shift as he smiled and turned to climb the tree while I swam to the edge of the spring to give him room. Before I knew it, he was swinging through the air, adding another flip to the fall back out of the loop.

I made sure he floated to an applause at the surface.

"Whew!" He shook his head and wiped the water from his face. "That was incredible!"

I wrapped my arms around him and pulled him close. We floated there together, with nowhere to be and nothing to do, in a world where time didn't exist and all that was needed was to *feel*. When his arms were wrapped around me from behind, I leaned the back of my head against his chest.

"Hey, Ramón."

"Si, Miss Scarlett?"

"Does the boy ever find his treasure?"

"Do people usually give you the shortcut?" His tease made me smile.

I glared at him, and he gave up.

"Yes, the boy finds his treasure. But it's not what he expected. It's far, far from what he expected."

That was clearly all I was going to get out of him.

A few minutes later, I dug a bit more in another direction.

"So, is that why your father doesn't want you to spend time with me? Because he doesn't want you to leave the village?"

"Ah, no. He knows I won't leave. I made my choice long ago. This is my path." Respect gripped me at the sound of his resolution.

I prodded, "So, what was he worried for then?"

"You, Miss Scarlett. You were his concern."

"What do you mean?"

"People come here to heal. We can't get in the way of that. He... he didn't want me to distract you or alter your path. We all have to choose a path, and I've chosen mine. It's time for you to choose yours. But, you have to choose it for yourself. No one else."

I marveled at the thought for a bit.

That grumpy old man who looked at me like he couldn't stand me... was looking out for me? A sense of duty and freedom swirled within as I felt a very unfamiliar control climb to my fingertips.

I have a choice.

After our fingers and toes had just about pruned and we'd had enough play time, we treaded up the side bank and pulled our clothes on.

Hiking back up the path around the volcanic mountain, we stopped when we heard a scream echoing through the trees. I turned to Ramón wide-eyed who was already trying to figure out the direction it came from. There it was again, this time rattling the trees.

That was no playful scream.

Ramón pulled me with him in the direction it was coming from, instructing me to stay low and quiet as we ducked around bushes. We followed a fresh scent of campfire and found a little red tent almost falling over where a body-sized bulge protruded.

There was a muffled female cry coming from inside it as a man emerged, fumbling and staggering angrily. He was at least six foot tall and skinny with a rotten beard. He grabbed a bottle of dark alcohol sitting on the nearby tree stump and pounded the last quarter of it before he smashed the glass into the fire and yelled something at the girl in the tent. We saw her hand and then her shoulder peek through as she pulled herself out. Under the blonde tousled hair, blood spilled from her mouth.

Ramón pushed my shoulder down further until I was on my knees. He leaned down and wrapped his hand behind my ear. "Look at me. No matter what happens, you stay right here, okay?"

"Ramón, no."

"Scarlett, I'm not asking."

Healing is a dirty process. It's not weightless.

"

Healing is a dirty process.
It doesn't feel like one of those sweet full moons.
It feels like broken bones and rotting flowers.
It growls and cracks and hurts.
It grabs the back of your neck and forces you to
stare at the shadows inside of yourself.
It strips you down until you're whimpering
and when it has you there, naked in the dirt
of your own undoing, and you think you'll
die at the feet of this process—it bends down,
puts its lips against your heart and kisses,
until something in you sews back together.

BROOKE SOLIS

Twenty-Four

"I'm going to go see if I can at least help. I don't care what happens. You stay right here. Promise me?" He took his keys from his pocket and wrapped my fingers around them.

"Ramón!" I grabbed his wrist and hoped my pleading eyes would keep him from leaving.

"Promise me!" he insisted.

"Okay, okay." I stayed low as he made his way around the bushes and down to the landing, barely making a sound.

I looked back to where the girl was, now completely out of the tent. It looked like she was crawling toward a backpack. When the man turned and saw her, he swung his foot into her stomach, flipping her entire body into a tree.

My eyes stayed on her, wondering if she'd be able to get up, until Ramón appeared from the trees behind the man and wrapped his right arm around his neck, holding him in a choke hold. The man squirmed to get out but after about a minute, his whole body fell limp and he stopped fighting.

With the threat handled, I rushed down and around the bushes to the girl. Turning her over, I saw that she was barely coherent. Ramón laid the man's body on the ground, came over to us, and searched for the girl's pulse.

"Ma'am, is this your bag?" Ramón held the bag in front of her. She nodded slightly and, in one swift movement, he flung the bag around his back and lifted her up to her feet. He ducked under one arm and I ducked under the other before we guided her up the hill.

"Did you kill him?" I whispered.

"No, no. But he'll be knocked out for a good while. Let's get her to the hospital."

We carried her to the back seat and laid her down. Noticing the sputtering of the blood pooling in her mouth, I decided to sit with her so I could hold her head up. She was drifting in and out of consciousness, and I tried to comfort her as best I could while Ramón drove furiously around the mountain.

"Shhh, shhh. It's okay. We're going to get you help. What's your name?"

"Andrea," she coughed.

"Andrea, was that man a stranger? Did he steal anything from you?"

She stared up at me as I brushed the hair from her eyes. "He's… he's my husband."

I couldn't control the pain that furrowed in my brows, and I felt his glance in the rearview mirror. Taking a deep breath, I nodded as I tried to separate her hair from the blood dripping down her neck.

"Okay, it's going to be alright. We're going to get you help." I placed my hand on her chest. "Can you try to steady your breathing for me? Follow mine, okay?"

Locked on her eyes, I began breathing slowly. She finally synced with me and her nervous system cooled beneath my palms.

Before I knew it, we'd pulled into the parking lot of a tiny local clinic and were unloading her into the care of the medics.

As I watched her roll on a gurney through the doors, I could feel Ramón's eyes on me. After a few moments, he grabbed my head with his hand and pulled me into his chest.

We walked to the car where he retrieved his water from the back seat and a towel from the trunk. Following his silent instructions, I stuck my hands out as he poured and then scrubbed them clean and dry.

"You were pretty great back there." His proud tone snapped my attention back from the trance that consumed me as I tried to make sense of her response.

"Huh? Are you kidding? You were the one who took that jackass down."

"No, really. You responded very quickly under that pressure, got her to relax and everything. You should consider some sort of emergency response work."

I shook my head at the thought, at how helpless I'd felt at the only other moment in my life when I was forced to rush to the emergency room.

This time, the memory of those last moments with him in the emergency room elicited something new. Gratitude washed over me as I recalled the papà I'd grown up with. He'd never laid a hand on my mother, none of us. I couldn't even remember a time I'd seen him that angry. I was so grateful I'd had such a strong, gentle man in my life and was able to watch him be the same type of husband.

"Gosh, I can't imagine ever being treated that way by someone—ever being in a situation like that."

I felt his eyes on me as I processed out loud.

"Yeah, it's not always simple, you know." His compassionate heart seemed to understand something mine did not.

"I suppose not." I shook my head and dried my hands with my sleeves. "So awful. That poor girl. She couldn't have been much older than me, could she?"

He grabbed them and gently brushed them with the back of his lips.

"I'm sorry. That wasn't exactly the morning I had planned."

I grabbed his hand and lifted it to my lips.

"Today was amazing. Really. Thank you."

We rolled the windows down and descended through the clouds and radiant blue sky in silence.

"You sure you can't come with me?" I shot him a playful look out of the corner of my eye. He smiled, a painful, dutiful smile, and pulled my hand up to kiss it.

Hours and several easy conversations later, we arrived at the wooden gates. When he stopped the car, he turned to me and smiled.

"I'll see you at the celebration tonight, right?"

"The celebration?"

"Yep, after every eclipse, we have a celebration for what is coming. The eclipse is a sort of portal. It takes us from the old and into the new. Tonight, we celebrate the closing of chapters. We celebrate the new."

"Mmm, and everyone will be there?"

"Yep, everyone!"

"Okay, I'm just uh…" I smiled and then looked myself up and down. "I'm going to go clean the blood off me before anyone wonders who I killed."

We laughed and I leaned over for another quick kiss. Slowly and sweetly, his eager lips slipped between mine.

A tear streamed down his cheek as I turned toward the bungalow, and I wondered what story of his I'd been part of during my time here. He was definitely part of mine.

I found Jenna sitting up, drinking from her coconut with a towel atop her head. She looked me up and down, taking in the splatters of blood on my clothes.

"Dooo I want to know?"

"Probably not. But everything's okay. How was your morning?" I grabbed a towel from my clothing rack and patted my damp head.

"Probably not as eventful as yours." Her sarcastic wince made me laugh. "So, I decided to tell my husband."

Her statement caught me by surprise and I tilted my head to inquire more.

"I just, I think it's right, ya know? I need to own up to my feelings, and he deserves so much better than that. Soon as I get back." Her voice quivered as she nodded, as though she were trying to assure herself more than me.

I sat on the edge of her bed and rested my hand on hers.

"It sounds like you put a lot of thought into it."

"Yeah." She dropped her chin.

"Well, just so you know… I didn't think poorly of you when you told me what happened, Jenna. But now, I do admire you so much. That's a tough choice and, if I ever catch myself in a similar situation, I hope I can find the same strength."

She cracked a smile. "Thanks, Scar."

Her eyes fell on my blood-soaked clothes again, and I remembered where I was headed.

Squeezing her hand, I said, "Well, I better go take care of this." I grabbed my toiletries bag and headed to the shower.

It felt good to wash my hair and get clean. Having another person's blood on me totally freaked me out, but I was glad Ramón intervened today. I was even happier knowing that woman was okay.

I hope she finds her way out of that situation. No human deserves that.

When I got back to the room, Jenna was gone. I grabbed my bag, shoved my journal into it, and turned to leave but stopped when I heard something fall.

The map unfolded on the ground before me. When I picked it up, I saw it was blank again. Stepping outside, I closed my eyes and took a long deep breath. As soon as I opened them, a path flickered across the paper and the jungle opened a pathway for me.

It really is like magic.

I recalled Shawna's ideas about the stars containing my map— my own personal map: *"A map that was made just for you. By god, by the universe, by destiny, or whoever you want to believe in."*

I brushed my fingertips across the fresh sketches on the parchment.

A Mapmaker.

I shook my head as I stepped out of the bungalow. Following the map to a familiar gazebo with two very lonely rocking chairs, I smiled on arrival and traced my fingers along the carving in the wood, *La Conexión.* I walked around and stared at them. This time, I didn't let myself think it over too long. I faced the vast beyond and sat back, rocking into the chair. Laughter as loud as my Portuguese blood was deep ripped through me and bellowed into the wide-open canyon.

I quickly fell silent when I heard a loud roar fill the valley and reverberate off the mountains, shaking the pebbles at my feet and vibrating the misty particles around me.

Everything stilled.

I wrapped my fingers tightly around my chair's arms as I braced for a pending earthquake. But, there was only silence. My heart had stopped completely.

I crooked my head at that timely coincidence and gazed down to my chest where my father's ring vibrated wildly. Stunned, I waited.

"Sounds like you've opened quite the portal, Traveler..." Sibú's voice was smooth, oozing from what appeared to be a proud grin as he rounded the second rocking chair and plopped right into it.

He didn't frighten me this time. Perhaps because I was already on edge.

"Did you hear that?" I stared into the distance.

"Oh Scar, the whole universe heard that." He chuckled and I wondered just exactly what he meant.

I sunk into my chair and tried to relax my body with some deep breaths. In a few seconds, our breathing was synchronized and the next time I heard his voice, I wasn't sure if it was coming from inside or outside my head.

"So, what parts of you have you chosen to let die, Traveler?"

I took another deep breath with my eyelids closed as I considered his question...

My rage. My responsibility. My hopelessness. My grief. My panic. My disappointment. My betrayal. My guilt. My shattered dreams. My self-neglect.

He continued as if he'd heard the response in my skull, "And, what have you remembered?"

Another deep breath and I watched the memories I'd made here swirl in my vision: my body twirling through the trees, my skin waking to the light, my tummy rumbling with hunger, dancing, resting in the safety of Ramón's chest, staying up late into the night with Jenna, awakening my desire in Aiana's touch, forgiving myself, grieving with Caleb, expanding at the speed of light through a field of eternity in the forest with Sibú. I remembered the pool of crystals, of falling into darkness with abandon.

What part of me hadn't come back to life here? Parts I didn't even know I had, had awakened.

I searched for a response and rested on the image of the sweet, glowing butterfly I'd rescued from the storm in the labyrinth. Her strength, her resilience, that grew brighter with every step I took forward.

Perhaps she rescued me.

I felt a smile creep its way to my lips and pull them back with gratitude as I thanked myself for letting my light lead me, for pressing on through the storm of these lessons, and finding my way back to... me.

"Sibú, I..."

But when I opened my eyes, he was gone.

Perhaps, I was just talking with myself after all. I looked down and laughed a bit more, but quietly this time. I wasn't trying to awaken any beasts out there.

Just then, that breeze rushed around me, through me, "Vita..." I let my head sway in its sweetness. I pulled out my journal, hoping to find some words that might make sense of all this.

"Remember..."

She had a laugh like her father's,

a cackle that carried on the wind.

Rich in passion,

fierce with drive,

she had sunrise in her eyes

and nations on her mind.

This is what he made her for.

She would never know

all the ways he knew her,

all the ways he loved her.

With summer in her curls

and adventure in her blood,

healing spoke on the wind.

There was no day

but today.

"

To the mind that is still,
the whole universe surrenders.

LAO TZU

The echoes of a distant drum ricocheted off the walls of the gazebo and I decided to head back to the center of the village. The celebration would be starting any moment. Somehow, with a faint breeze guiding me, I followed the tumbling of the trees and plants as they parted for me, past the main desk under the front canopy.

It was empty until, quicker than I could blink, a white-faced capuchin swung down and let the canopy slingshot back with the release of its grip. Wide-eyed, he stared back at me from upon the desk, still and curious. Eyes locked, I shook the surprise from my shoulders as he watched me tiptoe past him into the trees.

I laughed, picked up my skirt from the ground, and ran toward the music until I stumbled into an open field. The entire village stood in a crescent moon shape around the two stunning intertwined trees I'd driven through upon my arrival—the same ones which followed me to the labyrinth. This time, no door resided within them. But before them, logs of wood stood in a circle and were tilted to the center and tied at the top. Covered in dry brush, the pile stood at least twelve feet high.

The drums slowed to a steady pace. Two men on either side, dressed in white-laced garments, buttoned with gradient feathers, approached with a flaming cotton-tipped branch. All at once, flames shot to the sky and the people cheered in a collective chant. As I scanned the crowd, I watched knees drop to the grass and tears tumble in what seemed both like joy and mourning, relief and sadness.

Behind and around the fire, a group of men, masked with large wooden creature-like faces, spread out and started playing their congas. Others carrying skin drums joined. Together, they picked up their pace. Women dressed in similar style weaved through them, harmonizing ever so eloquently with reed flutes. Music filled the air and the wind danced through us.

Rectangular tables were draped in fine-patterned garment and topped with food of all kind. Every delicious thing I'd eaten in Costa Rica had been prepared for this one evening. My eyes grew wide and my mouth drooled in anticipation, scanning the gallo pinto, the fresh cilantro covered ajo, and tenderized chicken swimming in creamy sauce. The ceviche and chifrijo, lined with salty plantains. The mountains of tamales and lines of spongy refrescos. My stomach growled as I realized I hadn't actually eaten yet today.

I filled a plate and turned to the circle of other visitors, now friends, who gathered on the ground at the center of all the tables. I found a spot between Jenna and Sybil and made myself comfortable. As I looked around, I noticed it was more than just us. Many of the natives and Awas had joined us, too.

The ruby hair of the fair-skinned woman sat across the circle from us in very intentional conversation with the slow-moving, round-bellied older gentleman whose resting smile made me feel more at ease. The faces I'd seen tending the fields and scuttling around the kitchen... they were all in attendance. It was beautiful.

Nick, Aileen, and Caleb all joined us.

"Is this seat taken?" Ramón's voice sent an excited chill down my spine.

"It most definitely is not."

He dropped down next to me, two mugs in his hand.

"Try this out!"

"What is it?"

He sighed, "Must you know everything?"

I laughed and sipped the melted popsicle-like texture, a nutty mixture of alcohol and corn.

"Chicha! Isn't it amazing?"

"Whoa! Nice." I nodded, hiding my lack of enthusiasm over the mucky tasting wine-beer. Placing the cup on the ground in front of me, I picked up my fork and dug into the feast on my lap.

We ate and stared at the fire dancers.

"This ceremony is massive. They made so much food!"

"Oh yes. They make enough food for the entire three days so no one has to think about cooking and they can all stay present during it."

Two warm hands grasped my shoulders and Sol's beautiful glowing face dropped down from behind me.

"Para ti, mi bailarina pequeña" she said as she pulled my hair back and tucked a big white hibiscus in it.

"¡Gracias a ti, Sol!" I smiled and kissed her on the cheek before she bounced up and floated through the rest of the ceremony in her flowing fiery dress.

We ate into the night, sharing and basking in each other's company, sharing our memories from our time here and our excitement over future plans.

I kept my eyes open for Sibú. It was important to me that I thank him for all he'd done to guide me through so much that still made very little sense.

On the other side of the fire, I finally spotted his faint figure, almost materialized in the flames. He offered a soft smile and a wink through his moving silver locks, which melted into feathered wings through the haze of the fire. Outstretched, his vulture-like figure vanished into the evening air, joining the wind in the beyond.

I shook my head, my vision rattled with magic. I gulped my last bite down as the gears within me finally began to put the pieces together.

"Scar, come here! I want you to try this." Ramón waved me back over to where one of the drummers had joined us. "Sit on it!" He pointed to the long conga laying on the ground.

"Sit on it!?"

He bellowed, "Yes, sit on it!"

Realizing this was perhaps the most relaxed I'd seen Ramón in my entire time here, I followed his instructions and straddled the drum, and the masked man next to us invited me to follow his lead. The lack of rhythm in my hands was comical and eventually sent everyone tumbling back on the grass in laughter, knocking a couple of their masks right off their cheekbones.

It was a lively night under the high moon, shining in all its glory over the land. The soil glistened with those majestic, reptilian scales. Eventually, more dancers, acrobats, and fire-twirlers emerged from the trees, dressed in fewer white garments, revealing the silk of their caramel skin, gleaming with sweaty heat from the fire. Over their necks and arms, they twisted long pieces of wood flaming at the tips. They danced and spun their thrilling art into the air and tossed it between one another, alternating from their hands to their feet and back again.

We rejoiced into the sunrise, and I marveled at this culture so beautifully acknowledging and praising death, life, and the transitions in between that made us both human and utterly... so much more. A resonant hum filled the air—one of acceptance, of celebration.

Eventually, Ramón pulled me aside and reminded me that I needed to get on the road soon if I was going to make my afternoon flight. Sadness washed through me as I wrestled my newfound animosity toward time. Without arguing, I headed back to my bungalow to pack my things.

As I took inventory of each piece of clothing I placed into my bag, I wondered how exactly I would fit into it when I got home— how I'd fit back into my life.

Walking slowly out to the front canopy, I strained to memorize every flower and tree, every animal I'd encountered here. At the desk, I set my things down so I could say my goodbyes to the group, one by one.

Jenna might have been the hardest to part with. She let a few tears fall and stuffed a paper with her number on it in my shorts as she squeezed me tightly.

Ramón waited behind me until I gave my last hug to Nick.

"It was really, really nice to meet you, Nick."

"Yes. I have a feeling we will be seeing you soon, Scar." His sincerity was palpable, and he gave me a sweet wink as he pulled away with those last few words.

Hands in my pockets, I walked toward Ramón who moved the hair from my forehead and, hand tucked behind my ear, leaned his brow against mine.

"Come on, there's still time." He put his arm out and didn't move until I wrapped mine inside of it.

We turned a few corners to the wooden stairs of *La Transparencia*. He led me inside and dropped my hand so he could open the blinds covering every window. He clicked a button on his phone and a familiar rhythm beat through the speakers.

My cheeks warmed as he walked over to me and I laid my head in the crevice between his chest and neck. I threw my arms around him as his hands found the low of my back and began leading me to Prince Royce's *Stand By Me* once last time.

I bent my knees and stayed light on my toes as he carried me in circles, leading me by my shoulder blade at moments and the back of my neck at others. Every ounce of care in this man's body was palpable as he spun me just to pull me back for a dip.

We smiled and even chuckled through our tears.

I relaxed in his arms as words tumbled a trail of footprints across my mind, and I promised myself I'd get them written down in the car.

Here I am in the earliest hours of the morning,

dancing atop the fine lights of San José,

body relaxed in the presence of a gentleman,

a Love whose heart opens to this moment

though his mind knows I'll be gone with the rising of the sun.

Here I am in the earliest hours of the morning,

smelling the sweet sweat of tiresome laughter,

feet surrendered to the lead of a gentleman,

a Love whose arms welcome me with each turn

though his fingers feel me slipping closer to the door.

Here I am in the earliest hours of the morning,

staring into the eyes of Costa Rican moonlight,

hands locked in the tender grasp of a gentleman,

a Love whose spirit tickles me silly with joy

though his hands know they can't follow me home.

Here I am in the earliest hours of the morning,

dancing under the fine stars of Alajuela,

heart captivated by the touch of a gentleman,

a Love whose gentleness fastens me to this moment

though his lips ache of longing

and his breath of goodbye.

The song faded and Ramón brushed the hair from my shoulders, kissing my neck and cradling my jaw in his palms.

"I have something for you."

"Oh?"

I love gifts.

He led me by hand to the front canopy, where he reached under the desk and pulled a brown paper bag out. I bounced with joy and moved to open it, but he put his hand on it as he gave it to me.

"Open it in the car, okay?"

I pursed my lips, "You're not driving me to the airport?"

"No, Gitana will be driving you."

"Why?" I frowned.

He moved the hair out of my eyes and tucked it behind my ear.

"Because if I see you get on that airplane, I'm going to follow you."

Ramón pulled me in for another hug and kissed the top of my head. I slipped a small understanding glance toward his father who leaned against the cabin behind him. Looking back at Ramón, I shifted my weight to my toes so I could kiss him a last time. His lips were warm and wet with longing and love—and zero regret.

Already missing his embrace, I grabbed my things and walked to the car where Gitana waited by the Volkswagen. He followed and opened the door for me, placing a final light kiss on my forehead before closing the door and sending me back to my life.

As soon as we passed through the village gate, I wiped the tears away and opened his gift.

El Alchemista.

I chuckled as I flipped through pages covered in his ink. Halfway through, a piece of paper fell to my feet... I picked it up, recognizing his handwriting.

Her love left as quickly as it came,

much like the way lightning strikes,

piercing Its beacon through the chaos of my storm

with fury too determined for comprehension

in a language far too complex for translation.

Her love came crashing into my world,

teaching me this law of the universe,

awakening my faith in moments,

in how they pass as swiftly as the weather,

in how they linger as long as a lifetime.

Her love left as quickly as it came,

much like the way lightning strikes,

trailing a roar of thunder in its wake

with parts of me I didn't know I had

set afire.

I pulled out another heavier item. It was a coffee mug, with a waterfall painted on it. In rainbow print at the bottom, it read Costa Rica. Pulling it close to my heart, I let my head fall against the window.

I would keep my eyes open on this drive—open and free of fear and panic. I had my breath now, and that was all I needed.

We wound around the green hills and I marveled at the beauty of this land, the majesty of its bloom. Light fluttered through the low-hanging clouds and rainbows twirled on the road ahead of us.

A few hours later, we arrived at the airport and Gitana handed me my papers and plane ticket.

He was right.

I could not believe the date on this ticket was only seven days after my arrival. I shook my head and thanked Gitana with a warm hug before I walked into the airport and found my gate.

When I found my seat, and a few more deep breaths, I let the tears fall.

"Teaching me this law of the universe…"

La Presencia.

The way out, was in.

I pulled my journal from my bag and another, harder piece of paper slipped into my lap. Catching it, I saw the backside of the cards Rebecca had pulled for me. I turned it one over and on the front was a woman on a throne—the Alchemist of Cups, decorated in gold with a smoldering sunset sky painted behind her.

The card she'd placed on me. Cups. Truth. From the sad woman under the tree to the throne. I dropped my head against the seat as I reminded myself that not all of this was meant to make sense right now—perhaps not ever.

"Magic is not quite a matter of belief."

I'd found my portal. I'd found my power. That was all I needed in this moment.

I flipped to the first few pages I'd written on the flight to Costa Rica and smiled.

Perhaps… I was the answer I was looking for all along.

And he will tell the tale of the girl

with the sad eyes,

whose love would come to know pain

as her victory or her demise.

He will talk of her beauty,

of how the gold in her chest tarnished to a dark rust,

of how her sanity unwound

with her father's last breath.

He will talk of her light,

of how the fire in her fingers dimmed to ash,

of how she would never touch another man

with the desperation she felt in that emergency room.

He will tell of her pain,

of how her lips tasted of bitter salt,

of how he watched the rage rot her

from the inside out.

He will talk of her resilience,

of how her knees calloused

with the changing of the seasons,

of how her fists

pushed her body from the dirt

time and time again.

He will talk of her bravery,

of how her feet sought solace

in the blackness of despair,

of how her hands

created a sanctuary within the sadness,

welcoming all who might meet her there.

He will tell of her pain,

of how her lips tasted of sweet nectar,

of how he watched the rage grow her

from the inside out.

The best is yet to come.

About Alyssa Noelle Coelho

After sharing her first journey back to love in her 2016 #1 bestselling poetry compilation, *CHOSEN,* Death's breath sent twenty-one-year-old Alyssa on her first meaning-seeking mission around the world. Through her sociocultural anthropology training at UCSD and many seasons of disconnection with her soul and source, Alyssa unearthed some deeper truths behind the human experience and learned to alchemize her own tragedies into a greater sense of meaning and adventure.

A poet and novelist, dancer and world traveler, she has been passionately immersing herself in cultures worldwide, studying their traditions and transformations through the lens of meaning and purpose for years. A lover of novelty and a delighter in the extraordinary, Alyssa uses the power of words and stories to romance humans into falling in love with their precious existence. She reminds us of our wild potential, of our hungry spirits, and of the entire world awaiting our unique gifts.

As the Founder of Lionheart Creations, and Co-Founder and Lead Designer at Saved By Story Publishing, she serves messengers and enterprises on a mission to facilitate positive change in the world. She also co-hosts the savory, storytelling madness of Sips of Story 'n Sanity podcast, showcasing the journeys of other Seekers and Creators from around the world.

A Special Invitation

Hungry for More?

I'm excited to continue sharing Scarlett's journey through The Lionheart Chronicles, as well as offer various opportunities and experiences to help my fellow Travelers with their own Scar Work.

Visit *LionheartCreations.org/Chronicles* to find out how you can join me on these adventures.

Travel with Me!

Acknowledgments

To my Mapmaker, for every light and every darkness, for carving every path just as my soul craved it to be, and for so many sacred invitations to experience magic in different humans, cultures, and lands. My gratitude knows no bounds.

To My Family...

To my Mama, for remaining my rock through the years, the voice reminding me who I am and who I came here to be. Thank you for seeing me and loving me in all of my seasons.

To my sisters, for the panic calls, movie nights, and tequila-espresso cookie-crumble days; for holding space for my brokenness, and for seeing every best thing inside and before me; for pulling me through with so much unconditional love—always. A world without you two is no world at all.

To my brother, for being the only voice my heart could hear during a time when it needed it most.

To my nephew, for growing into the mad genius you are and propelling this project forward with your constant tyrannical deadlines when all I wanted to do was say "fuck it" and become a barista. I want to be you when I grow up.

To My Allies...

To my Peanut, for agreeing to come back with me in this lifetime and shake shit up. Our friendship has known more honesty, compassion, and growth than others ever get to experience. I am grateful to be on this journey with you by my side.

To my Kennedy, for always pouring so much love and faith into everything I do, for always showing up, and for dealing with so much crazy you never signed up for.

To All of My Past and Present Teachers, Mentors, and Coaches...

To Ryan Leonhardi, another acknowledgment for your collection (wink, wink). Your friendship over the years has meant more to me than words can do justice. Thank you for your humor, your light, and your encouragement.

To Joel McKerrow, I just wanted my book signed (ugly cry). Imagine my surprise when your beautiful soul broke through my antisocial tunnel vision. And, how grateful I am to you—for seeing every potential within me and treating me as a Friend, as a Poet, and as a Creator in all my mess and glory. For inviting me into your community and for offering your expertise and time with so much generosity. Onward, together.

To Dan Millman, I never would have guessed that week in the jungle would have paved the way for so much healing and transformation in the years to come. Thank you for creating the catalyst for me to begin my journey home to myself. May the wisdom you birthed that changed my world in so many ways continue to live on.

To my Writing Coach, where would I be without you? Probably on a beach in the Bahamas, dancing away all my tragedies and traumas instead of facing, healing through, and alchemizing them. You have taught me everything I know, and I am continuously grateful for your wisdom, support, safety, and tenderness.

To My Community and Team...

To the True To Intention Cocoon, I have not known a group of people as safe and nurturing as you. Thank you for all of the listening, the holding, and the believing.

To the Saved By Story Family, so much of this book would not have been possible without every single one of you. Thank you for being my team, my cheerleaders, and my family.

To Carly Ash, your intuitive talent captured every last detail my poetry craved. Thank you for pouring your heart into these paintings.

To Dawn Teagarden, this book is more beautiful than I dreamed it could be.

With Love, Gratitude, and All of the Espresso I Can Share,

Alyssa Noelle Coelho

Glossary

A

ajo
garlic

amor
love

¡Aquí tienes, ponte esto!
Here, put this on!

Aquí tienes, Señorita.
Here, Miss.

awa
shaman, medicine person

awapa
plural for awa

Ayyyye no seee. Estoy muy cansada. No sé cómo lo haces.
Oooh I don't know. I'm so tired. I don't know how you do it.

B

bailarina
dancer

¡Bien, bien! ¡Dime si hay algo que puedo conseguir para ti, pequeña bailarina!
Fine, fine! Tell me if there's anything I can get for you, little dancer!

Bienvenida à La Présencia.
Welcome to The Presence.

Bienvenidos.
Welcome.

Bolshevik
a member of the majority faction of the Russian Social Democratic Party, which seized power in the October Revolution of 1917

Bosque Nuboso
Cloud Forest

Buenas noches.
Good night.

¡Buenas tardes, Sol! ¿Cómo estás?
Good afternoon, Sol! How are you?

Buenas tardes.
Good afternoon.

Buenas tardes, mujeres.
Good afternoon, ladies.

¡Buenos Días, mi bailarina, pequeña! ¿Cómo estás?
Good morning, my little dancer. How are you?

¡Buenos días, Sol! ¡Qué bueno para verte!
Good morning, Sol! So good to see you!

Buenos días.
Good morning.

Buenas tardes, pequeña bailarina.
Good afternoon, little dancer.

C

Cazzo.
Fuck.

Ceibo Barrigón.
a tree in the Kapok family, meaning big bellied Ceiba

ceviche and chifrijo
a traditional appetizer from Costa Rica, made of beans with broth, pork rinds, pico de gallo, and tortillas

chicha
a fermented (alcoholic) or non-fermented beverage of Latin America, emerging from the Andes and Amazonia regions

chisme
gossip

Ciao, Luna.
Hi, Moon.

Ciao, Scarlett. Buongiorno.
Hi, Scarlett. Good morning.

Ciao. Uh perdóname, hola.
Hi. Uh sorry, hi.

Claro. Oh and Amor, open your eyes this time.
Okay. Oh and my love, open your eyes this time.

¡Clarooo! ¡Por supuesto que sí!
Of course! Of course you do!

¿Cómo sé dice en inglés?
How do you say it in English?

cómo sé dice... ¡la Présencia!
how do you say it... the Presence!

Cómo... increíble.
Like... incredible.

Con permiso, mujeres...
Sorry, ladies...

¡Cuidado, cuidado!
Be careful, be careful!

Cuidado, por favor.
Be careful, please.

Déjalo.
Let go.

Descansa, Miss Scarlett.
Rest, Miss Scarlett.

Dio Santo.
For God's sake.

E

¡El baile es vida, mi Corazón! ¡Te lo dije!
Dancing is my life, my heart! I'm telling you!

Entonces, los dos.
So, both.

¿Entonces, ok? Estamos listo.
So, okay? We're ready.

¡Entonces, una sorpresa! The big reveal… ¿estan listos?
So, a surprise! The big reveal… are you ready?

¡Espero que tengan un buen día!
Hope you have a good day!

¡Esssoooo!
Thiiis!

Está despierto.
He's awake.

Esta es Salsa, Señorita.
This is Salsa, Miss.

¡Estamos aquí!
We're here!

Estamos listo.
We're ready.

Estás lista.
You're ready.

Estás loca, you know that.
You're crazy, you know that.

Estás loca, pero muchas gracias.
You're crazy, but thank you so much.

¡Estoy muy contenta, Señorita! ¿Estás bailando esta noche?
I'm very happy, Miss! Are you dancing tonight?

G

gallo pinto
a traditional dish from Central America, particularly from Nicaragua and Costa Rica, consisting of rice and beans as a base

Gracias, Sol.
Thank you, Sol.

¡Gracias a ti, Sol!
Thank you, Sol!

Gracias por hoy.
Thank you for today.

Gracias por todo.
Thanks for everything.

Gracias... por todo.
Thanks... for everything.

Grazie. Grazie mille.
Thank you. Thank you so much.

Hay dios mío.
Oh my god.

Hay dios mío contigo.
Oh my god, with you.

¡Hermosa! ¡Tú eres increíble!
Beautiful! You're amazing!

¿Hey, cómo estás?
Hey, how are you?

hojas de palma suita
suita palm leaves

¡Hola, Sol! ¿Cómo estás?
Hi, Sol! How are you?

Hongo copas o copa de vino
[a type of mushroom] or wine glasses

𝓛

La Conexión
The Connection

La Encarnada
The Incarnate

La Piscina Sagrada, El Portal Del Presente
The Sacred Pool, The Portal to the Presence

La Presencia
The Presence

¿La salsa?
The salsa?

La sonrisa… la sonrisa del momento.
The smile... smiling in the moment.

La Transparencia
The Transparency

Lista?
Ready?

¿Lista? ¡Ahora, una vuelta!
Ready? Now a spin!

Lo siento. Linda, no puedes cambiar tú destino.
I'm sorry. Girl, you cannot change your destiny.

M

Me llamo Scar.
My name is Scar.

Menya zovut Scar. Kak vas zovut?
My name's Scarlett. What's your name?

Merda.
Shit.

¡Mi bailarina! ¡Vente! ¡Por favor, vente!
My dancer! Come! Please, come!

Mio dio.
Oh my god.

¡Mira!
Look!

Muchas gracias, Sol.
Thank you, Sol.

mujer
woman

N

Necesito practicar el español, pero el inglés me resulta más
fácil.
*Well, I need to practice my Spanish, but English is much easier
for me.*

No quiero salsa. ¿La música, qué es?
I don't want some sauce. The music, what is it?

No sé.
I don't know.

No, Sol, yo no bailo. No he bailado en mucho tiempo.
No, Sol, I don't dance. I haven't danced for a long time.

No te preocupes, mi bailarina. Nosotros vamos a cocinar.
Don't worry, my dancer. We are going to cook.

No, lo siento.
No, I'm sorry.

¡No, no, usted! ¿De dónde sacas toda tú energía?
No, no, you! Where do you find all this energy?

¿Oh, Sol, hablas inglés?
Oh, Sol, do you speak English?

Ok, entonces, escucha la música.
Ok, so listen to the music.

¡Otra vez! ¡1, 2, 3... 5, vuelta al derecha!
Another time! 1,2,3... 5, turn to the right!

Para ti, mi bailarina pequeña.
For you, my little dancer.

Perdóname.
Excuse me.

Perdone.
Excuse me.

¡Pero siii, Señorita! Tú eres una bailarina. ¡Tú eres una bailarina increíble!
But yesss, Miss! You are a dancer. You're an incredible dancer!

plátano
plantain – a low growing plant that typically has a rosette of leaves and a slender green flower spike, widely growing as a

weed in lawns

¿Por qué me llamas bailarina? No soy una bailarina.
Why do you call me a dancer? I'm not a dancer.

¿Prefieres inglés o español?
Do you prefer English or Spanish?

¡Puesss, no puedes cocinar con esa ropa!
Welll, you can't cook in those clothes!

Pura vida, Miss Scarlett.
You're welcome, Miss Scarlett.

Pura vida.
Pure life.

¡Pura vida! ¡Mucho gusto!
Great! Nice to meet you!

Pura vida, mi amor.
You're welcome, my love.

¡Que buenooo! ¡Ahora! ¡Vuelta a la izquierda!
So good! Now! Turn to the left!

¿Que estás haciendo?
What are you doing?

¿Qué hora es?
What time is it?

¿Que me haces, mujer?
What are you doing to me, woman?

¿Que? ¿Tú me dijiste qué?
What? What are you telling me?

¿Quieres beber algo?
Do you want anything to drink?

Reclinarse, por favor.
Lean back, please.

refrescos
soft drinks

Russian Ashkenazi
a Jewish person of central or eastern European decent

sabe-lo-todo
know-it-all

¿Sabes que hace que la comida sepa tan bien?
You know what makes food taste so good?

salsera
female Salsa dancer

salseros
male Salsa dancer

¡Salud!
Cheers!

Sei la mia vita.
You're my life.

¡Señorita! ¡Buenos días! ¿Cómo estás mi bailarina pequeña?
Miss! Good morning! How is my little dancer?

Señorita, en esto momento, nosotras cocinamos. Vamos.
Miss, right now, we are cooking. Let's go.

¡Señorita! ¡Que buena para verte!
Miss! How nice to see you!

Si, muchas gracias.
Okay, yeah. Thank you so much.

Si, nos vamos pronto.
Yes, we're ready.

Si, si. Todo bien.
Yeah, yeah. Everything is fine.

Sol, uhm estoy... confundida. Un poco.
Sol, um, I'm... confused. A little bit.

T

Ti... ti voglio... ti voglio bene, Papà.
I... I love... I love you, daddy.

Todo bien?
Everything okay?

¡Tú eres una bailarina! ¡Vive en ti!
You're a dancer! It's in you!

U

Uh si, prefiero un coco si tienes, por favor, Sol.
Uh yes, I prefer fresh juice if you have it, please, Sol.

¿Uh, Sol, cocinar? No sé cómo cocinar.
Uh, Sol, cooking? I don't know how to cook.

Un momento.
Just a moment.

Un perezoso.
A sloth.

Una pregunta. ¿Qué música es?
A question. What is this music?

V

Vamos.
Let's go.

Vuelta a la derecha.
Turn to the right.

Yo? ¿Cocinar?
Me? Cook?

Z

Zdravstuytye! Kak vas zovut?
Hello! What's your name?